ABOUT THE AUTHOR

Roland Curram was born and educated in Brighton and went on to a career as an actor for over fifty years, appearing in the West End in *Enter a Free Man, Little Murders, Grand Manoeuvres, Design For Living (1982), Noises Off (1984/5),* and *Ross (1986).* Many television plays and series include: *Nana, Z Cars, Avengers, The Crezz, Some Mothers Do 'Av 'Em, Bouquet Of Barbed Wire, Artemis '81, Big Jim and the Figaro Club, Till We Meet Again,* and *Eldorado.* Among his films are: *Dunkirk, Oh You Are Awful, Decline and Fall, The Silent Playground* and John Schlesinger's Oscar winning *Darling.*

His first novel, Man on the Beach was published in 2004
The Rose Secateurs 2007
Mother Loved Funerals 2010
The Problem with Happiness is his fourth novel.

The

PROBLEM

with

HAPPINESS

ROLAND CURRAM

Matador
9 Priory Business Park,
Wistow Road, Kibworth Beauchamp,
Leicestershire. LE8 0RX
Tel: (+44) 116 279 2299
Fax: (+44) 116 279 2277
Email: books@troubador.co.uk
Web: www.troubador.co.uk/matador

ISBN 978 1780884 127

British Library Cataloguing in Publication Data.
A catalogue record for this book is available from the British Library.

Typeset in 10pt StempelGaramond Roman by Troubador Publishing Ltd, Leicester, UK

Matador is an imprint of Troubador Publishing Ltd

Printed and bound in the UK by TJ International, Padstow, Cornwall

Money can't buy happiness, but I'd rather cry in a Ferrari.
Clare Booth Luce

Happy are those whose way is blameless.
Psalm 119

Happiness in intelligent people is the rarest thing I know.
Ernest Hemingway

Happiness sneaks in through a door you didn't know you left open.
John Barrymore

Some cause happiness wherever they go, others whenever they go.
Oscar Wilde

Some people walk in the rain, others just get wet.
Roger Miller

Happiness is a strange notion. I am just not made for it. It has never been a goal of mine; I do not think in those terms.
Werner Herzog

Happiness is good health and bad memory
Albert Schweitzer

Happiness is cuddling up on the sofa watching something recorded.
My daughter, Kay, Aged 9.

Family Tree

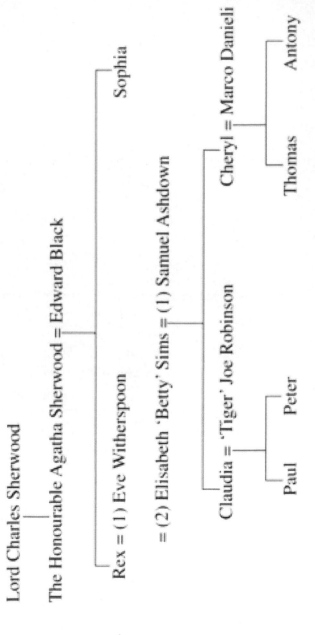

Lord Charles Sherwood

The Honourable Agatha Sherwood = Edward Black

Rex = (1) Eve Witherspoon

Sophia

= (2) Elisabeth 'Betty' Sims = (1) Samuel Ashdown

Claudia = 'Tiger' Joe Robinson

Cheryl = Marco Danieli

Paul

Peter

Thomas

Antony

Contents

Part One

Chapter One

The Wedding

Saturday 25th March 2008

"*I*, Elizabeth Estella Ashdown," says Betty, feeling a piercing stab of guilt knowing she is about to tell the biggest and wickedest lie of her life, "take you, Rex Franklin Black, to be my husband, to have and to hold from this day forward"... *but for how long, oh Lord?* "For better, for worse, for richer, for poorer,"... *at least there's no chance of that, the man's rolling in it,* "in sickness and in health,"... *I don't believe he's had a day's illness in his life,* "to love and to cherish, till death do us part."... *and may God forgive me. I will try to make him happy.*

Betty is taking her marriage vows for the second time round in her forty-five-year-old life, this time standing before the altar in the Church of Christ the King in Brighton, a city with a seriously tarnished reputation, which she is doing nothing to improve.

Her neat shapely legs stand in sensible high heels that match the cream taffeta dress her daughters assured her flattered her, which it does, for it is daringly low cut, revealing *la belle poitrine,* at which the more prudish in the congregation have raised eyebrows, but which Rex, and one or two other red-blooded gentlemen present, find delicious. On her blonde bob, freshly cut and coloured yesterday for the occasion, she wears a delightfully silly hat with a veil partially hiding her downcast eyes; she lifts them, treating Rex to the sight of the bluest eyes he has ever seen.

Sixty-six year old Rex Black, all 6 foot, 16 stone of him

perfectly fitted into an elegant morning suit, with his distinguished air and head of thick white hair looks robust, healthy and very happy. In fact, the pair appears the picture perfect epitome of senior happiness – but then appearances in life, as most of us know, are not always what they seem.

At this particular wedding, nothing is what it seems. Not that either party have lied to each other exactly, it's just that they have withheld the truth, consequently dishonesty is at work, each has a murky hidden agenda.

"You may kiss the bride," says the Rev Jones.

Relishing the occasion, Rex turns and plants his dry lips passionately upon hers. Betty squeezes his hand, half in an effort to restrain this public display of ardour, and half in an effort to turn him round to commence their walk back down the aisle.

Having delivered himself of such a legitimate smacker, Rex chortles victoriously. Betty knows better than to simper, so, like the game girl she is, she turns to face the congregation with a magic smile.

In the front row stand her two daughters grinning fit to bust, Claudia, a strong featured young woman with long brown hair, and Cheryl, a lovely looking girl with hair the colour of gleaming yellow straw. Both girls are the pride and joy of Betty's life, for she has a strong maternal nature and is fiercely proud of bringing them up as a single mother.

Alongside them stand 'Tiger' Joe, Claudia's slightly older husband, with their five-year-old twins Peter and Paul between them, and Marco, a shockingly good looking youth with a tumble of black gypsy hair who is Cheryl's boyfriend. Both men are tall, hunky specimens with carnations in their buttonholes, very bright ties and beaming white toothed smiles.

However, for each one, their exuberant expressions mask inner turmoil. Claudia has a drink problem, Cheryl is in love, 'Tiger' is in despair over his wife's drinking, and Marco, who is an actor, is out of work; the twins are exempt, for they have the innocent eye.

Across the aisle, a clue as to what is really happening at this ceremony is more visible. Here a more conservatively dressed group of witnesses regard the proceedings with long disapproving faces. Money is at the core of all their thoughts... *a pot of gold is going to the wrong sort of people.*

Two ladies sit alone in the front pew: Rex's eighty-five-year-old ramrod of a mother, The Honourable Mrs Edward Black, hard and unyielding, daughter of the late financier Lord Charles Sherwood, with her daughter, Sophia Black, a trim little body with a faint moustache, wearing the pinched expression of the headmistress of a Presbyterian girls' school. Seemingly as pious as they are respectable, they stand like black vultures, befitting their habit and nomenclature, in black fur coats, which flutter, like feathers, as they stand. As a concession to the joyful occasion, there is a peep of white lace circling their throats from the collar of their blouses. On their heads, they wear serious black hats, the brims shading their glinting eyes.

Beholding her son's happy face, Agatha purses her lips and Sophia inclines her head, such minimal gestures indicating resignation, rather than jubilation. As their bird like black eyes swivel to scrutinize the midlife interloper beside him, they glisten like voracious predators intent on feeding.

The wedding reception, on this windy Saturday afternoon, takes place in the ballroom of the Grand Hotel, a magnificent Victorian edifice standing on the coastal road between Brighton's two piers. The views through the full-length windows at the end of the room include the road, and over the esplanade the mesmerizing sight of the ever-crashing grey-green waves of the English Channel. The black skeleton of the West Pier, burnt and destroyed in March 2003, the present council unable to afford its removal, sticks up through the sea like the remnant of some long lost shipwreck, a perfect symbol of past glories and the harsh reality of life as it is today.

There are placement settings only at the top table, so the two hundred and fifty guests have been obliged to "sit as you please" at the twenty-five large round tables, where they sit feasting on a sumptuous spread.

There is a clear social divide in the room. The Black family consider the Ashdowns and their friends, composed of butchers, bakers, building workers and beachfront traders, as their social inferiors. The Ashdowns regard the Blacks as the town toffs, for they are an assembly of the senior burghers who run the city, the mayor, his councillors, a J.P., the Chief of Police, even the Deputy Lieutenant of the County, a lawyer, a dentist, and the family doctor, all accompanied by their wives decked out in their finest.

Nevertheless, with champagne constantly flowing and a general air of bonhomie, for everyone enjoys a wedding, there is laughter at the speech by the Chairman of the Golf Club, followed by ribald guffaws at the racier speech by the President of the Brighton Race Track, both speakers being lifelong friends of the groom.

No sooner has the final toast to the bride's daughters been drunk, than the orchestra strike up a selection from *Grease*, especially requested by the bride, indicating that the party can begin in earnest.

Rex leads Betty onto the dance floor, where they foxtrot rather inappropriately to the lyric "Summer Lovin', had me a blast." The groom suddenly suffers a coughing fit.

"Are you okay, dear?" asks Betty.

Choking and unable to answer, Rex lurches to a side table where his sister, Sophia, administers a glass of water.

Betty frowns: *Is that just a cough, or an indication of something more serious?*

Watching with interest and not a little amusement is his new son-in-law, 'Tiger' Joe Robinson, the husband of Betty's eldest daughter, Claudia. Turning to the concerned bride hovering on the dance floor he gives her a most unbefitting grin.

Joe is in his forties, with a well-shaped shaven head of salt and pepper stubble. He has merry twinkling eyes and enough charm and male testosterone about him to make every woman he meets check for a wedding ring on his finger and be just a little disappointed when they see the thick band of gold on his big workman-like hand.

Eight years ago, he worked as a brickie and road-mender, which was how Claudia first caught sight of him from her bedroom window, working on a pneumatic drill, stripped to the waist. She opened her front door and asked him in for a beer, and in the course of time, he became the father of both her sons. Joe has since become a very successful builder.

"Mind if I step in, mate?" he asks the choking groom.

Rex attempts speech, fails, but nods his assent.

Joe swiftly replaces him on the dance floor, grasping the soft rounded figure of his mother-in-law up in his arms and leading her surprisingly smoothly around the ballroom.

Mildly surprised, Betty recalls her mother's words: "If a man is a good dancer, he can probably do anything." *I believe Joe could.*

On the evening Claudia had introduced him, she had been surprised to meet a man nearer her own age than her daughter's.

"Ah, ha!" he'd said, with an exaggerated bow kissing her hand, "Now if I'd met this lady first, things might have been very different!" They'd all laughed and Betty had put the remark down to him ingratiating himself with her. Later on, when she learnt he was a foundling and had spent his boyhood in an orphanage, she guessed at the damage inflicted on him and forgave all his teasing. She has since grown very fond of him.

"Never got a chance to kiss the bride," he says, planting a kiss firmly on her cheek, then, somewhat abruptly, "So, y'gonna be happy with this old geezer, then?"

"Tiger Joe, you are dreadful!" she scolds, "He's a very sweet man."

"Paying for all this lot, I suppose?"

"Yes. Now stop it."

"Where you gonna be livin'? Moving in with him?"

"That's the plan. He has one of those beautiful Regency houses in Brunswick Square."

"Blimey, they're worth a bob or two. I worked on one of them once. Y'moving up in the world, gal."

"Rex says the square is one of the finest examples of Regency architecture in the country. Last year it was voted one of the top most picturesque squares in Great Britain."

"Well, whatever makes y'happy," he grins. "You'll be missin' y'old homestead though, I daresay?"

"No, not really, I have lived there twenty-five years after all, ever since I married Claudia's father. I admit it does get a bit lonely nowadays without the girls, but… "

Betty checks herself. Reluctant to admit just how miserable she's been these past months, she laughs and twirls gaily in Joe's arms wishing to avoid any further chat on the subject.

After the anxiety of ensuring her youngest daughter found a worthwhile husband, Cheryl took her totally by surprise three months before by announcing over the breakfast table, "I'm pregnant!"

Betty's stomach had lurched… *try to stay focused.*

"Now don't be cross, darling. I would never have allowed it to happen if I hadn't been prepared for the consequences. Marco and I are thrilled, really. He's asked me to move in with him."

"Move in with him!" Betty repeated, "Not get married?"

Cheryl's patient expression said, 'You are so old fashioned, Mum', but all she actually said was, "No, darling, just move in."

"It's a very different world from my day," sighed Betty, stirring her tea. "I don't know anything about him."

"I do, that's all that matters," answered Cheryl. "He's half-Italian, and I love him to bits. I want to be with him every day for the rest of my life. All my girl friends rate him number one on their Hot A list. You're going to love him. He plays guitar and is going to be a big star. I met him in the Line Dancing group at that fringe theatre in the north Lanes, remember, I told you?"

That dreadful place, full of dropouts and hippies. Wisely, Betty put on a brave face. "I'd better meet him, then."

The following afternoon Marco Danieli came to tea. He turned out to be a slim, hirsute youth with black hair and a piratical earring in each ear.

"Hi!" he said, shaking her hand. "Glad to know you."

Hardly film star material, judged Betty, but at least he spoke the Queen's English, and yes, he was young, attractive, and keen to make his way in the world, and who knows, one day he might. However, Cheryl's departure from home left Betty not only bereft but without anyone to cook or care for, something she'd done all her adult life. Desolate long years of loneliness seemed to stretch ahead. Living alone, she decided, in the home where she had always been so busy, was one of the trials of life she was not keen to prolong. Deprived of not only her daughter but her rent, she also experienced an alarming tightening of the belt.

So worried had she become about money, she had taken in a boarder. "It's either that," she'd joked to Cheryl, "winning the lottery or marrying a millionaire, and as neither of those are on the cards, it's a lodger." She also applied for a job as a cashier at Marks and Spencer's in the High Street, submitting to an interview. On the very morning she received their letter inviting her on a training session, Rex Black had telephoned requesting a rendezvous.

Rather as a duty, Betty was in the habit of meeting up occasionally with her husband's lonely old widower friend. Their habit was to stroll along the promenade and, weather permitting, take tea at The Meeting Place, a sea front cafe by the statue of the Mistletoe Lady. Such was the scene on the sunny, but chilly afternoon six weeks ago when Rex surprised her by popping the question. At that precise moment she'd been gazing out to sea admiring a young kite-surfer doing somersaults, unsure whether she'd heard correctly, she turned to him with a bewildered smile.

With his question hanging in the air, Rex placed his hand upon hers. "My dear, surely it can't come as that much of a surprise. Why do you think I chose today for our meeting?"

"Oh!" she exclaimed, "It's Valentine's Day. Rex, you amaze me. I never had you down as a romantic." Then, as the significance of what he had asked dawned on her, her heart skipped a beat, for her pragmatic nature sniffed security.

"If you say 'yes'," he continued, as if reading her thoughts, "I can assure you, you'll always be provided for, and," he paused, "I hope I'm not a totally dry old stick."

Snapping into focus, she acknowledged that though her daughters frequently teased her about her liaison with 'Uncle' Rex, it never occurred to her for a minute that anything serious would ever come about; Rex was from a different class and background, besides, he was an old man. Nevertheless, he was very comfortably off. *Hell! Rex Black is money, serious money. So best consider this seriously.* However, she found herself replying quite honestly, "I'm very fond of you Rex, but I don't love you."

Her admission did not dissuade Rex in his determination to make this warm hearted, efficient and very pretty woman, his wife; he had been a widower far too long. "Neither of us is getting any younger," he announced, ignoring the fact that Betty was twenty years his junior. "At our time of life it is important to have a pleasant companion by your side, to be warm and comfortable, and to be well looked after, and that, I can promise you, you will be."

As astonished as Betty had been by his offer, she did not wish to hurt his feelings by dismissing him outright. Besides, it was not every day an impecunious widow received a proposal of marriage from a millionaire. Not to appear too hasty and deeming a polite hesitation seemly, she replied, "Will you allow me to think it over?"

"My dear Elizabeth, of course, but for how long?"

"I'd like to discuss it with my girls. Let's say the same time next week. I'll give you my answer then."

Directly she arrived home, she lifted the telephone and dialled Marks and Spencer's administration department. "Elizabeth Ashdown speaking. Just to say I'm cancelling my appointment for tomorrow's training session... Yes, that is correct. My plans have altered. I am no longer seeking employment. Thank you." She replaced the receiver with a certain amount of satisfaction, and dialled up her daughters, summoning them to a family council.

Rather giving them the idea she had not yet made up her mind, she consulted them over a glass of sherry that evening. Both girls welcomed the news that their mother might marry 'Uncle' Rex, with enthusiasm, for not only would it relieve their anxiety about what was to become of her, but crucially, get her out of their busy and complicated lives. Besides, old 'Uncle' Rex was safe, he had been their father's friend and a part of their lives for as long as they could remember.

"Get that ring on your finger, Mum," Claudia advised, knocking back her Amontillado, then turning to her sister, "You too, if you've got any sense."

Coolly, Cheryl replied, "Marco doesn't want to get married. Anyway that sort of thing's not important these days."

"It will be to that illegitimate little bugger sitting inside you!" snapped Claudia.

"Now, now," admonished Betty, "We've been through all this. If Cheryl and Marco want to move in together, that is their business. Can we please confine the conversation to me for a change?"

The following week, once again over tea in The Meeting Place, Betty gave her answer.

"This past week," said Rex, extracting a small box from his pocket, "has been an eternity, but well worth it." Passing the box across the table, he added, "For you."

Betty opened it up to discover a diamond engagement ring nestling in the mock velvet. "Oh, Rex!" she cried.

"I did hope," he grinned, standing up and coming to her side of the table. Bending down and for only the second time in their relationship, planted a whopping wet kiss on her lips. The first occasion had been twenty-five years ago at a New Year's Eve party, attended by both their previous spouses.

This time, the experience was not as alarming as she had anticipated.

That was how today had come about. So, here she is, married again and dancing in Joe's arms. She glances across the ballroom at her new husband. His eyes are on her and she blows him a kiss. He is sitting between his white haired sister, Sophia, and Cheryl's handsome young boyfriend, Marco.

Rosa, Betty's next-door neighbour, a blowsy woman in a lizard-skin kaftan, jitterbugs past her. With a whooping laugh she cries, "This won't do me angina no good!"

Betty gives her a good-humoured laugh. Rosa has been a close and valued friend for years, a fellow widow, they have seen each other through many a crisis.

"If you like," says Joe, "I'll buy your old place off you. Tart it up, give it some posh fittings and sell it on. Make us a profit."

"Joe, that's very good of you. But I have to sell it at a good price. I couldn't possibly ask that from you, you're family. Actually, I've been meaning to tell you. I'm planning to give the money from the sale to Cheryl. I know you and Claudia won't mind, 'cause, well, Claudia has probably told you, Cheryl and Marco are expecting a baby in six months, and at the moment they're living in some grotty bedsit without two pennies to rub together."

"None of my business," he says, shrugging to the beat of the music.

"They don't have a lovely home like you do. Besides, if I give them this, they'll be able to get on the property ladder, have a place of their own, what with the baby coming and all."

"Mighty generous of you, luv, but what about yourself? Are you going to be okay?"

"Oh, Rex's stinking rich," she says, gleefully. "We're sailing from Southampton tonight on a cruise to the Mediterranean. I've never been on a cruise before."

"Claudia told me. But I meant are *you* going to be okay," he leans closer, lowering his voice, "moving in with that mother of his?"

"Oh, that won't be a problem. We're planning to turn the house into flats. Actually you might be interested in helping with the conversion?"

"Be glad to. Of course when I got married, I never had the opportunity of moving in with my mum-in-law… if I had… things might have been very different."

"Joe, really!" Leaning back she frowns at his grinning face. Used to his flirting, she decides to ignore it. "You can see the gardens and sea from all the front rooms. It's really beautiful. I intend having a blissfully happy old age."

"You're not old," says Joe, with a twinkle, his hands squeezing her waist, his mouth very close to her ear. "You're gorgeous."

Fully aware of her son-in-law's admiration, his masculine magnetism creates such worrying and disturbing thoughts in her, she extends her arms to separate her flesh from his gyrating body. *This whole wedding extravaganza is making me feel friskier than I've done for years. I do hope it's the champagne.*

Gaily waving to Rex again, she goes on dancing, her head telling her to ignore the apprehension she secretly feels in her heart, for she knows there will be no passion, no bliss, no love in this marriage, not like there was the first time round with Sam.

Chapter Two

Sam

"Throw us your bouquet," shouts one of the guests. "The bouquet, the bouquet." They all take up the chant. "Throw us your bouquet."

Laughing, Betty looks at the faces surrounding her. Spotting Cheryl, she thinks *no, too obvious*, so turns her back on them all and throws it high over her shoulder.

It lands on Rosa, Betty's next-door neighbour, who catches it and with a wickedly coy grin shrieks, "Now watch it all, you bachelors. I'll be after you!"

Upstairs in the bedroom Rex booked for them to change, Betty opens the balcony door and steps out on to the terrace. The wind has calmed, the cool sea air on her neck and arms is a relief from the heat of the ballroom, the exhaustion of having to be charming to everyone, of being in the spotlight, of pretending to be in love. *Blimey! Married again. After all these years!*

Looking out at the remnants of the burnt out West Pier reminds her of Eve, Rex's first wife. *She killed herself over there. 'Suicide while the balance of her mind was disturbed,' they said at the inquest, though no one has ever offered a reason to me why her mind was disturbed. She seemed perfectly sane to me. I cut out that article about it in the 'Evening Argus'…*

WOMAN'S BODY FOUND UNDER WEST PIER

Search divers found the body of a missing woman under West Pier in Brighton yesterday morning. Eve Black, 30, was last seen walking on the pier with her sister-in-law, Sophia Black, on Thursday morning, said her husband Rex Black, she has not been seen since. After an unsuccessful search Thursday night, authorities resumed their search Friday morning. Brighton Patrol dive teams found a woman's body matching the description of Eve Black underneath the pier shortly before noon. Family and friends of Black, who came to the pier early on Friday to assist in the search, were devastated when they heard the news. 'It doesn't make sense who goes. Life is so precious, that's why you have to enjoy each day, each moment because you never know when your card's going to be pulled,' said a friend who wished to remain anonymous. The medical examiner will confirm the identity of the body and is investigating the cause of death. Police do not know if it was accidental or if there was foul play. They are currently treating the case as a death investigation.

This newspaper cutting wasn't something Betty actually had on her, that was pasted in an album somewhere at home, but what we can't help remembering in life isn't necessarily what we have taken pains to learn.

That was in September,1989, just after Sam died.

Ironic that without meeting Sam, this new change in my life would never have happened.

Meeting Sam! Six foot two, thick yellow blond hair, with the body of a young Viking, just gorgeous. Life with Sam was heightened, brighter, better than being with anyone else, tastier... like his cooking. When it happened, I tried to numb the pain to forget, but what was the point? They were the best years of my life.

I was a nubile eighteen-year-old. It was the first Monday night screening of E.T. at the Odeon, West Street. Sam in a black leather jacket and grey T-shirt with the words 'Beam me up Scottie' emblazoned round a black and white Scottie dog. Standing next to him in the queue... flirting, buying our tickets and ushered into the back stalls as a couple... the musk of his masculinity. Hoping he'd hold my hand, but he was the perfect gentleman, until the end when I started crying. He slipped his warm hand into mine and squeezed. My emotions just fizzed. When the film was over, I longed for him to ask to see me again.

"Super film," he said as we stood up.

"Super."

Walking up the aisle: "Fancy a drink?"

"Yes, I'd like that."

Me going on about the film in the pub opposite over my lemon shandy, "When Elliot cycled over the moon with E.T, I just couldn't stop crying."

"When they said good-bye," he laughed, "I blubbed my eyes out, but then, I blub at most things."

I was astonished that such a manly type, leaning on the bar with his pint of beer, should admit to such a thing. "Such as?"

"Music. George Gershwin, Rachmaninoff, even the news, sometimes."

"You are funny. What do you do, I mean, for a living?"

"Training to be a chef, taking a cookery course at the City College. But I work in kitchens anywhere, go and cook for people wherever I can. How about you?"

"Doing a foundation course in nursing."

"The caring type, eh? What branch are you going into? Adult, mental health, or paediatric? Bet it's paediatric."

"How did you guess?"

"You look the Mumsie kind."

"Well, I do like babies. Is that good?"

"Sure, if a guy wants to be a Dad."

Oh, my God, seriously flirting. "Do you want to be a Dad?"

"Eventually," *he gazed into my eyes so coolly.* "Want to live a bit first." *He seemed to look right into me.*

"Me too," *I gulped my shandy.* "Trouble is the training takes another three years. Mum says it's poorly paid, she wants me to be a high-powered secretary, so I'm taking shorthand classes at Pitman's."

"Busy girl. I'd better get in quick. What's your phone number?"

I gave it and he wrote it down in his pocket book.

"E.T. phone home," *I said.* "Golly! Look at the time. Mum will be worried. I ought to be going, sorry."

"Would you like me to walk you home?"

No boy had ever offered to do that before. "Thanks. That would be nice."

"Not far, is it?"

I laughed. "About half a mile, West Drive by Queen's Park."

"Sorry, I suddenly had a vision of us walking miles. I know Queen's Park, I've played football there."

Walking along the sea front, he took my hand and linked it through his arm. It felt right somehow, walking arm in arm under the stars, under a new moon, heralding a new life. Did I sense then he would be so important in my life? I'd like to think so, but no. I just knew I wanted to be with him. "Where do you live?"

"A bed-sit in Hove," he answered. "My parents live in Barcombe near Lewes."

"Look at those twinkling lines of lights on the Palace Pier." I really meant 'didn't it look romantic'. I had the notion of us sitting together on the beach watching the moonlight on the sea, telling each other our life stories.

"We're lucky," he said, "the lights are usually out by this time. Someone's probably counting the pennies from the slot machines."

In the Old Steine we walked round the splashing fish fountain, water gushing up, spraying us in the floodlight. "This is the first time I've ever seen this working," I laughed.

"I told you, we're lucky."

Passing the onion-shaped domes of the Royal Pavilion silhouetted against the stars, walking home through the maze of streets. "You'll be glad to know this is my parents' house."

"I'm so glad I met you, Betty," he said. "You're lovely." Leaning in close he looked into my eyes before giving me the sweetest kiss. "'Night. Catch you later," and he was gone.

That night in bed, I thought he was the nicest boy I'd ever met.

Nine o'clock the next morning Mum calling up, "Betty, there's a man on the phone for you, says his name is Sam."

Rushing downstairs in my pyjamas to the phone in the hall, "Hello!"

"Good morning, Lovely! Fancy dinner on Wednesday? Seven thirty, English's, do you know it?"

"Of course, in East Street," I answered. "But it's very expensive. All the stage stars from the Theatre Royal go there."

"Well, on Wednesday it's going to be us. See you. I'll call for you at seven, okay?"

Dad, home from the shop, answered the doorbell. Sam in a blazer, looking so smart, but his mop of hair was still sticking up like a schoolboy. "My! You're a big lad," said Dad. "Mind you take care of her."

"Certainly will, sir. I'll bring her home by eleven o'clock."

"Think I might have seen your Dad somewhere before," he said, as we walked down the road. "What does he do?"

"Runs 'Sim's Newsagent's' in St James's Street."

"Of course! Know it well, that's where I buy my fags."

"Mum and Dad have run it for years."

In English's restaurant, half way through his lobster bisque: "What are you doing over the May Bank Holiday?"

"Don't know. Why?"

"Wondered if you'd like to spend it with me? My parents have a cottage in Barcombe. They're driving up to the Lake District over the weekend, so we'd have it to ourselves. What do you say? I've got my motorbike."

Carefully removing the spine bone from my Dover sole, knowing quite well what I was committing myself to... hopefully the loss of my tiresome virginity, I answered, "Love to, be fun."

Flying along on the back of his motorbike, holding him tight around the waist, which was about the most romantic thing I'd done up to then.

Reaching Barcombe, over his shoulder he shouted, "This village is mentioned in Doomsday book." We passed an old mill, then a pond, and reached a thatched cottage with roses round the door. "This is my parent's home."

Inside a low ceilinged living room, a great old-fashioned open fireplace. The armchairs and sofa all in the same chintz as the curtains; Sam's parents were obviously well off. Underneath the floor was a floodlit stream: through a thick glass window set in the floorboards we watched the water rippling over pebbles and an occasional trout swim past.

Sam with a box of tapes, playing "Duran Duran" and "Depeche Mode" on his parents' stereo.

"Got any Elton John?"

"Natch!" He put on "Too Low for Zero", and "I'm Still Standing". Fooling around, jiving. He cooked a whole salmon with spices wrapped in silver foil. After dinner, cuddling up with wine by the fireside listening to Rachmaninoff's Second Piano Concerto. For the first time the thrill of discovering a silver cord connection to another human being. That night making love and knowing I'd found him, found my fella.

Like the well-brought-up girl I was, I telephoned on Tuesday morning to thank him for his hospitality.

"Thanks, but over the weekend something terrible happened," he said, an odd note in his voice. "I told you my parents were driving up to the Lake District, well, I've just heard they had a car crash and... they're dead."

"Oh no! Sam, I'm so terribly sorry. I'll come over at once."

Dropping everything I rushed over to be with him.

From then on, we were seldom apart. At night, I always tried to get home to Mum, but I missed my period.

"Sam, I'm expecting. I'm going to have a baby."

His face grinning. "Marry me, Betty? I was going to ask you anyway, promise. Told you I wanted to be a Dad."

Seeing our engagement in print in the 'The Brighton and Hove Gazette', and a week later Sam getting that invitation.

"Rex Black and his wife are asking us to dinner."

"Who are they?"

"Friends of my Dad's. I've known Rex ages, since I was a boy *at Brighton College. Since Dad died, he's rather taken it upon himself to see I'm 'well placed', as he calls it, but he's awfully nice. He's the guy who proposed me for the East Brighton Golf club, remember? Said Dad would have liked it. Be good P.R. It's true, I've met some great guys there and it's opened doors. When I was a lad, he took me horseracing, right into the Premier enclosure! 'Please bring along your fiancée,' he says, 'we would all so like to meet her. Dinner will be at eight'."*

First meeting the Black family in their grand house in Brunswick Square: Rex and his wife, Eve, sweet smelling, with dark hair, she wore an elegant soft grey dress, I remember. "You're so pretty," she said, shaking my hand. But I felt uncomfortable with Rex's snobbish sister and mother, but with Sam around nothing was ever awkward for long. In the end the three hours we spent at dinner turned out to be very pleasant.

Hove Registry office a month later, the thrill of marrying Sam.

Rex and Eve came, with his sister, Sophia – all sitting smiling in the front row – but they never asked us again to their beautiful home.

Then on New Year's Eve, there was that party at the Golf Club. Rex invited us to join his table. I danced with Sam. Later we swapped partners... Sam with Eve, and I danced with Rex. On the stroke of midnight, he gave me that disgusting wet kiss. Oh, Lord! I thought, the old codger fancies me!

Moving into Holland Street, our dear little three up, three down, Sam bought with the sale of his parents' pretty, but impractical Barcombe cottage.

Settling down to married life and discovering just what a happy nature and fine character my Sam possessed. He was my teacher, my university, my everything. Encouraging me to read Orwell, Aldous Huxley, Dickens, Wilkie Collins, opening my ears to classical music and opera.

The excitement when he got the job of cook at The Albion.

Completing my nursing foundation course.

Completing my Pitman's secretarial course.

Giving birth to Claudia, and four happy years later pregnant again.

Sam saying, oh so casually, one morning, "A group of my adventurous chums at the Golf Club have asked me to join them on a skiing trip to the Austrian Tyrol. You wouldn't mind if I joined them, would you?"

"Sam, have I ever held you back from your sports? You must do your own thing. I have no desire to ski whatever, besides, there is Claudia to look after, and look at my tum, I'm cooking!"

A week later three husky lads arriving in a Shooting Brake with skis strapped on top to take him to Gatwick airport.

Kissing him goodbye. "Promise to send us a post card."

"I promise."

The last time I ever saw him.

That poor little bald man from the golf club arriving in a big car. On the doorstep, in sombre tones, "I am afraid I am the bearer of grievous news. I have something of a serious nature to impart regarding our skiing party that visited the Austrian Tyrol. May I come in?"

Knowing what was coming, gripping the banister.

"I am very much afraid to tell you Sam Ashdown has met with a fatal accident. He fell to his death at the ski resort of Bad Gastein yesterday. They have found his body; arrangements are being made for him to be flown home tomorrow. Please accept our profound condolences."

Sinking onto the stairs sobbing my heart out.

Suddenly alone in the world, and a mum. My own darling Mum and Dad had gone by then. The most terrifying time of my life. How could God be so cruel? Pregnant with Cheryl, raging with love and grief, and no idea what the future would bring.

Meeting his body at Gatwick, and the next day the crematorium, with Claudia. Will I ever forget it?

Writing letters to tell people.

Cheryl's premature birth. That awful fever and depression afterwards. The doctor's face, "It is a complication that means it is unlikely you will be able to have more children." How could he ever say that to me, a young widow?

Reading the article in hospital about Eve's death in the Evening Argus.

Writing to Rex to express my sympathy.

Him visiting me in hospital: "How very considerate of you to take the trouble, in your grief, to pen that kind letter to me."

"And of you to come and see me."

"When you get home, we must keep in touch. You must allow me to offer you tea sometime? There's a new sea-front cafe just opened on the promenade."

That's how our friendship began. Over the years we don't seem to have found much in common, yet here we are married.

"What the blazes are you doing out there?" Rex shouts. "It's cold. Close the door. Aren't you dressed yet? We're on a schedule here, get cracking, gel."

Chapter Three

Bon Voyage

25th March 2008

At the far end of the ballroom, a sunbeam, bright as a spotlight, catches Sophia Black's silver white hair as she sits looking out of the window. Absently fingering a slim gold chain round her neck, her bright, intelligent eyes gaze curiously at the guests assembling on the front steps outside waiting to wish the bride and bridegroom bon voyage.

"Look at those two girls," she says. "It's so strange. Well, they're grown-up women, now."

"Ssh, dear!" says her mother. "Don't upset yourself."

"I'm not upset. I just think it's funny, in a sick sort of way. I've been watching them all afternoon."

"I know you have, dear," Agatha sighs.

"The younger one, Cheryl, is so pretty, but I noticed Claudia has been drinking rather heavily. I wonder if she's unhappy."

"I knew we shouldn't have come."

"In the circumstances we could hardly have done otherwise. Besides, I'm curious. It's just so odd. There they are, and they don't even know who I am."

"And that is the way it has to stay," hisses Agatha, her eyes glaring meaningfully. "I knew this was a dreadful idea from the very beginning."

A muffled cheer reaches them from outside.

They turn to see the honeymoon couple arriving at the top of the steps.

"Oh, dear!" says Sophia, "she's changed into shocking pink. She looks like a pink blancmange. Oh no! They've tied tin cans to the back of the Bentley!"

Agatha closes her eyes in horror and moves away. "At least we can now leave. Come."

"She's not really coming to live with us, is she, Mama?"

"I'm afraid it seems very likely."

Sophia glances back to her brother with his bride by his side. *Look at the grinning, bovine woman. I could tell her a few home truths that would make her blood curdle, wipe the smile off her face. I might just do that. Drop a few hints there are a few weeds in the garden that she seems to think is so rosy.* "Well, of course," she says, "we have to support Rex."

Agatha shoots her a look, and departs.

Last month Agatha made it perfectly clear to her son that she did not approve of his marriage. "Why, of all the women in the world, you have to choose Sam Ashdown's widow to marry, is quite beyond me."

However, what she was particularly concerned about was his new wife taking up residence with them in Brunswick Square. Born in 1923, the late child of Edwardian parents, Agatha Black was a woman for whom the term "generation gap" might have been invented. Convinced she had the right not only to control her children's actions but their opinions and emotions, she had learnt many years before that Rex was his own man and, in spite of anything she might say, would do exactly as he wished. Nonetheless, her nature is such that she persists in attempting to dominate him.

"Mrs Ashdown," she asserted, embedded in her favourite Victorian armchair, "is not our sort. We are from two different worlds. She comes from a completely different background. Her education and milieu are dissimilar. We are poles apart. She will be unused to our ways. She will be like an alien, and if she has any sort of sensitivity, will feel most uncomfortable. Not to mention any feelings Sophia may have about her."

A heated discussion had followed during which Rex had pointed out that by converting their house into separate apartments it would solve the problem, avoid friction, and enable their lives under the same roof to be more convivial. Agatha argued that, "The whole character and beauty of the house will be destroyed if builders are permitted to knock it about." Reluctantly, she had acceded to his wish that an architect should draw up plans, after which they would think again.

All this had disheartened Rex, but like the imperious fellow he was, he was loath to share his misgivings with Betty.

Among the milling guests on the hotel steps outside, Marco Danieli throws a handful of confetti over a smiling Betty in her new pink travelling suit.

"The management said no confetti!" reprimands Cheryl. "Here, give us some."

He does, and she throws it over her mother. "God bless, Mumma!"

Ducking, Betty calls out, "You, young man! Mind you take care of her."

"Promise," shouts Marco. "Bon voyage."

"And eat sensibly," she urges her daughter. "Remember," she mouths, "you're eating for two!"

"Stop nagging! Have a super time. Love you."

"Me too," she mouths again.

"Get in, girl!" says Rex, holding the car door open. "Come on."

"Wait." Betty searches for Claudia among the crowd. She

catches her eye and blows her a kiss, only then does she step into the front seat.

Rex closes the door behind her and amid cheers and catcalls, self-consciously makes his way around the front of his Bentley to the driver's seat.

Joe watches him ruefully. "Bloody hell!" he mutters to his wife. "He's not driving, is he? I thought he had a chauffeur."

"Why shouldn't he drive?" Claudia rounds on him. "He's not drunk."

"At least he's more sober than you! Get yourself some black coffee, woman."

"It is my mother's wedding day, for God's sake. I am allowed to have a drink."

"Or nine!"

"You are sooo boring. I'm going back... " she stumbles over the steps, "for another drink."

Joe ignores her. He has eyes only for Betty in the shiny Bentley as it moves off into the main road, pulling the tin cans he and Marco have tied to the back bumper. Waving, he wonders... *however is she going to be happy with that old man?*

Chapter Four

The Honeymoon

"Where are my glasses?" asks Rex, settling in behind the wheel.

"In your top pocket," answers Betty.

He fumbles behind his handkerchief and finds them. "Well, gel, we did it!" He turns on the ignition and slaps Betty on the knee. "Whoops! Concentrate… I think I'm a little skwiffy." Grabbing the steering wheel, he manoeuvres out into the main road. "What the blazes is that racket?"

"Heavens! I think they've tied tin cans to the back of the car."

"Damn! I'll have to stop and cut them loose. Bloody row!"

"It's only a joke. They meant well."

"Your friends are all very noisy, catcalling and yelling at me like that."

"Well, they're young. Weren't you like that once?"

"Never."

Betty looks at him.

He melts. "Well, maybe."

After a beat she says, "Come to that, your Mother and Sophia were very quiet, they barely spoke to me."

"You have to make allowances for Sophia. She'll come round."

Betty puts her head on one side. "Why?" She considers Sophia and Agatha's aloof manner at the Reception distinctly rude. Not for one minute though has she considered the ramifications of marrying into such an upper middle class family such as theirs, a family defined by background rather than by a job or income; if she had, and not been blinded by greed, or as she saw it, her need for security, she might not have been so surprised. "Why should I make allowances for Sophia?"

Rex clenches his jaw. "Can we not talk about Sophia right now?"

A car comes level. The driver leers out of his window and gives them a wolf-whistle.

"Better cut these damned things loose," he mutters, stopping the car and getting out.

When Rex was a golden lad in Rhodesia, he learnt always to carry a Swiss army penknife, an ingenious gadget with awl, scissors, corkscrew, a file and so on; he has never lost the habit. These days it is a slim silver-plated two-blade job with a night light, which he now slips open to cut loose the tin cans, kicking them into the gutter.

"Litter lout," yells a passing white van driver.

Crossly, Rex gets back in the car.

Betty notices his jaw muscles flinching as he speeds up chasing the white van. At the King Alfred swimming pool in Hove, he succeeds, but nearly crashes into an oncoming lorry. "Fucking hell!"

Betty raises her eyebrows. Not that she is a prude, she is made of sterner stuff than that, but it occurs to her that in all the years she has known him can she cannot recall him swearing. She realises with a sickening certainty that she doesn't really know the man she's married at all. She doesn't know what makes him tick, nor seen behind the courteous *bonhomie* mask he presents to the world. Unsure how to react to this swearing, speeding, changed creature sitting beside her, she remains silent for a few miles, only her clenched white knuckles indicating her anxiety. After another near miss, she coos in a controlled voice, "There's no need to rush, darling. We have plenty of time."

"Do shut up, woman."

Stunned as if slapped, she stares ahead, crushed.

If Rex is aware of her discomfort, he does not show it; his silence may indicate regret, but he is not a man to apologise.

Her mother's voice echoes again in her head. *'Men change character once they get behind a wheel'.*

On reaching Southampton docks, the bags are unloaded, the car keys given to a parking valet, and they are ushered into a hanger-like reception area with hundreds of other passengers.

"Please wait till your colour is called, sir," says a female official, handing them a yellow card.

"Would you be so good," Rex replies with the utmost gentility and in a tone of authority, "as to allow my wife and myself on board immediately."

Betty smiles to herself. *This is more like the man I know.*

Rex is not a man to throw his weight about, no jumped-up *parvenu,* but on the other hand, he is used to getting his own way.

The official looks up at him surprised. Recognizing something... a person of quality perhaps, she stammers, "One moment, please," and leaves them to confer with someone behind a desk.

"Just one moment," Rex says to Betty.

Guessing Rex will come out on top, but intrigued to know what will happen if he doesn't, she watches with interest as a scowling official approaches from behind the desk. "What seems to be the trouble, sir?"

"No trouble at all," says Rex, magically transferring a ten-pound note into the man's palm, "we simply wish to board straight away."

Without so much as a glance at the denomination of the note in his hand, the demeanour of the official smoothly transforms. "If I may take a copy of your credit card and signature, sir, I'll see what can be done."

Rex passes over his card and, at the desk, signs his signature.

"James!" calls the official, handing it back with two key-cards. "Escort Mr and Mrs Black through security, will you. Thank you, sir, enjoy your cruise."

"My profound thanks to you, sir," announces Rex, ushering Betty ahead, and breezily proceeding to the boarding entrance.

That evening in the dining room, another "incident" illustrates the character of the man she has married.

Betty had been unprepared for the dress code required at dinner on board until Rex showed her the brochure. Only possessing one evening dress and unable to afford another (the cost of the pink travelling suit having emptied her bank account), she confided her problem to her next-door neighbour, Rosa, who opened up her wardrobe for her. "Don't worry, luv. Take a couple of my kaftans and this silver wool shawl; it's very effective, certainly covers up my multitude of flesh!" Betty had accepted her offer gratefully.

"People don't dress up on the first night," says Rex, "just go smart casual.'

Betty decides her pink angora sweater with pearls and tan skirt is the ticket. On the Booking Form Rex had requested the second sitting and a table for two. The plan at the restaurant door reveals they are at a table for six.

Reading his face, she recognises his fury. Notwithstanding, "Please change it," is all he politely asks the Head Waiter.

"Impossible for tonight's sitting, sir," says the Head Waiter. "If you follow me, I'll see what I can do for tomorrow."

Following reluctantly they take their seats. Their companions are two pleasant, and it transpires, extremely wealthy, middle-aged couples. One elegant lady from Maida Vale wears a black sequined dress, dripping diamonds in her ears and glittering jewels on her fingers, the other lady from Norfolk in a thick polo sweater, says. "I do apologise for wearing this, I've not had time to unpack yet."

Betty notices her wrists and fingers are crammed with jewels. Fingering her own single string of pearls, she forces herself to make small talk.

Disguising his feelings, Rex appears relaxed and full of charm, the perfect gentleman; but then comes another coughing fit, like the earlier one at the wedding.

"We'll have to take care of that," says Betty handing him a glass of water, patting his back and wondering again if this is an indication of something more serious.

"It's nothing," he splutters.

"I hope not, but you don't have to be an advanced registered nurse to recognize a bad cough."

"Oh, are you a nurse?" enquires the lady in sequins.

"Not anymore, but I can still tie a tourniquet and weald a hypodermic!"

On their way out, they pass the Head Waiter. "Tell him we're on our honeymoon," says Betty, "he's bound to give us a table for two then."

"It's our own private business," Rex mutters. "Where's the Casino?"

Betty loathes gambling. Sam had been a gambler and lost a great deal of their money on horses and cards, on many occasions accompanied by Rex Black. Careful not to sound a spoilsport, she answers, "Not just now, dear, do you mind? Maybe another evening?"

Rex looks at her and leers. "Wanting bed? Me too. Long day."

She realises he has misunderstood her meaning. Resigned to the inevitable, she allows him to take her hand and lead her to their stateroom.

Then occurs the most interesting and surprising development.

Rex proves himself, if not a dynamo in the bedroom, a most proficient lover.

"I never dreamed such things were possible," he whispers afterwards on their sumptuous double bed. "You banish my worries and make me feel a young man again."

"What worries can you have, Rex?" she murmurs.

"Ones I've had most of my life; finances, wheeling and dealing. Now it's hedge funds, derivatives, private equity companies, and these bloody banks collapsing. Still, nothing for you to worry your pretty head over, give us a kiss."

Years ago his condescension would have maddened her, now, older and wiser, she ignores it, and kisses him, bathing in the sinuous pleasure of being in a man's arms, of being on board a luxury liner, of being taken care of, of being rich.

The honeymoon night having proved a success, after breakfast they stroll arm in arm around the Promenade Deck. Betty is flushed with happiness, exalting in the immense ocean extending to the far horizon, the endless sky and clean oxygenated air. "We've just walked a mile," she says pointing to a placard announcing "Three laps, a mile."

"My bones," smiles Rex, apologising for his age, "that's me done."

Strolling through the shopping arcade, he stops at the jewellery counter and sits down. "Take a look, girl. Choose what you like."

"Rex! Are you sure? I'd prefer it if you choose for me."

"I'm no good at that sort of thing. The place is reputable. Go on. Choose the best. Allow me to spoil you."

Looking into his adoring eyes, she reflects that he does appear to love her with a passion. Perhaps the passion of an old man gathering the energies of his being into one last effort of tenderness? *Well, here goes. Make the most of it!*

For the next half hour, like a gleeful little girl in a toyshop, she sits happily trying on rings, earrings, necklaces and bracelets. She does indeed choose the best, at least her choices are certainly the most expensive, but she is careful to check Rex's approval. "Are you sure? This is so dear of you."

He finally pays the assistant a sum just short of six thousand pounds for four items: a Jasmine eternity ring, a gold eighteen-carat diamond ring, a diamond tennis bracelet, and a fine yellow gold necklace.

"Good morning's work," he remarks walking away. Then comes the kicker. "Mind you wear them tonight at dinner. Show those people at the table what you're made of."

It is only then she realises she has been bought; not that her feeling is hostile, after all, she did sell herself very willingly.

As the great liner cuts and crashes through the Bay of Biscay, they lunch high up on the eight floor at the self-service Belvedere restaurant. Sitting by a plate-glass window with nothing but the sky and turbulent ocean beneath, Betty decides to speak about something that has been bothering her. "Can you tell me about Sophia, now? It's years since I first met her with Sam and Eve. Remember that evening when we came to dinner?"

Rex stirs his coffee. "Indeed, I do."

"After all," she continues, "if I'm going to have to live with her, at least for a while, until we get this flat conversion sorted out, unless"… and this is what she really wants… "we get a place of our own."

"No, Elizabeth," he answers firmly. "That is not going to happen. I could never leave Brunswick Square. Never leave Sophia or Mother."

"No, no, of course not… " she pretends to understand, and yet… a man of sixty-six still living with his mother… "Why?"

Rex hesitates and pulls his ear lobe.

She realises he is uncomfortable but she wants an answer and waits.

"It's a long story, Elizabeth."

"We have nothing else to do."

Reluctantly Rex appears to come to a decision. "I'm only telling you this to help you understand. You are now part of the family, but… it must never be spoken of again, you understand?"

"Of course."

"How to begin?" he asks himself. "Sophia wasn't always the little old lady you saw yesterday, y'know, oh no… there was a time… " his eyes flicker to the horizon. "My goodness! When I first saw her… 'Cause we never knew each other, y'know, not while we were growing up. My parents separated when I was a boy, not that they were divorced, that would never have done, not in those days. I was only seven when Papa took me to live with him in Salisbury. That's Harare, as it now is, in Zimbabwe, then, of course it was Rhodesia. We had a farm and I had the most wonderful life. Grand it was, just perfect. Anyway, when he died, I had to come home and earn myself a living. Fortunately, my Grandpapa found me a place in the City."

"Was that Lord Sherwood, the big financier."

"Yes, he was my mother's father, Lord Charles, a dear man."

"I remember Sam telling me."

"I was only nineteen at the time, that's when I first met Sophia. She was seventeen and so pretty, had fluffy blonde hair. She was at Brighton Art College at the time and in love with some fellow student. An American, he was; this was in 1965, when America was drafting its young men to fight in the war in Vietnam. Anyway, marriage was on the cards, but along with so many other young Americans at the time, they repatriated him home, drafted him into the army and sent him to Vietnam. Sophia never heard from him again. Seven months after he left, she gave birth to a baby."

"Oh no!" gasps Betty. "Was it a boy or a girl?"

"A girl," answers Rex. "Of course, the disgrace at the time was harsh, humiliating. Mother, was on the board of some orphanage committee; she made enquiries and it was arranged that the baby would be adopted. However, there was a snag, a big one. The couple who adopted the child lived in Brighton. Sophia even knew the woman slightly; they'd been at Roedean Girls' College together, a Jewish girl by the name of Roberta, like the title of that musical with Fred Astaire and Ginger Rodgers."

"Oh, I know that. Irene Dunne is in it, too."

"Mmm, I'm sure." Only by the faintest blink, does Rex indicate his irritation at her interruption. "On several occasions, she told me, she passed her in the street, wheeling her very own baby in a pram. Once, she said, while she was out shopping in Sainsbury's. Other times when she was walking along Hove promenade, she always hurried by, unable to acknowledge her own child. I think the pain dried her up, she took to staying in, afraid to leave the house in case she bumped into them. Mother, all of us, tried to encourage her to get out, but... well, she became a recluse. Oh, she's okay now. She goes out and about, does the shopping with old Mrs Hunt, our housekeeper."

"Mrs Hunt? I don't think I've met her. Was she at the wedding at all?"

"Yes. Yes, I'm sure she was."

"I must make a point of saying hello. Sorry, go on."

"Anyway, my dear Sophia suffered for her indiscretion; that of having sexual relations before marriage. But at least, I've been able to provide a decent life for her. People have forgotten about it now, but it's taken a long time." Staring into his empty coffee cup, he says, "Do you want some more coffee?"

"How dreadfully sad." Despite her interruptions, Betty has listened intently, but has many questions, the least of which is...

why did this make her so cold with me yesterday at the wedding? She sees two large tears about to drop from Rex's eyes and she checks herself. As he turns his face away from her, searching the horizon for who knows what, she thinks maybe she should leave him alone. Let him have some time to himself, after all, they have been in each other's company now solidly for well over twenty-four hours. "I think I've drunk enough coffee, bless you," she answers, putting her hand on his. After a moment she adds, "I think I'll pop down to that theatre and film quiz on Deck Three, they were telling us about. It's starting up in a minute. You'll be alright on your own for a while?"

Rex nods. "Bit pooped! You go and enjoy yourself. I'll put my feet up out on deck."

Betty kisses him and leaves him to his thoughts.

Chapter Five

Rex

*R*ex lies in a deck chair on the Promenade deck congratulating himself. *That seemed to go off all right. She believed me. Could never have told her the truth, of course. It was the truth killed poor little Eve.*

For the ten thousandth time he remembers his first wife Eve. Her youth, her sweetness, the pain and shock he gave her that caused her death. *Heaven knows I don't deserve it, but God has been good to me. Let's pray he allows me to enjoy all this for as long as possible. If last night is anything to go by, this marriage with Elizabeth could work out better than likely. Two to three years, he said. Lou Gehrig's disease! Whoever heard of such a thing? Old Lou himself, I suppose.*

Smiling, he fishes in his pocket for his pills, Riluzole, to slow the disease's progression, so Dr Woodcock had said, and diazepam, to treat the muscle stiffness. He takes one of each pill, downs them with whisky from his silver hip flask, readjusts the rug over his knees, and closes his eyes luxuriating in the combination of warm liquor trickling down his throat and the chill fresh air in his lungs.

How long will I feel this good? How many days do I have left? Make the most of them. Can't go on. His thoughts slip back two months to the interview with Dr Woodcock in his well-appointed consulting rooms in Harley Street.

"Rex, you have what is called Amyotrophic Lateral Sclerosis."

"What the hell is that?"

"Also known as Lou Gehrig's disease. It is a degenerative disease for which, I fear, there is no known cure."

"But... how... why? How did I get it?

"It could be genetic, but 90% of patients suffer for unknown reasons."

"Tell me... " he stumbled, "what in God's name is going to happen to me. I must know what to expect."

"It is a neurological disorder characterised by muscle weakness that gets worse over time. This would explain the recent swallowing difficulty you've been having. The symptoms include breathing troubles, gagging, speech problems. It will spread to the rest of your body. You will have weight loss, trouble lifting and walking, and eventually it will lead to paralysis."

"What the hell are you telling me, Doctor? Bloody hell! Excuse me, but...

"I understand. It is a difficult thing to take on board."

"So how long do I have?"

"Two, maybe three years."

Numbly he stared at the desk unable to feel or think clearly. After a moment, through a blind haze, something told him to be pragmatic, for Rex was always a businesslike fellow. "So... what can I do about it?"

"I can prescribe certain medications; you could try some physical therapy, low impact exercises. In a year or two you may require a brace and certainly a wheelchair to move about, and of course, you will need careful nursing."

"I see... "

Receiving such appalling news did not make Rex angry; the single thought in his head as he continued to be civil and shake hands, was how much he loved his life, his family, Sophia and even Agatha. *But I cannot tell them. It would make what time I have left unbearable for them.*

Outside in Harley Street, he closed Dr Woodcock's glossy black front door with the brass nameplates and stood on the doorstep. *I'm a dead man.* Taking a deep breath, he walked toward Oxford Street. Through the bewilderment and confusion in his head, he sought some practical solution. *How the hell can I go on living with Lou bloody Gehrig inside me growing stronger, while I get weaker? I will not be sorry for myself. I hate that. I will just have to fix it so I'm looked after properly. Can't expect Mother or Sophia to nurse me, be too much for them, especially for Sophia's delicate sensibilities. I need someone strong, efficient, yet sympathetic. None of the staff at home are suitable. There really is only one candidate... Sam's wife. Elizabeth Ashdown. She mentioned to me once she had nursing experience. But how on earth do I ask her to do such a thing?*

"There you are!" Betty's laughing voice cuts through his thoughts. "I've been looking all round the deck for you. Sorry, darling, did I wake you?"

"Elizabeth, my dear. No, no, I was just dozing. How did you get on?"

"I won! All my theatre going and telly watching finally paid off. Look at my prize, a P and O fountain pen!"

"Such riches! I always knew you were a clever girl." He clasps her hand and she sits down in the deckchair next to him. "I was just thinking, my dear, you and I have never discussed money."

"I was taught that was rude."

"My Grandpapa taught me the opposite," says Rex with a grin. "For money to work, options have to be discussed. I'm going to make you an allowance. On the 25th of every month, my bank will transfer £1000 into your bank account. I hope that will be satisfactory?"

"Rex! That is so dear of you," she says, embracing him. "I only hope I'll prove worthy of it."

"Oh, you will, my dear. You will."

Chapter Six

Homecoming

8th April 2005

"*Y*ou're back!" cries Cheryl, standing at her ironing board. "How was the cruise, and how are you?"

"Just great," laughs Betty, always keen to strike a positive note. "More importantly, how are you doing?"

"Right now, being a domestic goddess ironing." Clamping the cell phone to her ear to block out the sound of Marco's keyboard playing on the other side of the room, she waves at him to stop. "I just want to lie in bed and eat popcorn all day. I've started throwing up in the mornings!"

"Oh, darling! But it is par for the course, I'm afraid. Any work for your boy friend yet?"

"Nothing, but he's working hard at his music, as you can probably hear."

"Is that what it is? Listen, darling, I been thinking. I've been such a ninny. I should have asked you to housesit while I was away. You could have moved back home. I only thought of it after I'd given the estate agents the keys, and then I forgot all about it. I've just spoken to them and there's still not a sign of a sale. They tell me 'there's a down turn in the market.'"

"Are you serious? I mean about us moving back home?"

"Why not? It's just sitting there empty. It seems crazy when the two of you are having to rough it in that wee studio of Marco's."

"Studio is something of a euphemism, Mumma!"

"How would Marco feel?"

"I'll ask him." With her hand over the mouthpiece, she shouts, "Shut up!" Marco stops playing. "Mother's asking us to house-sit. You'd love to, wouldn't you?"

"What?" asks Marco, trying to hang on to a tune in his head.

"Move into mother's house till she sells it?"

"Long as she's not in it."

"He'd love to," says Cheryl.

"Let's arrange it, then," says Betty. "Have you seen Claudia?"

"Not since the wedding. I think there's some kind of drama going on with her and Joe."

"Oh dear! Why, what's happening?"

"She'll tell you. Can we meet up tomorrow at the house then? Say at eleven? We'll talk it through?"

"Let's do that. 'Bye, darling." Betty clicks off the connection and speed dials her eldest daughter. *Whatever's been going on with Claudia and Joe? What's wrong with me? Let them go. Stop being mother and father to them. Growing up without a Dad is probably why she married a father figure like Joe. She always was the difficult one, making dramas out of nothing. Kicking those legs of hers inside me. Sneaking through my handbag, little devil!* Claudia's answering machine clicks in.

"Claudia, pet. Just to tell you I'm back safe and sound. Hope you and the boys are well. Give us a buzz. Love you."

Next, she tries Claudia's landline.

Joe hears his wife's mobile ringing in her handbag, ignores it and continues staring at her lifeless form lying in their bed. Having given his sons breakfast, taken them to school, he is now back, but Claudia is still out of it.

The bedside phone rings. Reluctantly he picks it up. "Hello!"

"Joe!"

"I know that voice. How's my beautiful Mum-in-law, and how was the honeymoon?"

"Fabulous! The cruise, that is."

"Well, I didn't think you meant the old man."

"Tiger Joe, now you stop that! I want to talk to Claudia. How is she?"

Joe hesitates. When he had told his wife of Betty's plan to give the money from the sale of her house to Cheryl, Claudia had hit the roof. "She promised me half that money!" she wailed, "promised the money would be split between us. Why should Cheryl get it all?"

"Because we have a house and Cheryl hasn't."

"That's just an excuse," she barked, "not the reason!" Grabbing a bottle from the sideboard, she'd been off again on one of her devil-may-care immersions in gin. "Cheryl always was Ma's favourite. She's given in to her all our lives. Ever since schooldays, about clothes, food, holidays, everything, now this. Our own home, the whole bloody caboose. It makes me sick. If I hadn't got so used to it over the years, I'd be crying my eyes out, I really would. Never mind how we've had to struggle to hold things together with the twins. Oh no, it's 'Cheryl must have this', 'Cheryl must have the other.' Bloody Cheryl, she makes me sick!" She filled her glass with gin and sank on to the sofa in misery.

Ever since Claudia had cut Cheryl's blond curls off at the age of six, their relationship had never been good. When Cheryl was born, Claudia had been four and a half years old and spoilt. As they grew up, chubby Claudia, with her long face and lank brown hair, grew envious of her sister's slim prettiness and curls, but most of all, of her mother's lavish love for Cheryl. Cheryl, in turn, became jealous of Claudia's friends and toys, which Claudia never allowed her to play with; consequently, the two had seldom enjoyed a loving sororal affinity.

Claudia's excuse for drinking was that Joe messed around with other women. Joe's excuse for messing around was that his wife drank… a chicken and egg situation. So far, he was the only one who had guessed Claudia was an alcoholic.

"This love affair you are having with the bottle is poisoning your life," he'd told her, "and our marriage is heading for the rocks. Go get yourself to AA, they'll help you."

"AA!" she'd shrieked scornfully. "How dare you! Take the beam out of your own bloody eye before blaming me for our marriage being a failure."

Joe had considered asking Betty for her help… *but how do you tell a mother her daughter is a lush?*

Her eyes flutter open.

Joe covers the mouthpiece, "It's your mother, can you talk?"

She moans and buries her face in the pillows.

"I'll get her to call you when she surfaces," he tells Betty.

"Thought I'd pop round this afternoon," she continues, "if that's alright? I have some gifts for the boys."

"You're a dear! Look, luv, sorry, but I'm already late for work. I have to dash. 'Bye. Claudia will call you back."

Looking at his wife's bloated face he doubts she will.

Betty pops her mobile into her handbag; she is in Rex's private study, the room next to his bachelor bedroom where she has slept her first night under his roof in Brunswick Square. She noses round the knick-knacks on his desk reluctant to go downstairs, for she knows Rex is taking coffee with his mother in the morning room. Now that the architect's plans for the flat conversion are available, Agatha has had time to reflect and has demanded another meeting.

With the drawings spread across the table, Rex, looking well and tanned after his cruise, is explaining the crucial difference, from his mother's point of view, will be that her sleeping quarters will change from the Master suite on the second floor, to his own smaller suite on the third.

"Certainly not!" she snaps from a high backed Victorian armchair, her features compressed like an uncrackable walnut. "My bedroom is my inner sanctum. I do not intend being moved about like a piece of furniture to accommodate the whim of a shop girl. Move upstairs indeed, after all these years! Who does she think I am, a serving gal?"

Rex's features set like granite. He glares at her with his formidable Chairman of the Board glare.

It has no effect whatever.

"Mother," he says, retaining his composure, "I will not have you refer to Elizabeth in that way. She is my wife."

"Betty Ashdown has been a shop girl since I first set eyes on her when you brought your Sam Ashdown to dinner, and she still is. I did not like her then and twenty years later, I see no reason to change my opinion. She's a gold digger and you're a fool for marrying her."

"So you have told me before Mother, but life changes. So do people, surely I don't have to tell you, of all people, that. One has to adapt. The house is large enough, goodness knows, for two, even three families."

"Don't tell me you intend starting a family?"

"I hardly think that likely."

"Thank heaven for that, at least."

"By dividing the house in two we will avoid getting in each other's hair, it will be easier all round. By moving up a floor, you'll only lose the front balcony, which you never use anyhow, and my rooms are just as comfortable."

Agatha's mouth twitches sulkily.

"If you persist in this attitude," Rex continues, "I see no solution but to sell the place."

With a fierce glare, Agatha intones, "Sell the house?"

"In order to finance the purchase of three other properties."
Ticking off a proposed shopping list with his fingers, he elucidates.
"a) An assisted home for you... "

Agatha is mute, but her eyes dilate with a mix of fury and fear
at the mention of such a horror.

"b) A flat for Sophia.

And c) A house for Elizabeth and myself. I fear I could never
afford three such expensive transactions any other way."

Barely audible, Agatha murmurs, "That will be not be
necessary." She clears her throat. "This has been my home since
your father brought me here as a bride over sixty years ago. If Herr
Hitler could not get me out of it, Elizabeth Ashdown is not going
to succeed. I do not intend leaving here until I'm carried out toes
first!"

"Mother, for goodness sake!"

Agatha's head nods like a Chinese doll. It is a recent affliction
beyond her control. "Give up my suite, indeed! Your first wife,
dear Eve, never made any such demand of me."

"She was scared stiff of you."

"Rubbish. She was a thoughtful and respectful girl. I still grieve
daily for her loss. Neither did you, and it would certainly have been
your right to do so when you came home after your poor father
died."

Ever since Agatha's husband, Edward Black deserted her and
died of malaria forty-seven years ago in South Africa, she has
referred to him, as 'your *poor* father'.

"I wouldn't have dreamt of asking you for the master suite.
Anyway, I was too busy working my socks off for Grandpapa.
Besides, after the farm in Rhodesia, this place was a palace."

"Then why are you asking me now?"

"Because that way we, Elizabeth and I, and you and Sophia can each be on separate floors and not trouble each other. By dividing the house our lives will be happier, surely, you see that? You and Sophia can have your separate living and dining rooms upstairs; your bedrooms could be on the same floor, as they are now, if you like. You'd like that, surely? You'd never even have to see Elizabeth, if you didn't want to."

"You carry on as if you expect me to insult the woman. I'm sure I've never been impolite."

"No, Mother, not by anything you've said. Your expression is enough."

"I'm sure I don't know what you mean."

"I think you do." Adopting a conciliatory tone, he continues, "If I'm honest, I'm just afraid that, in time, your hostility will surface and life will become difficult. I think we stand more chance of happiness if we live separate lives, in separate apartments, albeit under the same roof. I just want the three people I love most in the world to live in peace together."

Agatha looks up surprised; his tact placates her. "Well, I must say, this honeymoon cruise of yours certainly seems to have tempered your usual acerbic tone towards me. I suppose we have Elizabeth to thank for that, at least."

"At least, Mother," Rex smiles. "And in truth, I would be loath to sell our magnificent home."

"On that, we are agreed." After a moment, she says, "What if I were to agree to exchange suites, would that satisfy her?"

"This isn't her idea, Mother, it's mine. And yes, that would help." After a beat in which he appears to weigh the projected cost of the conversion, he adds, "and it would certainly avoid the inconvenience of builders in the house, not to mention, the expense. However… "

"Then it's settled," interrupts Agatha, "that is what we shall do. I will tell Mary to take all my things up into your room and Robert can do the same for you."

He regards his mother for a long moment. "That still leaves the dining and drawing rooms as possible battle grounds. If that were to be the case, Mother, it would pain me dreadfully." Refraining from repeating the words 'assisted home', he merely states, "I should be forced to re-think our situation."

Agatha holds his look, fully aware of his unspoken threat. "I think, my dear, you are exaggerating the situation somewhat. I'm sure that with a little effort on both our parts we shall get along famously. Sophia will be only too happy to relinquish the administration of the house to Elizabeth, if that is what this is all about."

"That is not what this is about, Mother. Though Elizabeth is an exceedingly practical woman, she has run a boarding house and brought up two daughters."

Flinching at the very mention of *boarding house*, Agatha closes her eyes at such distasteful social implications. "Running a house of this size will prove slightly more demanding than that," with a bitter smile she adds, "However, I'm sure she'll get on excellently well with Mrs Hunt."

By teaming his wife's name with that of their cook/housekeeper, Rex is unconvinced his mother has fully understood his conditions. "That is just the sort of needling, condescending remark, Mother, that could lead to hostility between you. I wish you to accept Elizabeth and be kind to her. You can be a most delightful companion, you know, when you choose. She is most anxious to please you."

Agatha's eyes rest thoughtfully on her clasped liver-spotted hands. She twists the rings on her fingers. Once a great lady, she is wise in the ways of the world, and very conscious of her diminishing strength. She is also a convincing actress. Realising that she needs the support of her son if she is to remain living in his house and stay out of a retirement home, and who knows, one day may need the help of her new daughter-in-law, she looks up at her son with a disarming smile. "Forgive me, Rex. I'm a silly and fractious old woman. I expect I'm jealous. If she makes you happy," she shrugs, "then… "

"She does, Mother, very happy."

"In that case I must accept and welcome her. I promise to do my very best. Please ask her to come down and see me."

"Thank you, darling." Rex kisses his mother on the top of her head.

Upstairs in his study, Betty picks up the silver framed photograph of Eve, Rex's first wife. She remembers meeting her at dinner years ago; *she was so nice to me.* Wondering what kind of life she and Rex had together and what drove her to suicide, she replaces the picture, checks her reflexion in the mirror and leaves the room, unaware that the conversation concluded downstairs has set her and the Honourable Agatha Black on a collision course that will bedevil the rest of their lives.

Chapter Seven

Brothers-in-Law

July

Betty's old home in Holland Street does not sell.

"I'm afraid the market is very down," says the estate agent on the phone. Betty replaces the phone and glances at Rex reading the paper, "No luck yet."

"Well, you can wait. You're hardly hard up!"

Chewing her lip, she wanders to the window and glances out at the rusty old pier. "Rex!"

"Mm?"

"You know Cheryl's baby is due in September?

"Yes, you told me. Your new grandchild."

"Marco's place isn't at all suitable for a new born baby. Supposing instead of waiting for my house to sell, I was to give it to her? I mean that's the priority, isn't it? A home, not the cash? And after all, thanks to you, dear, I can afford to be generous."

Rex puts down his paper. "It's a big thing giving your house away. Still, you're settled in here nicely," he grins, "and if you have no use for it. It's up to you, Elizabeth."

"How would I go about doing such a thing? I mean to give it to her legally?"

"You'd have to go and see Henry, my solicitor. He'd make you out a Deed of Gift and have the transfer recorded in the land registry."

So that is what Betty does, she visits Mr Henry Williams, and signs her whole house, lock, stock and barrel, over to Cheryl.

Young Marco Danieli is not happy about it; it affronts his Italian machismo, a quality his beloved Cheryl admires in him, but in this instance mocks. However, being out of work and having nothing better to do on this warm Saturday morning, he assembles a ladder, paint and brushes, and sets about turning Cheryl's childhood bedroom into a nursery.

A stone's throw away, Joe, in the double-fronted house he practically re-built from the cellar to the roof tiles, places a CD of *Beethoven's 7th Symphony* into his sleek Sony Hi-Fi system and flops on to the sofa. He tries to immerse himself in the stirring music, but his thoughts return to the problem of his wife, or rather his wife's drinking problem. His eye roams his living room. He has taken a great deal of care to bring a certain amount of the rural mansion into his home; by mixing antiques with modern contemporary pieces, he has achieved a room with the look and charm of a comfortable country pile. Building shelves along one entire wall for books (Dickens and C. S. Forester adventures are among his favourites), and a collection of recordings by Beecham and Von Karajan among his pop and easy listening C.Ds.

Sunshine streams through the front windows tempting him out into the warm air. He decides Beethoven is not right for his present mood, what he really needs is some man-to-man therapy. He abruptly snaps off his CD player, leaves the house, and strolls up the hill to Betty's old house to have a chat with his chum, Marco.

Cheryl answers the door in an apron. "Tiger! Come in." Greeting him with a kiss, she adds, "Marco's upstairs, decorating. Like some coffee?"

"Ta luv, that'll be grand," and he strides up the stairs two at a time.

Seeing Marco shirtless, perched up a ladder, chinos clinging dangerously low on his slim hips and fiddling with a paint roller, he asks, "Looks like you need a professional."

"Gratefully accepted," says Marco, who is one of the few people who perceives in Joe a sensitivity at odds with the merry Bob-the-builder persona he presents to his customers. "But beer will only be served at lunch."

Joe grins as he examines a pot of paint. "What have we got here? *Dulux undercoat.* That'll do. Right!" Stripping off his shirt, he reveals impressive biceps and a hairy torso. Throwing the shirt aside, he pokes a brush around in a jam jar. "So, Marc, you know any alcoholics?"

"I work in show business, man, of course. Why?"

"Just wondered. Does AA work, do you think? I mean, do they ever really kick it?"

Marco studies him.

He looks as if he is concentrating extra hard on cleaning a brush.

Sensing something, Marco considers. "Is it Claudia?"

"Shit! Is it that obvious?"

"No, but it is part of my job to observe people. Study human nature. I notice things. Hell! I watch people the whole time, make up stories about them."

Joe remains silent.

"Do you want to talk about it?"

"Not much." He stops, sighs and looks up at his friend. "I just don't know what to do about it, Marc."

Marco recognizes his anxiety, knows what a big deal it is for Joe to admit this. Carefully, he considers, "The actors I know love being drunks, but there are clinics, y'know. That guy Woody Walsh, on the telly, he has a place. Google him."

"Thanks. I will."

Appreciating Joe's confidence, rating him and enjoying his companionship, Marco feels able to speak his own mind, for it is not in his nature to bottle up his emotions for long. "You know our Mum-in-law has given this place over to Cheryl."

"I heard."

"It bloody neuters me, man, I tell you. Oh, I'm grateful, don't get me wrong. We certainly couldn't afford it ourselves, but it totally castrates me."

"Hope not, old boy," says Joe, dipping his brush in the can and applying paint to the wall. "Thought Cheryl would be thrilled."

"Oh, she's over the moon. Keeps telling me what happened here, what happened there, when she and Claudia were kids. Riveting, I don't think!"

Cheryl suddenly opens the door carrying a tray with mugs filled with coffee. "It's only Nescafe. The blue one's yours, Joe. I have sugared it. I know about your sweet tooth."

"Ta, luv," and he takes the tray.

"I'm in the middle of trying to organize the kitchen, so won't stop. Have fun!" She blows them each a kiss and leaves.

In silence, Joe passes a mug up to Marco.

"Ta." In a hushed voice he adds, "You know it's her name on the title deeds now. No mention of me. Apparently, the lawyer's fee for fixing it up was two thousand quid. Rex paid, of course, not bloody Betty."

"She told me she wanted you to have it before the baby was born."

"Don't look a gift horse in the mouth, I know. But what happens if we have a row? Cheryl could turf me out."

Joe's eyebrows shoot up.

"Well, she could. What comeback would I have? I'd be homeless!"

"You'd have to shack up with me, wouldn't you? We'd have

some fun if you did, eh? Mind you," he adds, his voice suddenly serious, "you'll have to change that round, mate. You wouldn't catch me standing for that, no. A man has to have his name on his own house."

"But how? It's all signed and sealed."

"Get married, man! That's why she's not included you."

"You think so?"

"Of course, dummy. She wants to make sure you stick to her."

"Well, of course I'm going to stick to her. Cheryl's the best thing that ever happened to me. But marriage… " Marco shakes his head. "I'm not getting into that. Live the sort of life my Dad lived. When my Mum left him he collapsed, couldn't take it, committed suicide."

"Bloody hell! How old were you?"

"Eleven."

"So you were brought up by your English Mum?"

Marco nods, "Mm, she was great. She was a fashion editor. I loved her to bits. She taught me to be independent and not to take life too seriously. To laugh at myself, 'cause I'm inclined to get a bit intense sometimes. She died a couple of years back." He takes a sip of coffee. "Cheryl said you were brought up in an orphanage."

"Yup! In Folkestone. Wasn't that bad, really. Makes me appreciate my own two boys now." Joe rubs his bald head and surveys his work. "You should talk this house business over with Betty. She's reasonable."

"To you, maybe," Marco hitches up his chinos, "to me she's always so damn disapproving."

"Naw! Sweet as fudge. I quite fancy her."

"You fancy everyone."

"True," concedes Joe.

"She's still practically living here. She's at the door every morning." Impersonating Betty's tones, he coos, "Morning, Marco.

A wee giftie for the baby. When will you be finished decorating?"

"That's a bloody marvellous imitation, mate" chuckles Joe. "Cruel, mind. You gotta get on the telly."

"Tell me about it," says Marco. "But I'm more than just a mimic, I'm an actor."

But an out of work actor is a lost, frustrated man. To fill the time while he waits for his agent to call with a job, Marco follows Cheryl everywhere. He pays £139 out of his precious dole money for joint visits to an antenatal clinic. Channelling his considerable vitality, he writes songs on his guitar, and sinks himself in domesticity, redecorating Betty's old home from top to bottom, finishing on the very morning Cheryl cries out...

"Marco, I think this is it. It's coming. Get me to the hospital PDQ."

Chapter Eight

The Christening

9th November 2008

*M*arco and Cheryl stand side by side before the font looking as stunningly beautiful as only twenty-year-olds in love can look. Gazing at their baby son, seeds of parental responsibility stir in their minds. Cheryl, with her perfect retroussé nose and blonde tulip haircut curling charmingly under her chin, turns to smile up at Marco, whose deep green eyes sparkle with pride, as he tosses his thick black hair from his brow.

Beside them stand Cheryl's family, gathered once more with the Rev. Jones in the Church of Christ the King.

The Reverend Jones is keen to show that at a time when forty-four per cent of children are born to unmarried mothers, the church accepts the reality of more liberal attitudes to sex outside marriage, offering baptism to all, irrespective of the marital status of parents. When Betty telephoned to make the booking a fortnight ago he requested a meeting with Marco and Cheryl. He spoke to them for twenty minutes on the blessing and security of marriage, but to no avail.

"Do you reject the devil and all rebellion against him?" he now asks.

Tiger Joe gulps. "I reject him."

Claudia repeats, "I reject him."

A stranger, Michael Barrington, a tall, good-looking stiff in a formal suit and sumptuous glossy tie, repeats, "I reject him."

All three godparents are standing before the font holding small, lit candles, which is awkward for Claudia who is also holding the baby. Carefully she passes the candle to her mother so she can lower her nephew over the water. Everyone watches spellbound as the Rev. Jones pours holy water over the infant's head washing him free of sin.

If only it were that easy, think Joe and Marco. Each of whom have a high libido, which, over the years, has led them into some singular relationships.

Marco glances across the font at his old friend and Michael's hazel eyes meet his, crinkle and give a blazing smile.

Instantly Marco is fifteen again, the wind blowing in his hair, he is happy, his arms wrapped around Michael's waist on his motor bike as they fly along, riding pillion to Maidenhead. *When we arrived at the river, we rented a sailing boat and took a week sailing up the Thames, sleeping overnight in our tent. On that first night, I lost my virginity. We lay there side by side, in each other's arms and swore eternal friendship.*

God, I was a randy little bugger! I was so determined to get laid.

After the euphoria following the birth of his son, Marco had fallen into a pit of depression. In the last six months his agent has had only two TV commercials for him, he's had no work in the theatre at all. On top of that he had the distinct impression Cheryl was giving him the cold-shoulder. Maybe not deliberately, but so absorbed had she become in her new maternal role, she was excluding him. They had not had sex for four weeks. Her world now seemed to revolve around the baby, whereas no such "motherhood" hormones had flooded his brain to make him care as much. He had tried, offering to change nappies and take on midnight feeds, but was aware he was not having much success in his new father role.

His passion and talents were for the theatre, music and singing, acting in movies and plays. Ambitious for success, he was going crazy with frustration. One evening after hammering new shelves into place, he had taken a shower and joined Cheryl in the nursery.

She ignored him, leaning over the cot she picked up the baby and carried him to the wicker nursing chair Betty had bought.

Marco bent to kiss her.

"Ah!" she sighed, her nose resting on her baby's downy head. "It's time for your feed, isn't it, my lovely?" Hauling out her breast, she murmured, "Leave us be, luv, do you mind? I so love our bonding time together."

Marco had grabbed his leather jacket and gone for a long walk along the sea front culminating in a visit to a pub. Sitting alone, a man smiled at him and he realised he was in a gay bar. Wistfully, he recalled his schooldays with Michael, the only person, apart from his mother, to whom he had ever felt close. When they had bidden each other farewell on their last day at boarding school, he had wondered if their friendship would survive, wondered if it belonged too intimately, too delicately to the past. It seemed his suspicions had been right, for now he only had Michael's polite Christmas cards and his own guilty memories. His passion for Cheryl, for heterosexual sex, was as all consuming as ever, but boredom, and maybe curiosity, propelled him to unearth his old address book and next morning make the call.

"Michael!" he gushed. "Guess who? Voice from the past."

"I beg your pardon," answered a business-like voice.

"Mickey! It's me!"

"Good God! There's only one person in the world who's ever called me that, Marco Danieli. Is that you?"

"Of course. How are you, mate?"

"Well, um… Surprised!"

"Guess what? I'm a Dad."

"I hope that means you're married, old boy?" Michael laughed.

"Very much so," he lied, "and very happy."

"Me too. Did the deed two years ago. Ain't life grand? She's beautiful and the best thing that ever happened to me."

"Congratulations!" he called out mechanically, though perversely the news depressed him. Wanting some sort of renewal of their one time closeness, and because he didn't know who else to ask, he said, "Mickey, why I've called is, would you stand as godfather? It would be so terrific if you could."

"Of course, old boy," answered Michael smoothly. "Be proud to. Send me all the bumf and we'll fix it up."

Marco disconnected his mobile wondering why he felt so dejected. *He sounded so square, so unlike himself. 'Old boy' indeed! What the hell was that about?*

His son's bawling at the font re-focuses his mind.

Claudia passes the infant to Cheryl, who nestles him in her arms, "shhh, darling... sshhh." The baby quietens down and Cheryl straightens the lace gown Betty had given her yesterday. "This is the very gown," she'd said, "that you and Claudia were christened in."

Across the font, Marco regards Michael's wife, Georgiana. She reminds him of a younger version of his mother. She is very beautiful, classy and chic, befitting the wife of a successful financial adviser. *She looks as if she has it all. I wonder if she has? I wonder if Michael is true to her, if he is as straight as he gives out, or it is a pose?*

When they drove up in their Porsche Cayenne this morning, meeting each other for the first time in five years, Michael clapped him on the back saying, "They tell me you're an actor. Good God, man, couldn't you find anything better to do than that?"

Instantly, Marco realises the man is a prick. *He's become a stuck-up prig. Whatever did I see in him?* Understanding that they no longer have anything in common, he even regrets asking him to be a godfather. However, Michael's handsome gift of a silver Georgian christening mug endears him to Cheryl who is also impressed by the elegance of Georgiana.

As indeed is Joe.

Leaving the church, he scuttles after her. "Do you have children yourself?"

"Regretfully, no," she replies with a cool smile. "Do you?"

"Just those two," he answers, nodding to his six-year old twins running to the car ahead. "Little buggers!"

"Just like their Dad," chips in Claudia, hooking her arm smartly though his. Claudia prides herself on saying things as they are; besides, she is very aware of her husband's susceptibity to a pretty face.

Georgiana graciously inclines her head. "What handsome boys."

Cheryl and Marco, who are following with their baby, had originally intended having a small party after the christening in their new home. However, Betty has insisted on throwing them a slap-up christening "do" in her new home in Brunswick Square.

Standing with Rex by the church door, she is chatting animatedly to the Reverend Jones. Marriage has unquestionly brightened her life. Now the possessor of a black mink coat and an entirely new wardrobe; her hair is more convincing lightened by an expensive hairdresser, her nails are polished by a professional manicurist, and diamonds twinkle in her ears and on her fingers. Delighted by this boost to her femininity, she displays it in her shining eyes and glowing cheeks to anyone perceptive enough to notice. That person is definitely not Mr Jones, of whom she asks, "Will you be able to join our little celebration?"

"My duties," he answers with a charming gesture, "unfortunately prevent me."

The suave Michael Barrington hovers by his giant Porsche

studying his invitation. (Betty had insisted it was embossed and had gold edges, but in fairness, had paid for it.) "Which is the best route," he asks, "to this reception of yours?"

"Take the coastal road," calls Marco. "It'll be easier if you follow us. This is me," he indicates his dusty second hand Honda.

Parked next to it stands a gleaming silver Mercedes.

"I'll take this one," jokes Georgiana.

"That's mine," says Joe, trying not to grin.

Georgiana dilates her nostrils, as if smelling money. "Well, as we're all going the same way," she grins, "we'll follow you."

"And you, young man," commands Rex to Joe, holding his finger imperiously in the air, "follow me."

Rex's chauffeur, Robert, stands waiting. He opens the door for Betty, and she climbs in.

"Home, Robert!" calls Rex, "and don't spare the horses."

Rex is in a high good humour with no regrets whatever regarding his decision to re-marry. Of late, he has been experiencing inexplicable moments of elation, relishing each new day, grateful for each new healthy bright morn the Good Lord sees fit to grant. *Is it because I'm going to die soon? Is it a reminder of how I used to be? A last minute vision of how marvellous life is?*

As he merrily settles in his Bentley beside Betty, he calls out to Robert. "The sooner we're home, the sooner you can crack open the champers!"

Chapter Nine

The Party

On the morning of the never-to-be-forgotten christening party at the big house in Brunswick Square, Rex, who had some qualms about it, had remarked to his mother and sister after breakfast when Betty had gone upstairs, "I trust you will welcome Betty's family into the house in the appropriate manner."

"As long as they don't smoke or put their feet up on the furniture," answered Agatha.

"Mo-ther!" he warned.

She shut her eyes, waving away his reprimand with a vague gesture.

"I have told them not to smoke," assured Rex.

"I'm looking forward to it," announced Sophia, brightly, "meeting Claudia and Cheryl properly. I barely spoke to them at the wedding."

Rex's nostrils dilated, but he remained silent. Yesterday there had been a brief discussion about whether Sophia should attend the christening. "I'd love to be there," she'd said. "Do you think they'd mind?"

"Inappropriate, dear," Agatha had muttered.

"I don't see why. If the baby is Rex's grandson then I'm his great aunt!"

"You're no such thing, and you know it," Agatha responded. "Can we please drop the subject."

Now as Sophia sits at the breakfast table conscious of her mother and Rex's eyes observing her, she tidily covers the pot of

Mrs Hunt's homemade marmalade with the cut-glass lid, carefully adjusting the silver spoon in the grove. "After all, we've not had a party in the house for goodness knows how long."

Sophia was once, as Rex had told Betty, a very pretty girl. Agatha had seen to it that she had had a good education and upbringing, but she had always suffered from a sense of inferiority, never quite attaining the *savoir faire* that her mother had hoped for. Her fringe may now be white, but her dark eyes still sparkle and one suspects that beneath her timid manner there lies hidden steel, perhaps an acerbic tongue and possibly a long lost love. Her hobby, which has become an obsession, is Graeco-Roman Egyptian history, and her bedroom has become a veritable museum of the Hellenists. She has a collection of ancient coins, statues and busts of Ptolemy, Arsinoë II, Cleopatra, and Alexander the Great, even a miniature Rosetta stone plaque, and she has absorbed everything there is to know about the Macedonian kings. "The silver has all been polished," she continues, "and Mrs Hunt has prepared some fine canapés. I believe they are all quite excited about it."

By "they", she referrers to their servants: Doris, their elderly serving maid, and Mary, Agatha's personal maid, both of whom live in and have bedrooms on the top floor. Mrs Hunt, the cook/housekeeper, who lives a bus ride away in Portslade, and Robert, Rex's chauffeur, secretary, and general factotum. Robert once lived over the mews at the bottom of the garden, but since Rex sold it last year to a garage repair company, he now lives a bus ride away in a flat with a bachelor friend in Hove.

Although Rex is semi-retired as Chairman and Managing Director of Sherwood and Black Consolidated, his presence is occasionally required up in London. When, on the rare occasions, some accountant, or other business person calls, Rex conducts them to his magnificent library on the ground floor.

To admit to any weakness was to Rex an anathema. To admit

to feeling uncomfortable sleeping in the very same bed with Betty, as he had done for years with Eve, was unthinkable. Deviously, he had therefore used the flat conversion plans as a ruse to acquire, at long last, the master bedroom for himself. To Betty, his reasoning for ousting his mother seemed generous. "My dear, you will need the larger sitting room next to the master bedroom for all your things, your books, your television and treasures from your old home."

As the aforementioned flat conversion had come to nought Agatha, Sophia and Betty have had to rub along together.

So far, no problems – a least of a visible kind – have arisen, both parties taking scrupulously care to be polite to one another. Betty and Rex are now established on the second floor overlooking the gardens, and Agatha, as she reluctantly agreed, on the third floor in Rex's old suite. Sophia, however, has remained in her room on the second floor next to Rex and Betty. Rex told Agatha, "It's too much to expect Sophia to move all her statuary and antiquities up a floor. If you want to see her in her room, you'll just have to take the lift."

The aforementioned lift, installed shortly after the First World War, when, no doubt, it was an impressive and luxurious addition, now appears ancient and very shaky. It reminds Betty of the lift in the film *Thoroughly Modern Millie*, she almost has to do a tap dance to get the thing moving.

Anxious to please her in-laws and sensing their coolness, she occasionally brings them flowers and trinkets, which they accept with grace. Thankfully, in such a spacious house, (there are ten bedrooms, five with their own en suite bathrooms and sitting rooms), they are not obliged to endure each other's company for every minute of the day.

Agatha and Sophia are in the habit of keeping to the morning room after breakfast; and only the one meal a day, dinner at 7.00, is taken *en famille* in the dining room. Agatha seldom leaves the house, except once a week when Robert drives her to see her retired concert-hall pianist friend, Joyce Heron in Worthing. When she returns from these visits, she holds forth at great length about the fame, skill, and charm of her friend, sometimes bringing back a CD of one of her recordings.

Sophia, as Agatha had foretold, was relieved to relinquish her, what she considered, "tiresome" shopping responsibilities over to the new Mrs Black, which allows her more time for research.

Betty, who was always a resourceful housekeeper, ensures she keeps on good terms with the retainers, who, after an initial period of resentment, have warmed to her.

The relationship between Agatha and Sophia can best be summed up as that of Dowager Queen Mother and Princess Royal, devoted to each other, only once in their lives have they had a serious disagreement, which this tale will eventually unfold. They adore Rex and are exceedingly proud of his achievements, regarding him as king of their palatial, if fusty little kingdom.

At fifteen minutes past midday, they retire to their separate suites to dress for the christening party.

Forty minutes later Agatha emerges wearing a high-necked dress with three-quarter length jet-fringed sleeves, an amethyst and diamond brooch, a triple string of pearls, and matching pearl drop earrings. Outside Sophia's room, she knocks and simultaneously enters, "Are you ready, my dear?"

Sophia rises from her dressing table and executes a twirl to show off her ensemble. Both women are wearing a variation of their usual black with the addition of jewellery. Sophie wears a pair of exquisite dangling marquisate earrings.

Agatha, astonished, stares at them, "Not appropriate, dear. Long, only for evenings."

"But in honour of the baby. I've not worn them since I don't know when. Grandmamma left them to me, do you remember? It is time they had an airing, don't you agree?"

"Well, of course. They do look very fine. As you see, I'm wearing my usual pearls."

Together they leave the room, taking the lift to the seldom used, but impressive first floor reception room, which today looks especially handsome. The fire in the marble fireplace is burning and generous vases of flowers (delivered care of B. D Saunders, the florist in the Old Shoreham Road), are on tables and bureaux.

There is a good deal of curiosity in Marco's eyes as he is ushered by Robert to the elegant winding staircase. Betty's daughters, too, peer around inquisitively; they have never been in such a grand house before. Taking in the black marble refectory table with a white marble bust of Marie Antoinette, various gold framed paintings and Regency prints of old Brighton on the staircase, they refuse, perversely, to be impressed. "Bit gloomy," whispers Cheryl.

"Fancy polishing all those," whispers Claudia, pointing to the gleaming brass stairs-rods in the carpet.

In the reception room, Agatha has chosen her usual high-backed armchair beside the fireplace from where she can meet, greet and bestow her unique brand of detached friendliness. Sophia stands slightly to one side, behind her.

Betty effects the introductions, which become like a Court presentation. Agatha graciously nods and smiles a greeting to all. She undoubtedly makes a regal figure with her sharp features, silver hair and glinting black jet, but there is something disconcerting in her manner, particularly her smile: it never wavers, even, one might think, when ordering an execution.

"You've already met my daughters, Claudia and Cheryl."

Sophia steps forward shyly. "Hallo. We did meet at the wedding, but... "

"Of course," interrupt Claudia and Cheryl in unison, taking turns to shake her hand.

"And this is Joe," says Betty, "my son-in-law, with his twins, Paul and Peter. Say hello, darlings."

"Hello," they shout confidently.

"Georgiana and Michael Barrington. Michael is an old school chum of Marco's and the other godfather."

"What a delightful home you have," says Georgiana trading graciousness with the old lady.

Agatha continues nodding.

"And here," says Betty, "comes the proud Papa, Marco, with the man of the moment, Master Thomas."

Agatha inclines her head to take in the baby's face. "Ah!"

With the introductions over, Betty takes charge of the baby.

Rex's man, Robert, circulates with a tray of fluted champagne glasses. Once everyone has one, Rex taps the side of his glass for silence. "My dear wife wishes to say a few words."

Betty steps forward. Thoroughly enjoying herself, she takes her place in the centre of the room before the blazing fire. "I would just like to propose a toast to welcome my grandson into this crazy world. To Thomas David… " she cannot bring herself to utter what she considers his ridiculous double-barrelled surname, Ashdown-Danieli, so instead raises her glass saying, "May his life be a long, happy and merry one."

All raise their glasses toward the wicker crib with a blue satin bow on top, where, oblivious to all, lies the sleeping focus of the day's event. There is some confusion about the toast, some say "Thomas David," others "a long and happy life," but suddenly there is a happy, more relaxed feeling in the room and everyone drinks and laughs.

The elderly maidservant, Doris, formally dressed in black, with cream lace at the collar and wrists, circulates offering canapés.

Georgiana Barrington's eyes roam admiringly around the room, at the mouldings surrounding the ceiling, the magnificent pillars framing the floor to ceiling windows, the views of the lawn in Brunswick Square gardens to the sea beyond. Intrigued by Rex's wealth, she casually probes, remarking, "What a divine view. Have you lived here long?"

"When the sky changes," says Rex, "which is nearly every moment, it makes it all look quite different!"

"Delightful. How long have you been here?"

"Since I was nineteen. I misspent my youth in Rhodesia before it was made independent under Ian Smith."

Joe, fascinated by Georgiana's dangerous beauty, hovers by her side, his arm resting casually around the shoulder of his son, Paul.

Marco, anxious to avoid a one-to-one with his one time lover, Michael, but curious about Rex, joins his group, hoping to learn something about his long and interesting life.

The lean and sophisticated Michael Barrington bent on making himself charming, approaches Sophia. "This is a fantastic house!"

Shocked that someone so polished should talk to her, Sophia shakes her head almost ushering him away. "No, no. Please don't bother talking to me. I'm nobody. Talk to someone else."

Astonished that anyone could be so self-effacing, Michael pleads, "Please, I'd like to talk to you."

"No, no," she says, cringing, "talk to my sister-in-law, she's far more interesting."

Bemused, he drifts away and joins Betty on the sofa, where he receives a much warmer welcome. "Michael, come and sit beside me. Tell me how wicked Marco was when he was a little boy."

"Well, I was pretty wicked, too."

"I don't believe that for a moment."

For Cheryl, sitting alone on the other sofa devouring smoked salmon canapés, the whole business of choosing godparents had not been as cavalier or impulsive as it had been for Marco. Having insisted, to Betty's surprise, that Joe should stand as godfather, she had wanted her best friend, Myra, to be godmother.

When Betty heard of it, she was appalled. "You can't possibly not ask your sister, especially when you're asking Joe to be godfather. She would be terribly upset. Besides your dear Myra is a single Mum and hardly a shining example of virtue. Neither has she two pennies to rub together. They'll be no extravagant birthday presents from the likes of her!"

So reluctantly and rather hoping the request would please and placate her moody sister, Cheryl had asked her.

Claudia had accepted but commented to Joe, "I know perfectly well why she's asked us to be godparents. You watch out, she's been dying to get her claws into you since the day we were married."

Today, however, in the spirit of Pax, the Roman goddess of peace, Claudia, clasping a large gin and tonic, sinks next to her sister on Rex's buttoned old sofa, but cannot resist a dig. "Tell me, darling, has Marco got any work yet?"

"Not yet, poor lamb."

"Lamb, huh! I think you're marvellous keeping him the way you do. If Joe didn't bring home the bacon, I'd chuck him out. But at least Marco doesn't have to pay rent anymore, thanks to Mother. Now, are you doing those exercises I told you about to get your figure back?"

Cheryl is so busy dealing with her sister, she doesn't notice Sophia tentatively creep up on her baby's crib.

But from her chair, Agatha watches.

Sophia's lined face takes on an odd expression as she peers at the child. If anyone, apart from her mother had been observing her, they might have thought she had never seen a baby before. Her eyes become moist and her expression softens. Glancing across the room at her mother, she smiles.

Agatha's fixed expression fades and something flickers across her face. She shakes her head ever so slightly and Sophia straightens up and moves away toward Claudia and Cheryl. "He looks a fine little boy."

Cheryl and Claudia both look up at her surprised.

"May I join you?"

"Please do," says Claudia, making room for her on the sofa.

Agatha's eyes have followed her, her own social mask firmly in place. She turns her gaze to observe her son.

Rex is standing like a Victorian paterfamilias with his back to the fire holding court. "There is no explanation that I know of," he explains. "I just took to it, like a duck to water," he shrugs in his quasi-modest manner. "As a kid I enjoyed playing Monopoly, buying and selling hotels on Mayfair, which to me in Rhodesia was thrilling. When Grandpapa left me his fortune, I just carried on, but this time with the real spondoulix!" and he roars with laughter.

Georgiana joins in, looking, oh, so radiantly amused.

Marco regards her cynically, seeing through what he interprets as her affected social performance.

Joe turns to his son, "See, Paulie, there's hope for you."

Paul wriggles away to join his brother, who is investigating the pendulum of a grandfather clock on the other side of the room.

Georgiana takes out her leather cigarette case. Turning to Marco she says, "Do you have a light?"

"I do, but the old lady will throw a fit!"

"Oh dear, well, we can't have that, can we?" Leaning towards him she whispers, "She does make that chair look rather like a throne, doesn't she?"

Marco's dark face bursts into a delightful white-toothed smile.

Conspiratorially she adds, "Do you suppose we could sneak on to the balcony?"

"I don't see why not?"

"Would you be a dear, there seems to be a catch."

Marco slides the bolt of the balcony door and politely holds it open.

Holding up her case, Georgiana offers him a cigarette.

"Thanks." He lights hers with his old-fashioned lighter, then his own. "We'd better shut the door," he does and turns to face her.

She meets his eyes. "I hear you're an actor. I have many friends in show business. Sometimes, when I have a good tip, I have been known to invest."

"Are you an angel?"

"Absolutely. What are you doing at the moment, are you working?"

"Afraid not."

"But you do have an agent?"

"Yes, but these days it's hard. Overcast… too many actors around."

Georgiana smiles. "You're a good looking boy. I'd have thought producers would be beating down your door. Michael tells me you're Italian."

"Half. My mother was what my father used to call 'La Rosa Inglese'."

"Charming." Georgiana inhales her cigarette devouring the glamour of him through half-closed eyelids. "An Italian with perfect English manners. We really must find something for you. Do you have a card? Here, take mine." She fishes in her handbag. "Michael probably has your number. I sometimes represent people."

Marco reads: "Georgiana Barrington. Entrepreneur". "Are you serious?"

"Of course. It's not what you know, but who you know in show biz, any business, come to that. Ask your, what is he? Father-in-law, grandfather-in-law, in there."

"Actually, Cheryl and I aren't married."

"But madly in love. Any fool can see that. I'm flattered to have got you to myself. She's very pretty. Has she ever done modelling?"

"Yes, she has actually. Didn't like it, said it was a superficial world."

"She's right there, but it can be very lucrative if you're successful. Oh dear! She's heading this way to rescue you."

Through the window, Marco sees Cheryl making "come in" signs.

Opening the door, she whispers, "Rex is going to make a speech."

After extinguished their cigarettes, Marco ushers Georgiana back into the room as Rex, by the fireplace, squares up to make his address.

"I have been requested by my dear wife here, who you all know has an excellent eye for a bargain," there is a smattering of laughter, "to pass on to our young guests some sound financial advice. A contentious request, however, I will be brave." He clears his throat and adopting a comic pomposity, continues: "Given the uncertain economic outlook, the deceleration in China, the fiscal austerity in Germany, and the downright exigency in Greece, the euro will be weak... but don't write off the United States." There is more laughter. "While remaining cautious, I am confident investment in Sherwood and Black Consolidated will withstand all prevailing headwinds."

Amid laughter and light applause, Rex dramatically clutches his chest. Thinking he is joking there is more laughter.

He groans.

"Rex!" Sophia shrieks.

The laughter abruptly stops.

Betty, alarmed by Sophia's shriek, turns. It is clear something is wrong. "What is it, dear?"

He shakes his head, "Been overdoing it!" He staggers and Sophia helps him to a chair.

Rex's mouth droops to one side and he appears to be having trouble speaking, "Pain," he chokes, clutching his jacket.

Marco stares at him. "I think he's having a heart attack." Marco once played a male nurse in *Holby City* and remembers the three steps known as FAST: face, arms, speech test. "Lie him down on his left side. I'll call the paramedics." As he speaks, he takes out his mobile and dials 999.

Betty falls to her knees and fumbles with Rex's shirtfront in an effort to locate his heart.

Chapter Ten

Life Changes

One's whole life can change in a minute like the passing of a cloud, thinks Betty, staring unseeing at the floor in a corridor of the Nuffield Health Hospital. *Whatever will happen if he dies?*

Sitting bolt upright at the other end of the bench, seemingly in another world, is Sophia. Since screaming out her brother's name when she recognized his condition as serious, she has barely spoken, controlling her features, her dark eyes reveal nothing. Standing beside Betty is Joe, leaning on the wall badly in need of a cigarette. Marco sits on a chair opposite them studying their faces. Suddenly Betty looks up at him.

"I dread to think of what might have happened if you hadn't called the ambulance when you did."

He smiles weakly. It occurs to him to take this opportunity of asking her to add his name to the deeds of Cheryl's house, but the occasion hardly seems appropriate. He looks at Joe, sturdy reliable old Joe, and makes a glum face.

Joe raises his eyebrows and returns the gloomy look.

The four wait, listening to the echo of hospital noises.

Eventually a doctor in a white coat appears.

Betty and Marco stand up.

Taking in the group, the doctor speaks. "Mr Black has suffered a heart attack. I am afraid his prognosis is not good, but you may go in. One at a time, please."

Betty's legs go weak. She sinks back onto the bench, saying to Sophia, "You go in first."

Sophia, without acknowledging her, rises and follows the doctor.

Joe, by Betty's side, rubs her back. She turns to him with a half smile and holds his hand.

Half an hour later Joe is driving them all home in his Mercedes. The sisters-in-law sit silently next to each other in the back seat, the memory of Rex's waxy white face, tubes going into his body and his unfocused eyes, still in their heads. Betty cannot think what to say to Sophia, and since Sophia blames Betty and the party for Rex's heart attack, not a word passes between them. Marco and Joe also sit in silence, Marco contemplating his own mortality.

It becomes clear after ten days that Rex's heart attack has left him with a paralyzed right arm and leg, severely doubled over, and unable to control his urination.

"He'll only be able to get around in a wheelchair," Betty tells Joe over the telephone.

"I'll come round tomorrow; fix some planks over the front steps for easier access, be ready for when he comes home."

"Joe, that is so kind of you."

Betty visits the hospital every day. Christmas is approaching, but along with Rex, her own life seems to be on hold, even thoughts of Cheryl and the new baby diminish; her life seems as if frozen.

Sleeping alone in Agatha's magnificent old double bed with the carved bed head in the master suite, is uncomfortable, and knowing Rex's heart attack will mean the end of their sex life... *he'll need to sleep alone when he comes out of hospital.* She decides to sleep on the divan in the sitting room next door, it has become her nest, the one room in the house where she feels most at home. There she has her own telly, books and C.Ds, and the armchair Sam bought when they first moved into their home in Holland Street.

On the morning the hospital discharge Rex, they loan him a

wheelchair, which Betty promises to return after she has bought a new one. The sloping platform Joe erected over part of the front steps makes for easier access, but there are other awkward steps, one down to the sun lounge and another to a toilet. Betty telephones Joe to ask him if he can come over and cover them.

"Bit busy at the moment, luv. Big contract up at Horsham. I'll pop round in a week or two when I'm done, okay? See you."

She purchases a new wheelchair and Rex's chauffeur, Robert, returns the old one to the hospital.

Every morning she pushes Rex, wrapped in a rug, along the chilly sea front toward Hove, taking care to avoid the Meeting Place cafe where he proposed only nine months ago.

"Why are we going this way?" he demands. "Go down on the low level. I want to see the girls sunbathing."

"Rex, no one is sunbathing at this time of year."

In his new situation, a more brutal side to Rex's character emerges; "Bloody hell, woman!" he shouts, "I'm dying, can't you move quicker than that. I haven't got all day." He becomes a cantankerous old man. His mental processes become slow and ponderous; he cannot swallow properly, and he needs help with eating, drinking and going to the toilet. He is constantly tired, but worse hit are his emotions. In turn, he becomes depressed, angry, and anxious and seems to have lost all his self-esteem.

Betty becomes his carer, ministering to his every need, feeding him, bathing him, drying his wrinkled body, and even wiping his bottom after his toilet. All the do's and don'ts of her teenage nurse training come back, even the jokes. *'The definition of stress is when you wake up screaming and realise you haven't fallen asleep,'* and *'You see stress as a normal way of life'* best of all, *'You're a nurse if you've ever said to yourself, why am I here?'*

Agatha suggests employing a professional.

Rex barks, "Not necessary. I'm not paying some stranger to

come and boss me around." He even gets angry when Sophia tries to help. "Stop fussing, girl, for goodness sake, leave me be. Can't stand fussy women about. Betty will do it. She knows what to do. I want my wife to do it."

Fearful that his remarks will inflame Sophia's resentment of her further, Betty does everything without complaint. *This is the cross I must bear, my punishment for marrying for money.*

Christmas is a dismal affair. Betty doesn't even bother sending out cards. No one in the house has a mind to cheer it up with Christmas lights, there is no Christmas tree, holly, mistletoe or decorations, just a few lonely cards sit on the mantelpiece. It is the worst Christmas Betty can remember, even worse than after Sam died twenty years ago, then, at least, she had Claudia and baby Cheryl by her side. This year there is none of the usual noisy family gathering around her dining table, she doesn't even see her daughters on Christmas Day. This year they have to make their own Christmas.

Mrs Hunt tries, producing a turkey with all the trimmings, but Rex sits at the dining table in his wheelchair picking at it: Betty has no appetite. Sophie, with a yellow paper hat on her head, eats in silence. Agatha has pleaded a cold, her meal is taken upstairs to her room where she eats alone watching television.

Early in the New Year, Joe arrives in his van with some wood and his electric saw. He is sympathetic and warm and Betty is thrilled to see him, his is the first friendly face she has seen in weeks. She shows him up to the second floor to point out the steps leading down to the rear sunroom, called by the family the loggia.

"No problem," he says, measuring up.

As he works, Betty makes him a cup of tea in the kitchen and brings it up to him in the lift with some milk chocolate digestives.

"Bless you, luv," he says, sipping from the mug. "Tell me now, how are things? How are you managing?"

"Oh, Joe," she sighs. "I never dreamt it would be like this. This heart attack has completely changed him. He's no longer the sweet man he used to be. He's become a monster." She claps her hand to her mouth to take back the words, looking fearfully at the door at the end of the corridor, the master suite where she knows Agatha is now sitting with Rex. "God forgive me... what am I saying? I didn't mean that. It's because he's in so much pain, you see."

"'Course he is, poor bugger, and so I'm thinking are you?"

"I know I must be strong for him, and I am trying, but I don't think I'm quite as strong as I thought I was."

"You're just having a bit of a wobble, girl, that's all. You're a good woman, Betty; I've known that for a long time."

She looks up at him and gives a hesitant smile.

He bends down to put his mug on the floor. "Come on here, luv, give us a cuddle; you look all in."

For the first time in eight weeks, Betty gives way. "I'm feeling so trapped, Joe. I know, it's terrible of me, because he's the helpless one, poor man. I know I shouldn't talk this way."

"You talk as much as you like, luv. Who have you got to look after you, eh? You just talk as much as you like."

She looks up at him, "You're so understanding, Joe. So kind and thoughtful. Forgive me."

"Of course, luv." Looking into her eyes, he wraps his arms around her, leaning forward he kisses her softly on the lips, then more deeply.

Betty closes her eyes and allows her body to melt into his.

His kiss becomes more passionate, shattering her melancholy, thrilling her very soul with joy.

At that moment a door in the corridor opens. Sophia emerges with a book, she notices them, and watches them embrace with considerable interest.

Betty is lost; her heart beats faster, her senses reel, her world is

Joe's mouth, his kiss, his body. Dimly she hears the clunk of a closing door. She breaks away and looks up, but sees only the empty corridor, all doors are shut. "What was that noise? Did someone see us?"

Joe shrugs.

She moves stealthily to Sophia's door, puts her hand on the doorknob and opens it.

Inside, Sophia is reading, standing beside a white statue of an Egyptian pharaoh. Calmly she looks up, taking off her spectacles, "Yes?"

"I didn't know you were in here. I'm sorry."

"I hope you are," Sophia's meaning is plain. She holds Betty's eyes with a steady gaze.

After a beat, Betty closes the door.

When Joe finishes his work, he packs up his tools and in silence, the pair, standing side by side, descend in the lift.

Joe turns to her. "You know I care for you very much."

"Don't, Joe, please. We just had a kiss… that's all," she says with a light laugh, "just as if we had been under the mistletoe."

But she knows it was a good deal more than that.

Reaching ground level, she opens the lift doors and walks him to the front door. *I am a sensible woman, now behave sensibly.* "Take care, Joe, and thank you so much."

He stands looking at her for a moment.

Opening his arms he gives her a bear hug, she clings to him recklessly obeying some primal need. Forcing herself to break away, she opens the door and stands aside, her eyes down.

He looks at her for a brief moment, then, without a word moves away.

From the doorstep, she watches his van drive down beside the gardens to the seafront and turn into the main road. *What the hell just happened? I must be mad… but I wish to God I could go with him. Get away from all this. What am I thinking? That is Joe, Claudia's husband, my son-in-law! Do not go there!* Turning back into the house, she rides up in the lift to her sitting room and goes into her bathroom.

She washes her hands, splashes cold water on her face, combs her hair, dabs some Cologne on her forehead and prepares herself for whatever may be said when she visits Rex.

Opening his door, she sees Sophia sitting on the bed grasping both his hands. Agatha is sitting by the window working on her sampler; glancing over her spectacles, she immediately looks back at her work. Aware of an atmosphere, Betty is convinced Sophia has told them what she just saw. She notices Rex withdraw his hand from Sophia, but she tightens her grasp.

"Joe has just covered the steps to the loggia," she says. "It'll make it so much easier for you with the wheelchair."

Sophia turns and asks sweetly, "How long has your daughter been married to your carpenter?"

Betty regards her evenly. *Venom from such a mouse.* "Nearly nine years now," she answers, taking pains to add, "I count it a blessing that both my daughters have happy marriages."

"I thought you said Cheryl wasn't married?"

Agatha looks up.

"Not yet, but they have plans to." This lame cover-up brings the conversation to a halt, but convinces no one.

Agatha's eyes return to her sewing.

A flush of embarrassment covers Betty's face. *If Sophia did tell Rex, he would say something. Wouldn't he?* "Anything I can get you, dear?"

"Not at the moment," he says avoiding her eye.

She hesitates, vaguely tidying up. *Should I retreat, or brazen it out? Oh, for goodness sake, it was just a kiss.* Idly she picks up a book. She sits in the armchair and turns a page.

Sophia looks back to Rex. She wipes some drivel from his chin with a Kleenex, which she throws away in the bin, then sits and clasps his hand in hers.

Betty cannot stop thinking of Joe. *Will he tell Claudia what just happened… laugh about it, maybe?* She knows he will not.

The three women sit in silence round the bedside. The tension in the room is palpable.

The only sound is Rex's wheezing breath… in… out, in… out, in… out.

Sophia frowns.

He seems not to see her. He lifts his eyes to the ceiling and stares. He seems to have given up all hope, all desire, all illusions. He closes his eyes and waits for death.

Chapter Eleven

Claudia

January – April 2009

*B*etty was correct in assuming Joe did not tell his wife about their discovered embrace, but not for the reason she supposed.

Claudia was not at home to be told.

For the last two weeks, she has been a voluntary patient, virtually under lock and key, in a private rehab detox centre outside Horsham with the cryptic autonym of 'Prospect'. Joe did not share this vital information with her mother because he thought, what with one thing and another she had enough on her plate, besides, Claudia had asked him not to.

For Claudia things had come to a head after Christmas.

"Our busiest time of year," commented Woody Walsh, psychotherapist to the stars, who, thanks to his frequent appearances on television had become something of a celebrity himself.

On the 5th of January, which was the first working day after the New Year celebrations, Joe had received a curious telephone call. It was from a certain Sylvia, the supervisor at Claudia's place of work, the Liverpool Victoria Insurance Company.

"Is Mrs Robinson available, please?" she enquired.

"No, afraid not. Can I help? This is her husband speaking."

"Oh, I'm so glad to talk to you. Are you quite well?"

"Never better," he replied, mystified. "Why?"

"Mrs Robinson told me you were in hospital."

"Well, I'm not… and glad to say never have been."

"How odd. This is Mr Joe Robinson?"

"That is correct."

The line went silent while Sylvia thought the thing through. "It seems I have been misled; sorry to have bothered you. Do you know where she is, by any chance? Her mobile doesn't answer and I need to talk to her?"

"I thought she was with you at work."

"No, she's not in today. As I said, she told me she was visiting you in hospital."

"What was supposed to be wrong with me?"

"She told me you had taken an overdose of barbiturates, and were at death's door."

"Oh, I see!" exclaimed Joe. "Not that I do see exactly, but I appreciate your concern. I'll ask her about it when I see her."

"Do, and tell her to call me, please. Thank you."

Joe replaced the receiver and thought.

It didn't take him long to figure out his so called suicide attempt had been a dramatic excuse, an invention of Claudia's to get off work so she could go to a bar for a drink. *Trust her to invent something dramatic. Nothing simple, like, the children have mumps, no, it has to be a big story. Suicide, indeed! Huh! She always was a drama queen.*

Joe was learning the hard fact that an alcoholic will say just about anything to get a drink. Knowing that combing Brighton's bars looking for her would be a hopeless task, he Googled Woody Walsh's web site, as Marco had suggested. He made a note of a contact number and waited for Claudia to come home.

When she eventually showed up, it was 1.30 a.m. and she was drunk.

Joe patiently undressed her and put her to bed, choosing to sleep in the spare room.

The next morning he cooked his boys breakfast, took them to school, called up his second in command to take charge on the site they were working on, made a strong pot of coffee and tackled Claudia in their bedroom.

From Woody's web site, he had learnt the key element to beating alcohol, or any addiction, come to that was accepting that you had an addition. "Acceptance and then action," it said.

Claudia's mood was at least one of contrition. "God is punishing me!" she moaned clutching her head. Then she became maudlin, confessing she hated her life. "I want to die," she grizzled. "What use am I to anyone? I might as well be dead. I'm nearly thirty and crap at everything."

"You're twenty-seven," Joe corrected.

"Oh, Mr Precise!" she sneered. "I'm cooped up in that bloody insurance office cubicle all day listening to people's woes, telling me their houses have been burnt down, they've been burgled, lost their limbs, their husbands, smashed their cars, making unbelievable claims, nothing but an endless itinerary of misery. It's no wonder I can't get through the day without a drink. My Mother hates me, my sister despises me, my children drive me dotty, and you don't can't bear the sight of me anymore, fucking everything in skirts that comes near you!"

Joe looked at the bloated harridan his wife had become. He had seen her in many roles in their nine years of marriage, sex kitten, friend, wife, mother, and latterly, bitter unhappy bitch, but he had never known her express such self-excoriating thoughts before. The intense passion, which had brought them together, had diminished long ago, but he had not lived with Claudia, a sensitive, intelligent woman, with whom he (occasionally) shared affection, without forming a strong emotional bond. She was, after all, the mother of his two handsome sons. He was fourteen years her senior and had realised some time ago that he no longer loved her, he'd been making excuses not to come home for too long, but he did still care for her. Patiently he talked to her for an hour, trying to make her understand and accept the fact that she needed professional help. After tears, harsh words, and much soul searching, she admitted to wanting to be a better person, and eventually agreed to see Woody Walsh.

Joe set up the meeting. He never discovered exactly what Woody had actually said at their interview, but his words and personality had a profound effect on Claudia. From then on she was "mad about Woody... such a wise man... so sensitive... he understands people with drink problems because he was once one of them."

With instructions to Joe that he should not on any account tell her mother or Cheryl, she agreed to a stay at Prospect. Hoping and believing it would cure her addiction, she submitted to the strict discipline imposed there, which included the surrender of her mobile phone and complying with Woody Walsh's unique brand of drama-role therapy.

Joe agreed to abide by the rule that there was to be no contact with her for four weeks, and to engage a Nanny/Housekeeper to look after Peter and Paul. To cover the considerable cost he was obliged to cash in £7,000 of BNY Mellon Asset stock he had invested.

From the six young girls and women who applied for the job from Bunnies Nanny Agency, he chose to employ the most experienced and plainest. Experienced, because he knew his sons well enough to know whomever he selected would have to be strong enough to deal with their boisterous behaviour. Plainest, because he knew himself well enough to know if she were plain, he would not be tempted to seduce her.

Mrs Elliot was indeed very plain, and by no stretch of the imagination a bunny. From her C.V. he noted she was the most experienced, but when she walked in to the interview, she appeared formidable and not very likable. Pointing out that one of her jobs would be to collect his boys from school, she answered, "Excuse me, sir, but I'm used to dealing with the mothers of my charges. It saves so many misunderstandings. I prefer to take my orders only from the lady of the house."

"As the lady of this house is in a clinic for alcoholics," he replied, "I confess to you frankly, Mrs Elliot, I am at my wit's end. I am a working man and trying to hold my family together without her. So I am asking you, please, to take your orders from me. You seem to be a wise and warm woman of the world, I trust you will adapt to this change and be able to help me."

Mrs Elliot had looked at him and seen a handsome, masterful yet helpless male pleading for her help, there was also a very well appointed flat at the back of the house that went with the job. She had melted, and from then on had been at his feet. She would gladly even have washed them for him, if he had so requested

For Claudia, the turning point came after she had been at Prospect for ten weeks. Summoned to an afternoon "role play" session with Woody, four other staff members were in attendance, three women, and a man. She knew all the staff well by this time, but when she spotted two life-sized dolls propped up on the sofa, she knew some new therapy was afoot.

"I want you to imagine," explained Woody, in his warm Irish brogue, "that in this room are the most important people in your life. The family that we have discussed in our sessions together. I want you to go up to them, and tell them exactly what you think of them. Dress 'em down. Let rip. No holds barred, you can say what you like, but try to be honest, honest to yourself. Tell them why you think they've let you down. I don't care if you swear, say anything you like, let yourself really go. I want you to get rid of all the shite that's been clutterin' up your head for all these years. Off you go now."

The next twenty minutes were an emotional rollercoaster for Claudia. She let rip. One by one, she cleaned the key people in her life, swore, accused them of being selfish, unloving bastards, even admitting to her own mistakes; each staff member took it in turn to represent Betty, Joe, Cheryl, and her boss, Sylvia. The dolls stood in for her twins.

When it was over she was an exhausted wreck. Meekly, she muttered, "Well, I let them have it."

"Yes," agreed Woody, "but there's another person in the room you've not noticed yet. Look again."

She looked, but saw no one. Then behind the sofa, she spotted a doll, smaller and prettier than the life-sized ones on the sofa. This was a real doll, like the ones of her childhood, it had dark hair like hers, and on a label was written, "I'm Claudia".

"It's me!" she gasped, clasping the doll. "It's me!" She started sobbing uncontrollably. "I didn't see you before. I'm so sorry. Oh, God! I love you. Love you more than anyone in the world, you're beautiful, the most important person in the world. I promise to take better care of you. I'll love you always. Forgive me for being so bad, so bad. I love you so much." She collapsed on the sofa, weeping and cuddling the doll.

Woody nodded wisely, "Well done, you're getting the idea of it at last. Maybe you'll get to love yourself a bit more now, eh? Stop pressing that self-destruct button, start listening to the wise, protective side of yourself. We might well be losing you to the halfway house soon."

Two weeks later, she moved into a halfway house in Horsham presided over by a matron. Joe took the boys to see her and they went out in the town for tea. Claudia behaved beautifully and was more like her old warm funny self.

Ten days later, Woody released her on the promise that she would never touch another drop of liquor, not ever. "If you do," he warned, "You will be hooked forever."

Chapter Twelve

Marco

January – April 2009

Márco stands dejectedly by the sink doing the washing up in Betty's redecorated old kitchen in Holland Street.

His mobile on the kitchen table buzzes.

Drying his hands, he quickly answers.

"I have a meeting for you," says Judy Pearl, his agent, calling from London Management in Mayfair.

"Great!" he grabs a note pad from the dresser. "Pencil at the ready. Shoot!"

"It's for a new play. They want to see you at the King's Head, in Islington."

"Isn't that a pub?"

"Yes, but it's the smartest Fringe theatre in London and always gets reviewed by the nationals. There's not much money, I'm afraid, but I hear the part is excellent. Be there at ten, tomorrow morning."

"What about the script?"

"No time to send it, and it's too fat to fax. You'll just have to read it on sight."

"But…

"I know, dear, it's an absurd situation, in an absurd profession, but go with the flow."

"Can't you tell me anything about the part?"

"Only that he's a vampire! I know," she adds in a dry voice, "don't ask. Call me back afterwards. Good luck. 'Bye, darling," and she is gone.

Marco bounds up the stairs to share the news with Cheryl, who is sorting through baby clothes at the airing cupboard.

"At last," he gasps, "an interview. After all these months of frustration, now it's all hectic rush. Typical! I have to be bright-eyed and bushy-tailed at ten o'clock tomorrow morning in Islington."

"You'll do it, darling," says Cheryl "I know you will. You'll charm the pants off them. It's your turn, it's only fair."

"But life isn't fair, honey, we know that, but I'm sure going to try."

All the way up on the early morning train from Brighton, he wonders what the part and the play are like, and how it has come his way. *Don't be too desperate for the job,* he reminds himself, *just be cool.*

He arrives at Victoria station at nine thirty, makes his way to Islington on the tube, walks up Upper Street, finds the dingy looking pub and pushes open the Lounge Bar door.

A bald unhappy barman in braces is behind the counter cleaning.

"Where are the auditions being held?" he asks.

Miserable baldy nods to a door at the back.

He opens it to discover a dusty little theatre. At the end of a 120-seat auditorium, a working light shines on a tiny stage. Sitting in the stalls, smoking, a mink coat over her shoulders, is Georgiana Barrington.

All is suddenly clear.

"Darling!" she says, rising to kiss him, "How lovely. Sorry this is so last minute, but our original actor fell out, and I only thought of you yesterday." Turning to the writer and director, she introduces him. "This is the boy I was telling you about."

Two intense intellectuals look him up and down. They talk a while about the play, which they politely inform him is a comic gothic thriller concerning the love life of a twenty-first century vampire, entitled *The Reluctant Vampire.*

"It's a fun mix of Anne Rice and Martin Sedgwick. Here," says the director, tossing him a script, "have a read. Page one, first speech, the part is Zak. We'll call you back in five minutes."

Marco returns to the bar with Miserable Baldy to absorb his lines. Reading greedily, he smacks his lips and grins. It's good stuff.

Half an hour later, he walks out of the pub into Upper Street having landed the leading role.

During the next hectic four weeks, travelling back and forth to rehearsals from Brighton, Marco burns the lines into his head; along with costume fittings, he researches everything there is to know about vampires, reads Bram Stoker's novel, eats and drinks the play, hypnotizing himself into becoming the part.

On the opening night, Cheryl leaves baby Thomas with her next-door neighbour, Rosa, who asks, "How's Betty? I do miss her. Is she enjoying her new life? It's champagne all the way now, I suppose."

"She's fine," answers Cheryl, handing over the baby things. "Thank you so much."

This is the first First Night she has ever attended; excited and nervous for Marco, she travels up to London alone, for Marco left this morning. It is the first time she has been out without her baby, it's an odd feeling, but she likes it, she begins to feel more buoyant, more like her former dainty self.

In The King's Head bar, Georgina and Michael Barrington greet her warmly and buy her a drink. She takes her seat, and when the curtains part she has her heart in her mouth as Marco, hypnotic in a black evening dress coat comes on stage to confide to the audience his "little problem". There is laughter and later, in the eighteenth century flashback scene, the agony of his initiation is deeply moving. At the curtain call, there are wolf whistles and enthusiastic applause. Afterwards there is barely time for a drink before they have to dash to Victoria station to catch the last train home.

The next morning the highbrow press condemn the play as trash. The red tops carry sexy photographs of Marco stripped to the waist, his dark mesmeric eyes glinting through tumbling black hair; under his picture they describe the play as "erotic", "witty" and "deliciously macabre". By the end of the first week the show is a sell out and it becomes apparent they are the latest hot ticket in town. The play is a fashionable success. Marco acquires hoards of female fans and becomes a much-talked-about actor in circles where that sort of talk matters. The production runs for four weeks, and at the last mid-week matinee, just as Marco is beginning to wonder how he is going to cope with unemployment again, Georgiana pops her head round the door of the cramped little dressing room he shares with five other actors.

"Marco!" she calls, "Free for tea?"

"Sure," he answers, covering his nakedness with a towel. "Give me two minutes, and I'll be with you."

Walking arm in arm down Upper Street, Georgiana says, "I have news."

"What?"

"Wait till we're sitting down."

At Madam Chi's Tea Room, the smartest teashop in Islington, they find a table. "Well?" he asks, grinning, "what's up?"

"We're going to New York. Broadway!"

"What?"

"Well, actually, Off Broadway. The entire production."

"But how? Why? When?"

"We've been invited to be part of a short four-week 'Brits on Broadway' season. We open ten days after we close here."

"You're joking!"

A waitress arrives to take their order. Georgiana asks for "Smoked salmon and scrambled eggs, please and a pot of tea." Charmingly she lifts her eyebrows to Marco, "You, too?"

"Sure," he says, then, not waiting for the waitress to leave, "This is fantastic! But what happens about flights and hotels? I'll never be able to afford those?"

"Don't worry! All airfares and accommodation are paid for, part of your per diems. All taken care of, darling," she laughs.

"By whom?" Marco always wants his i's dotted and t's crossed.

"The management, of course."

"But the management is you, isn't it?"

"Not entirely. It's sweet of you to be concerned, but it's not all coming out of my pocket, I assure you. We'll have some fun together, eh?"

"New York, wow! We sure will!"

Cheryl, wise girl that she is, announces, "I'm coming too," when Marco tells her. "I'm not letting those New York floozies get their talons into you. They'll eat you up alive. Thomas and I will be by your side every step of the way."

Her plan, however, is not to be.

"The company can't afford to fly our families out as well," he explains. "But don't worry. We'll only be apart for a month."

It is not until after the show has closed in Islington, the preparations and packing complete, after the excitement of arriving at Kennedy Airport and riding down Broadway in a taxicab, that Marco discovers his bedroom is in the same downtown hotel and in the adjoining suite to Mrs Georgiana Barrington.

Chapter Thirteen

Coping

Coping with Rex becomes Betty's full time job. There are no visits to the cinema, no outings to theatres or concerts these days, caring for Rex becomes her life. It has its own small reward, he looks up at her from his bed like a grateful spaniel, she hasn't felt so valued since nursing Claudia and Cheryl through the measles. However, no such feelings of gratitude emanate from his mother or sister. Since her discovered embrace with Joe outside the loggia, her relationship with Sophia has utterly disintegrated: though her sister-in-law has never mentioned it, she insists on regarding Betty these days with a superior smirk.

Agatha, who cannot help her personal prejudices, now barely bothers to conceal them. She never says anything to Betty of a personal nature, addressing her only when telling her what to do for Rex, how to do it, and when, and in her inimitable frosty aloof manner. Obstructed from helping her son by her fragility and age, as well as by Rex himself, she observes Betty feed her son with the steely look and the pursed lip of a lemon-sucking witch. "Make him finish up those greens. The last bite is your strength."

"Mother, you've been saying that to me for years and look at me, I'm dying."

"Because you never listened to me," she snaps, insisting, as always, on having the last word.

Rex is now more or less bed bound, he has lost a great deal of weight, as he no longer shaves, his beard grows out white, his face assuming the deceptive countenance of a old sage. Because he is unable to swallow properly, Betty has to liquefy all his food and medication, at least she has Mrs Hunt to help with that, and Robert to help turn his heavy body over in bed.

In her involuntary inner life, her feelings at letting herself go in Joe's arms still torment her. *It was only a kiss, for heaven's sake. Stop making such a mountain out of a molehill. We didn't commit adultery!* Nevertheless, in her bed at night she relives that kiss too often. *Such a fuss! So it was nice kiss, but no more than under the mistletoe at Christmas. Such foolishness, how could I have behaved so stupidly? Weak, that's what I am. It was the circumstances, because I was so depressed.* But she cannot forget the feel of his warm body wrapped around hers, his words, "I care for you." *What the hell does that mean? Care? That's what I do for Rex.*

Fearful of her guilty emotions, she avoids contacting Claudia; she cannot bear the thought of meeting her daughter's eyes. In an effort to keep straight, in trying to live a decent honest life, she refuses to return any of Joe's calls, ignoring his pleas to meet up. She deletes every one of his messages and texts on her mobile, but try as she may, she cannot delete her thoughts, imagining what might be, imagining escape from this, her trapped, wealthy new life as the second Mrs Rex Black of Brunswick Square.

The few crumbs of happiness she does experience are when she can spend a few hours with Cheryl and the baby in her old home; though even then, she feels she cannot leave Rex, without asking his permission.

"Will you be alright while I pop round to see Cheryl and my grandson?"

"Must you?" he asks, his surrendered eyes looking up pleadingly from the pillow. "Don't be too long, will you? Get Robert to take you in the Bentley."

Never having learnt to drive, this is a bonus; however, she feels most uncomfortable returning to her pokey little street sat behind her smart chauffeur in the Bentley.

Robert is good at his job and knows his place, preferring to wait in the car outside the house.

Cheryl greets her warmly. "Mumma darling! Claudia said she'd pop round this afternoon, too."

Betty's heart skips a beat. She realises she will have to go through some sort of test. In spite of being in the heart of her family, she will have to put on an act and guard her tongue.

In the kitchen, she spoon-feeds baby Thomas in his high chair.

Cheryl watches fondly, "You don't have to do that, Mumma."

"I enjoy it, don't we, Thomas? Open wide… in we go!"

"I'm feeling a bit guilty about Claudia, actually," says Cheryl, "I've not set eyes on her for weeks. She said she had something particular to tell me. Did you speak to Joe at all?"

"Only when he fixed the platform over the steps for Rex's wheelchair."

"Did he say anything? I mean, about anything being wrong with her?"

Keeping her eyes from her daughter, she goes on feeding Thomas, "No. I don't think he even mentioned her."

"How odd. You know they never went to see Marco in his play."

"Well, neither did I, for that matter," she says, not feeling in the least guilty. Starved of culture she may be, but the thought of travelling up to London to see her daughter's layabout boy friend playing a vampire in an Islington pub, was a definite no-no.

"You're excused: you were busy looking after Rex."

"You will explain to him, won't you, when you speak to him. How's he enjoying New York?"

"Excited, he calls me nearly every night. He's staying in a

fabulous apartment, he says. They have their first night to-night, probably about right now, actually."

"Pity you're not there to cheer him on," says Betty.

The front door bell rings and Cheryl admits Claudia.

Hearing her elder daughter's voice in the hall, Betty goes cold with guilt. *What's the matter with me? It was only a kiss, for goodness sake.*

"Mum!" exclaims Claudia, in the kitchen doorway. "I might have known I'd find you here. You never come to see me."

Betty smiles and greets her daughter with her usual hug and kiss. "You're looking well, dear. I do declare you've lost weight."

"I have," says Claudia, "I'm a new woman!"

"I'm pleased to hear that!" says Cheryl, dryly, wiping Thomas's mouth and lifting him out of his high chair. "This is Aunty Claudia. Say hello Aunty Claudia."

Claudia beams at the boy. "Hello, Thomas. You're going to be as good looking as your Dad, aren't you?"

Cheryl, holding Thomas on her hip, says, "So what's this news you have to tell us?"

"Patience. Let me get settled, first," she says, taking off her overcoat. "Do I get a cup of tea?"

"I'll make it," says Betty.

"Mum! No," says Cheryl, ushering them away down the hall. "Go and sit in the front room and talk to Claudia while I put Thomas down."

In the living room, mother and daughter face each other in armchairs.

Outwardly cool and unperturbed, Betty squares her shoulders, determined to behave naturally.

Claudia smiles, "How are you, Ma? I've not seen you in ages. You look a little peaky. How's Rex?"

Betty makes a face. "Not good, I'm afraid. But you're looking well." Not daring to enquire after Joe, she says, "What have you been up to? How are my handsome grandsons?"

"They're fine, thanks to Joe and this new nanny we've got. Mrs Elliot, she's a marvel. At last that 'Granny' flat he built at the back has come into its own; but, oh Mum!" She bites her lip and wanders to the fireplace. "Where on earth do I start?"

"How do you mean?" she asks, suddenly fearful. "What?"

"I didn't want to tell you before, but... I've been ill. I'm all right now," she adds hurriedly. "But I've been away at a rehab centre. I'm an alcoholic, you see. Now, don't get yourself upset, I'm not anymore. At least, I am, but I've not had a drink for nearly three months, and I never can again, not ever."

"Darling girl!" exclaims Betty, rising, full of maternal concern, her own indiscretion forgotten. "I never knew you were having to deal with all this."

Claudia looks at the door, "I wanted Cheryl to hear this."

"Why on earth didn't you tell me?"

"I couldn't, Ma," she says, allowing her mother to hold her. "My head was too muddled. I was ashamed. I wouldn't even admit it to myself. Joe's been marvellous. He fixed up the clinic and everything. I'd be nowhere without him, nowhere."

Betty shuts her eyes and hugs her daughter, feeling like a betraying Judas.

"But while I was in the clinic, or rather since, I've done a lot of thinking. One of the things I've come to realise about myself is," she holds her mother at arm's length and looks her in the eyes, "I have to stand on my own two feet and not rely on Joe anymore."

"Whatever do you mean?"

"Let's face it, Mum, I married Joe for all the wrong reasons." She slips back onto the arm of the armchair. "He's that rare combination, a stud muffin and father figure. At least, he was to me. At the time, he was exactly what I was looking for. I was mad about him, well, you know I was. With him I could remain a little girl, be looked after, and still have glorious sex. Not that there's been much of that around lately. Now that I'm a woman. I have to grow up, and I think I have in these last months. I think I've leant how to take responsibility for myself, and I like it. I'm not that spoil little girl anymore. I want to carry on, and I don't think I can go on doing that being married to Joe. So I've decided to leave him."

Betty looks at her dumbfounded.

"I want a new life for myself, Mum. I'm full of enthusiasm about it and hope."

The word hope hangs, not entirely convincingly, in the air, as Betty carries on looking at her.

"Do say something, darling. Back me up."

"Claudia, you take my breath away. You've always told me what a wonderful man Joe is, how lucky you were to find each other."

"He is, and we were, but that was then, now is different. Oh, I'm sure we're going to go on being friends. I intend to anyway. I'm determined to be civilized about it. But I must be on my own for a while. I have to be."

"But what about your boys? You can't just turn your back on your children."

"Don't worry. I've got it all worked out. They will stay at school, Joe will look after them at home as usual, with the help of Mrs Elliot, and I'm going to leave. I've still got my job, and I've been looking at flats. I need to look after myself for a while. I never have, well, you know. I left home to get married, and I've never had to fend for myself. I want to do that, to find out about myself. I need space."

"You need space! But what about your children? What does Joe say about all this?"

"I haven't told him, yet."

"Claudia!"

"So don't you say anything."

"As if I would! Oh, my dear girl! When are you going to tell him?"

"Soon. When I've found myself a flat."

"Darling… " Stunned by Claudia's lack of responsibility to her sons, her "wanting space", she is at a loss to find the words to put some sense into her, all she can manage is: "Do think things through properly, I implore you. Make sure it's what you really, really want, before you do anything you may regret. What a thing!" she sighs, "I had no idea you were going through all this, no idea. I've been so wrapped up in my own life, my own miserable little problems."

"Of course you have, pet." She caresses her mother's cheek fondly. "Like the chauffeur-driven Bentley outside. Poor old Mum!"

Betty attempts a smile and Cheryl comes in carrying a tray of tea things, "Should we ask that nice driver of yours in for a cup of tea?"

"He's quite happy out there," says Betty, absently.

"Oops! You're too late," says Claudia, glancing out of the window. "Look, Rosa's got him."

They join her at the widow and smile as they watch their flamboyant neighbour on the pavement chatting up Robert with a mug of tea.

"Typical Rosa!" says Claudia. "She's never slow in coming forward. Let's hope it's not gin."

Chapter Fourteen

Off Broadway

Marco walks down 42nd Street to his theatre feeling more alive and elated than he has ever done in his life. During the last week he has been operating on all cylinders, he has given four newspaper interviews, made two television appearances, had a two hour photo session, and all in between rehearsing *The Reluctant Vampire* in the new space. The electric billboards flash their advertisements on the high buildings, and looking up at the skyscrapers of the Great White Way it seems Woody Allen's *Manhattan, Rhapsody in Blue, On the Town, The Sweet Smell of Success*, and all the New York movies he has ever seen have come to life and he is starring in every one of them. He revels in the commotion, the noise and adventure. New sexier costumes have been made for him (courtesy of Georgiana), and he feels more confident and in control on stage than he ever did in Islington. As the hours to his first night approach, every inch of his body tingles with excitement.

There is only one problem… Georgiana.

Oh yes, she's beautiful and in every way the most thoughtful producer, but her husband, Michael, has remained in London, and Marco has the uneasy feeling that any moment she could pounce. Mercifully, the connecting door between their bedroom suites has remained locked, but on his side of the door, there is no sign of a key.

Reaching The Little Shubert Theatre, his theatre, at 422 West 42nd Street, he is thrilled to see the title of his play up in lights. His name, however, is nowhere to be seen. Only if he looks very closely at the small print on the alphabetically listed cast on the pamphlet can he spot, "Marco Danieli".

The auditorium is larger than The King's Head; but not too much, it seats 499. The buzz backstage is electric, the cast, who have bonded over the last two months, are enjoying a strong camaraderie, wishing each other "good luck", "break a leg", and "a big hand on your opening".

In his No 1, dressing room Marco hums and warms-up his voice as he makes up and oils his hair. He gets dressed in his First Act costume and at last, the moment arrives... "Places please," comes over the tannoy. Standing up, he takes one last full-length look at himself in the mirror. His black hair gleams, his kohl eyes blaze green, he has become "Zak".

He leaves himself behind and walks to the stage.

Since he is in nearly every scene, he goes through the evening aware only of the audience and his fellow actors; timing his laughs and when necessary, controlling the house. Being Zak is like being on a razor's edge, living his emotions but simultaneously keeping the customers quiet.

In the final scene, when the Zak dies and the heroine is doomed to walk the earth in eternal misery, there is dead silence, ultimately leading to a crescendo of applause. As the cast assemble at the curtain call, they are bathed in glory.

Backstage, slews of strangers pack the tiny corridors to congratulate them. Georgiana arrives with hugs and kisses saying, "You're a star! Bless you, Marco. Thank you so much. I've arranged a table for us all at Sardi's. It's the only place to go after a Broadway first night!"

Sardi's opened in March 1927 and has since been described as "providing a transient home and comfort station for theatre folk for 20 years". As Marco and his "Brit" company excitedly enter the celebrated restaurant, they spot hundreds of cartoons of famous faces decorating the walls, but disappointingly no live ones eating. The place seems full of out-of-towners and tourists, hoping to spot celebrities.

The waiters are cool; the reputation of the place so secure they don't bother much. The meal is fair, but the cast chatter excitedly and say complimentary things to him. Reaching the coffee stage, they wait for their newspaper reviews, just like in the movies Marco has seen… but times have changed, these days actors can read their reviews on iPods and mobile phones.

"The New York Herald says you're 'the new Colin Farrell,'" calls out one of the actors reading from his Blackberry, "Get you, dear!"

"I don't want to be the new anybody," laughs Marco. "I wanna be me!"

"You are, dear, and apparently 'a thrilling new talent,' so it says here."

"Listen to this, 'Strikes a fresh note of intimacy to a classic genre'."

"'Don't hate him, he's beautiful,'" quotes someone else. "That means you, Marco, cookie!"

"My production," quotes Georgiana, pulling a comically modest face, 'delves into the magical world between dreaming and waking in an unexpected twist on a classic franchise.' Well fancy that!"

The reviews, overall, are good, ranging from 'a fun evening' to 'classic Brit acting'. The Daily News even paraphrases a famous Robert Benchley quote: 'Where will the people come from to keep this going? You won't see them out in daylight!' All single out Marco, describing him as 'possessing a dangerous sexuality,' 'a talent to watch,' and 'Brit shines'.

After midnight, in the taxi returning to the hotel, two other cast members pile in with Georgiana and Marco. When they have gone, she cuddles up closer. "I forgot to tell you. Michael said particularly to wish you good luck for tonight. He's so fond of you, you know."

This comes as news to Marco. Whenever he met Michael in the bar at the King's Head, he had hardly spoken and then only in platitudes, almost as if he were embarrassed. Marco guessed it was because he remembered too well what had once been between them.

In the corridor outside their rooms, Georgiana tosses her hair out of her eyes and kisses him on the cheek. "Good night, darling. You were quite, quite wonderful. I am so proud of you. Sleep well, you deserve to," and they go their separate ways.

Once in his room Marco considers calling Cheryl. He looks at his watch. *Ten past one, she won't appreciate being woken at six in the morning. Leave it till tomorrow.* He has a quick shower, flops naked into bed and turns out the light.

There is a light tapping on the connecting door… it opens.

Standing silhouetted in the moonlight is Georgiana in a thin nightdress.

Oh, God what do I do now? I can't say 'no' to the boss. Oh well! Rise to the occasion! I've had the husband, now I guess it's the turn of the wife.

Georgiana closes the door, slips off her shoulder straps and lets the nightgown fall to the ground. Without a word, she gets into his bed.

Chapter Fifteen

Michael

*G*eorgiana had been unable to temper the excitement in her voice when describing to her husband on the telephone how her 'first night' had fared, particularly regarding Marco's brilliant performance.

Michael, who is a sharp cookie and has a possessive nature, had experienced something of the sort before with his wife. Instinctively grasping the situation and quietly seething about it, he decides to call the pretty little girl friend of his former school friend in Brighton.

"How's my godson?" he merrily chirps down the phone.

"That's Michael Barrington!" exclaims Cheryl, "What a surprise. How are you?"

"Feeling rather a spare part, actually, which is why I've called. I wonder if you would allow me to take you out to dinner. Our better halves seem to be having such a whale of a time across the pond; I thought it might be appropriate if we were to do the same. What do you say?"

"What a super idea. I think that'd be fun. But I'm afraid it would have to be a lunch; in the evening I'd have baby-sitting problems."

"No problem."

So it came about that two days later, Michael, wearing an impeccably tailored navy blue suit and shiny striped tie, accompanies Cheryl, in her best summer frock (and the pair do make a handsome couple), into Terre à Terre, an award-winning vegetarian restaurant in East Street, just around the corner from the Palace Pier.

"Table for two, Barrington," confirms Michael to the headwaiter at the door.

Shown to a banquette by the window at the back, they settle at their table and are handed massive menus.

"I know this place of old," confides Michael, "we'll have a superb meal." Turning to the waiter he orders, "A bottle of Picpoul de Pinet, please."

Never having been to a vegetarian restaurant before, but delighted to be out with such a sophisticated man of the world. Cheryl gawps at the menu. "Goodness! What a vast array of choices! What would you advise?"

"Would you prefer me to choose for you?"

"Please, I'm totally lost."

"I've been a veggie most of my life, leave it to me." Addressing the waiter, he's off on one of his favourite pastimes. "We'll start with an order of three types of mushroom, sautéed, creamed and pickled, a micro-shoot salad with spiced Jerusalem artichokes, with your red mulled port liquor, dusted with hazelnut and salt praline. For our main course, we'll have gnocchi," Turning to Cheryl, he checks... "All right with you?

Cheryl nods. She has no idea what he is talking about... *knocky?*

"Potatoes!" he says aside, in answer to her pretty frown. "Your fluffy rosemary infused potato pillows," he continues to the waiter, "pan fried after blanching, golden and crisp, accompanied by butternut squash puree with orange zest and crispy fried sage leaves cooked your three different ways. That will do for now. Thank you. Oh, wait, would you like Perrier, Cheryl?"

"No, thanks," she says, wondering if she could ever acquire his enviable sangfroid, "The wine will be sufficient."

"Thank you," he says, dismissing the waiter and leaning back, "So... What do you make of all this 'carry on' we're hearing from the other side of the Atlantic?"

"It sounds thrilling. I just wish I was there."

"I was in New York two years ago when Georgie had another show on the go. I get a bit bored with it all, to tell you the truth. Don't look so shocked," he laughs, "Show business isn't my bag. My hobby is more sports. Tennis is my game. Ask Marco, I used to play him at school."

"Who won?"

"We were fairly evenly matched," he says, adopting a modest demeanour.

Cheryl knows Marco to be a fierce player, so doubts Michael is telling the truth. "I love tennis, too. Both of us are glued to the telly over Wimbledon. I think it starts in about a fortnight."

"It's Ascot, this week, so yes, next week it'll be Wimbledon. Would you like to go?"

"I'd love to. I've never been."

"Right, it's a date," he says grinning. "I'll fix it up. Be my pleasure."

"Marco says there are celebrities out front at nearly every performance in New York. The other night, he said, there was Martin Scorsese. You know the film director, *Goodfellows, The Aviator* and *Blood Diamond* with Leonardo Di Caprio?"

At that moment, the wine waiter delivers the Picpoul, which to Michael is far more interesting. He reads the label, feels the temperature of the bottle, and nods to the waiter, who pours some into his glass. Michael swirls it, smells it, and takes a sip. After the savouring, he nods appreciatively, "That will do nicely, thank you," and the waiter pours wine into Cheryl's glass.

She takes a sip, "Nice."

Michael regards her with a steady smile.

"Marco said Georgiana took them all out to 'Sardi's' after the opening night."

"Yes, well, that's what she does. She gets these crushes on her artists. Her 'boys', as she calls them. It never lasts long. Once the show is over it's forgotten, it's up and on to the next project. Usually the next good looking young actor," he flips casually, taking another sip. "I've learnt to live with it, to look the other way. I advise you to do the same."

Confused for a moment, Cheryl is about to ask what he is getting at, when another waiter arrives with a platter of delicious looking hors d'oeuvres.

After taking a bite, she is compelled to ask, "When you say, look the other way? What exactly do you mean?"

"I've always believed that what the eye doesn't see, the heart doesn't grieve over, know what I mean?"

"You mean… you think… they've having an affair?"

Michael grimaces and attempts a cool philosophical air. "Who knows? Probably. Marco's a handsome fellow, Georgiana a lovely woman, and she told me herself she finds him attractive, but don't worry, it'll blow over. It always does." He shrugs and forks a piece of artichoke into his mouth. "This is superb. Eat up, but leave room. The puddings here are divine."

It is only with the greatest difficulty Cheryl continues her meal. *Why did he have to tell me that?* Despite such a shaky foundation, her tender young heart is breaking. Doubts escalate to certainties in her mind; painful thoughts of a forced separation from Marco crowd her brain. *Is that why he's asked me here? To warn me? He can't be serious about taking me to Wimbledon. Is Marco really having an affair? Georgiana is very attractive. Please God, pray let everything be all right. I couldn't live without Marco. I couldn't bring up Thomas alone, not like Mumma did with me and Claudia, I couldn't be a single parent, I just couldn't.*

She endeavours to hide such thoughts from Michael, who, to her amazement, chatters on about the necessity of keeping to a healthy non-meat diet and taking twice-weekly exercise in his Kensington gymnasium. Whether he is oblivious to the pain he has delivered, or, having accomplished his aim, is content to behave as if nothing has happened, is beyond the limits of her judgement.

Later, when in his giant Porsche he drops her off outside the house in Holland Street, he kisses her farewell on the cheek. "Take care. I promise to call you in a couple of days about our Wimbledon assignation."

No way, she thinks, as she waves him good-bye. She rescues Thomas from Rosa, next door, and retrieves the toy truck that Michael had given him earlier as a present. She would like to throw it away, but as that would upset Thomas, she only hides it. *Beastly thing! Beastly man! How could he suggest such a vile thing?*

So much for Michael's good intentions, and incidentally, the cost of his sixty-six pound luncheon.

With her tummy churning and her imagination painting unspeakable pictures of Marco and Georgiana on her retina, Cheryl finds it impossible to settle to boring domestic chores. She flings down the ironing bag and bundles Thomas into his buggy, setting forth on a long walk along the sea front to blow away the horrid pictures in her head.

Chapter Sixteen

Sophia

On the other side of town, Sophia looks out of the window absently fingering the slim gold chain round her neck. "What a heavenly afternoon."

"Go for a walk along the sea front," suggests Agatha, ensconced in her armchair with her needlepoint. "The fresh air will do you good."

"I'll get Rex into his wheelchair, it'll do him good."

"You'll only get an argument from Madam." Agatha glances up meaningfully, "She's the only one permitted to take him walks. Just go. It's so warm, I don't think you'll need an overcoat."

"Mm, I think I will." So saying, she leaves Agatha, eschews the lift and trips lightly down the two flights of stairs to the front door, not forgetting to pop her purse and key into her dress pocket.

The warm air makes her feel ten years younger. Sophia may be sixty-two, but her heart is young and she still possesses a child-like naivety. She walks down to the sunny promenade taking in the joyous sight of the blue sky and calm, greeny-blue sea. Crossing the road, she grasps the rail overlooking the beach and takes in a deep breath of fresh air. She forces herself to look left, as she has done a thousand times before. There may be a brilliant sun but there is that ugly skeleton of the West Pier sticking out of the water, a constant reminder of the day and way Eve died. Defiantly she lifts her head and walks towards the wreck.

The beach is crowded. Day-trippers are swimming in the sea and sunbathing on the pebbles. People pass, licking ice cream cones, groups of girls wearing such flimsy clothing that Sophia shakes her head in disbelief, reminding her, as if any reminder were necessary, of the narrowness of her own little world. There are couples in love, gangs of young men in shorts, bare-chested with tattoos covering their arms and legs, people from all walks-of-life: everyone comes to Brighton in the sun. Below her on the underpass children splash in the shallow paddling pool, the smell of chlorine drifts up; and there, as always, rising from the sea, is that damned rusty reminder.

A piecing scream.

Eve's face appears.

Sophia puts her hands over her ears.

She opens her eyes. A child in the paddling pool below is bawling her eyes out. She has been hit by a ball and her mother is comforting her.

Sophia walks on.

Coming towards her, she sees a young woman with a pram. Her thoughts flash back to the time she passed her friend Roberta from Roedean. *Wheeling my baby in her pram and I had to pass by without a word, without even a glance at my own son. Why did I ever allow them to take him away? We should never have done that. Never to know my own boy until he was grown up and married, and even then, he never knew me.*

Will I ever be allowed to know his daughters? Or rather will they ever be allowed to know me? God willing, one day...

In front of her, sitting alone on a bench under a covered promenade shelter, is Cheryl, forlornly gazing out to sea, her hand absently rocking a buggy containing a sleeping Thomas.

Hardly believing her eyes, Sophia slowly approaches her. *The Lord has answered my prayer.* "Cheryl, is that you?"

Startled, Cheryl looks up. "Oh, hello, I was miles away. It's Sophia, isn't it. How are you?"

"Very well indeed, thank you. May I join you?"

"Of course."

Sophia sits beside her and looks about excitedly, not knowing quite what to say. "What a fine day, it is." Taking in Cheryl's sad expression, she frowns. "But you're looking sad, if I may say so. Is anything the matter?"

"No… it's just that, well, Marco… you met him, do you remember?"

"Of course. Thomas's father, your young man."

"He's away in New York doing a play, he's an actor, you know, and I'm missing him."

"Of course you are. New York! My! How exciting for him. And you're missing all the fun, yes?"

Cheryl nods and suddenly busts into tears.

Shocked, Sophia stares at her. "Oh dear! Whatever is it? What have I said?"

"Nothing. I'm so sorry, forgive me. It's nothing you've said. It's just that he… he… "

"What?"

Cheryl shakes her head, fishing for a handkerchief in the pocket of the buggy in front of her, but she can only find a used baby wipe.

"Here," says Sophia, "don't use that. Have this." From her purse she hands her a folded lace handkerchief.

"Thanks," says Cheryl, wiping her eyes. "You're so kind."

"Have a good blow. Make you feel better."

Cheryl blows her nose.

"It's only natural to be sad with your boy friend away," says Sophia. "Wondering about all the pretty girls he's meeting… "

Cheryl starts a fresh bout of crying

"Oh dear! Is that what this is all about? Him meeting other girls?"

Cheryl nods and blows her nose again.

"Ah well! I understand that. I remember a time when my boy friend met a pretty girl. He even married her."

Cheryl's eyes look horrified over the handkerchief.

"I was heartbroken, but you know what? In the end, it didn't matter. He came back to me. It was all horrible at the time, but we survived it and got back together. Nothing lasts forever, you know, that's the problem with happiness, it flows through your fingers like water. I'm perfectly certain your Marco would never desert a pretty girl like you, nor such a bonnie lad as this young sleeping prince here."

Cheryl smiles and hands Sophia back her handkerchief. "Thank you."

"No you keep it… as a memento of our meeting."

Looking at an embroidered S in the corner, she says, "But it's so pretty."

Sophia nods and smiles.

"Thank you."

"You're nearly twenty-one, aren't you?

"Yes, next month. How did you know?"

Sophia gives a half shrug, "I just knew."

A seagull lands and hops around at their feet looking up at them optimistically.

"He's hoping for some crumbs," says Cheryl watching.

The sunlight falls on her glowing, clear young cheek. Sophia drinks in her beauty, *skin like the petal of a sweet pea.* "What I wouldn't give to be your age again."

Surprised, Cheryl turns to her, "That's funny, because I can't wait to be older. To be wise and sensible, not have to worry about money and stuff. To have what you've got."

"What have I got? I have no son, like you. I've never been a mother, well, not like you. I've no position… No, that's not quite true, I am on the committee of several charities, but I don't count them. I'm only there because of Mother and my brother. I don't have any prospects. I don't even have a house of my own, like you."

"Well, my mother arranged that for me."

"So I heard, with your stepfather. He told me he wanted you to have security."

"Did he? How very kind of him."

"My brother is an exceptional man. A wonderful man. He's clever and been all over the world. I wish you could get to know him."

"I'm sorry he's so ill."

Sophia flicks a quick smile to cover the pain in her heart. "Thank you. Maybe you'd like come over to the house one day for tea and see him. I know it would cheer him up immensely. And your Mother would be pleased, wouldn't she? I have a fine collection of Graeco-Roman and Egyptian statues, you might like to see them, too?"

Cheryl thinks about that for a moment. "Yes," she says, politely. "That would be nice."

"What about next Tuesday? I'd ask you to come this afternoon, but Mother's always rather put out when someone arrives unexpectedly."

"Next Tuesday would be nice. Yes, I'll look forward to it. At tea time?"

"Perfect!" says Sophia, brightly. "Actually, it's tea time right now. Supposing I buy us an ice cream at that cafe over there? Would you like that?"

Cheryl nods, cheered up by their meeting, "Very much." Readjusting the buggy and checking Thomas is happy, she sets off by Sophia's side to the Meeting Place cafe, where Rex proposed to Betty.

Sophia is in heaven. *What I wouldn't give to see Mama's face.*

Chapter Seventeen

'Tiger' Joe

Towards the end of May, Joe comes home late one evening to find his wife has left him.

"Mrs Robinson asked me to tell you she's gone to look after a sick friend," says the nanny. "The children are both in bed."

"Thank you, Mrs Elliot." He walks thoughtfully up the stairs to shower. In his bedroom, lying on the pillow of the marital bed is an envelope with the word 'Joe', written in Claudia's handwriting. He tears it open and reads…

Dearest Joe,

I had hoped to be able to sit down and talk things over with you in a civilized fashion, but we never seem to get the time. By the time you're home, it is always late and you're tired, and by then, so am I.

So I am writing you this letter, it is the hardest I have ever had to write.

You must be aware that since I came home from 'Prospect', things between us have not been good, even though I have stopped drinking. The spark, or whatever, in our marriage seems to have gone out.

Our relationship has undergone a change over the years, and I don't think it is for the better. I am sure you will agree. After all, I was barely eighteen when we married, and far too young to know what I was really doing.

So, after much soul searching, I have decided to leave.

I must assure you there is no one else involved. I just need to be on my own for a while, to stand on my own two feet and not rely on you.

I have rented a little flat in Kemp Town from a friend at work. I have told Peter and Paul that my leaving has nothing to do with them, it is my own problem and I still love them. The flat is not far from their school, so some evenings they could come and be with me. I have told Mrs Elliot I am going to look after a sick friend. I just thought it was easier that way.

Try not to worry about me, as I am sure I am doing the right thing, at least for me. I have to concentrate on myself for a while or I will go crazy. I shall probably regret it and come home crying, who knows, I just know that right now I need some space.

Try to be patient, and not think too badly of me, I know it's for the best.

We did have some lovely times and laughs in our early days, but right now, I just don't think we fit anymore. Thank you for all the fun and the good times.

Love Claudia.

He sits on the bed with the letter in his hand, pole axed. For Joe, this is a first. He has never been dumped in his life. In every affair he ever had, he did the dumping first. So he is both, shocked, hurt, angry, and although reluctant to admit it, having guessed their time together had run out long ago, in his secret heart of hearts he is just a tiny, tiny bit relieved. He's off the hook. A slow grin creeps over his face to the back of his ears. Alone again, naturally... as Gilbert O'Sullivan sang, but Joe had learnt he was that, at a very early age.

The boys!

He leaps up and goes into his sons' bedroom. Quietly opening the door, he looks in. They are both sound asleep; he creeps in and stoops down in between their beds. Tousled heads on pillows, both out for the count, deep in the land of Nod. He softly strokes their heads, and tips toes out back to his room.

He picks up the letter again and reads... *The spark, or whatever, in our marriage seems to have gone out.* You're telling me. No sex for months!

On her first day back from Prospect, Claudia had bravely emptied the contents of every liquor bottle in the house down the drain; no longer on the gin, she had at least been easier to live with. But she had become so used to talking about herself in her therapy sessions with Woody Walsh at Prospect she could not stop. She insisted on broadcasting her dramatic cure with everyone they met, even to neighbours shopping in the grocery store. "I'm a recovering alcoholic," she boasted, to Joe's cringing embarrassment, "so I can never touch another drop of liquor, not even a sip of wine. Its fruit juices all the way, so don't tempt me! But I won't go on about it."

But she did go on, on and on.

Joe knew he had to careful with her, just out of re-hab was a delicate time, she was vulnerable and genuinely trying to move on, but he was still her caretaker, which didn't make for much fun in his life.

Although he realised that he no longer loved his wife, theirs was the only family he had ever known. The orphanage had brought him up with strict middle class morals and while he might philander, he would never walk away from his marriage or leave his sons. Since the one woman he desired refused to have anything to do with him, he became deeply depressed, an unnatural state for such a normally buoyant fellow. By nature a glass full, sort of guy, even if the glass was only an inch from the bottom, Joe would still think it overflowing, but in this particular case, no.

So he buried his never-ending ache of love in work and his emotional life stagnated.

He drove to whatever building site he was working on like an automaton, worked hard, had lunch in a pub, or ate sandwiches with his work mates. Came home late, showered, had dinner with his sons (if it was not too late), snoozed in front of the telly, and so to bed… without nookie. He didn't even want sex, which for a man like 'Tiger' was a very bad state of affairs indeed.

No wonder she left me!

For a third time he reads the letter. *I shall probably regret it and come home crying.' No mention of a solicitor or divorce. She's keeping the door open. A trial separation.*

So Joe adapts to life without a wife.

Ensuring he gets home earlier from work, he makes a special effort to spend more time with his boys, saving Saturday mornings and Sundays to play football with them at Queen's Park. The household functions efficiently, rather more so, in fact, than with Claudia, the fridge is full, the washing and ironing done, and the place is spotless, all due to the professionalism of Mrs Elliot.

Two weeks later, Peter and Paul visit their mother.

"How was she?" Joe asks on Sunday evening as he's tucking them into bed. "What was her place like?"

"Bit small," says Peter, scowling.

"It's a basement," says Peter.

"She hasn't even got a bath, only a shower room."

"I had to sleep on the floor in a sleeping bag. Paulie got the sofa, 'cause we couldn't both fit on it."

Joe glimpses some of the sacrifices Claudia is making to live alone.

Burying his own unhappy heart in manual labour, he is so exhausted when he gets home he doesn't even listen to music, neither classical nor his favourite Frank Sinatra/Nelson Riddle recordings. But as Shakespeare says "The man that hath no music in himself/ Nor is not mov'd with concord of sweet sounds/ Is fit for treasons, stratagems, and spoils." *

So Joe evolves a plan.

He telephones Claudia at her workplace.

"Claudia, luv, wonder if we could meet up and have a chat one evening?"

"Oh Joe, it's you. How are you?" she answers, apparently cheerful. "What do you want to talk about?"

"Us. How are you getting on one your own?"

"Fine," she says, with a just little too much bravado in her voice.

"Could I come round to see you?"

"No, no, not there. Somewhere neutral, a pub, say, or restaurant."

"O.K. How about our old Regency, opposite the West Pier?"
"When?"
"Eight o'clock, tomorrow?"
"Fine. I'll be there."

When Joe arrives, showered, with clean clothes, she is already at a table by the window overlooking the sea front. He kisses her and sits beside her.

* The Merchant of Venice

"I've ordered the plaice," she says.

He notices she is wearing new clothes, at least he doesn't recognize them. *This used to be our favourite table.* In happier days they had sat here holding hands and pressing knees under the table, planning their life together looking out at the faded grandeur of the entrance to the old West Pier, now all that remains is a rusty carcass against the darkening evening sky.

A familiar waiter appears.

Claudia looks up and smiles in recognition. "Hi!" Turning to Joe, "Will you have your usual scampi and chips?"

"Yes," says Joe, nodding to the waiter. "Thank you, with tartar sauce and a carafe of white wine... No, no, sorry," he avoids Claudia's eye. "Just an orange juice and beer for me. Thank you."

The waiter leaves.

"Sorry, luv. I forgot."

"Really!" says Claudia in disgust. "You are truly amazing. How could you do that? After all I've been through, I thought you had more sensitivity."

"I've said I'm sorry. I just forgot for a moment."

"That just proves to me how much you're thinking about my problems," she says, nostrils flaring. "The daily fight I have not to drink. What was it you wanted to talk to me about?"

"Claudia, honey! Come on."

She shrugs and flaps her hand in a sulky dismissal.

Joe takes a breath and looks at her. "I've had an offer of work from one of my old customers. He's bought a property in Fuengirola on the Costa del Sol, a beachfront cafe. He wants my help in licking it into shape. He says he has an apartment with a swimming pool he can let me have while I'm working. The job will take three months, maybe more, and I was wondering if you want to move back home while I'm away? The thing is, the boys' school summer holidays are coming up soon, from the 24th July to the 2nd

September. I was hoping they could fly out and be with me, but you'd be left on your own. What do you say? Would that be agreeable?"

With a half smile, Claudia looks at him thoughtfully. During the last few months living in her tiny one-roomed basement, she had begun to learn that the grass away from home was not as green as she had hoped. When she left Joe, she had imagined an exciting new life of parties or suppers with her young work mates, maybe a new romance, but it turned out everyone had partners of their own and wanted to get back home to them after work. There were certainly no more visits to the pub in the evenings, and the expense of running the flat solo was proving astronomical. She was beginning to wonder if the price she was paying for her independence was worth it, the loneliness, the smell of damp in the basement, missing her comfortable home... *what exactly have I done, throwing it all away?*

Therefore, the offer is fortuitous. "Joe," she says. "I must say, I think that is pretty good of you. I've always knew you were a forgiving man. It's an excellent idea. Thank you."

"You're sure won't mind the boys coming out to me in Spain to spend the summer holidays?"

"Of course not. They'd love it."

"I could then let Mrs Elliot go. The bank pays all the household bills by standing order and direct debit, so there shouldn't be any problems there."

The waiter brings their food. They talk of dates, and continue their meal in peace and pleasantry.

The following morning Joe visits his bank manager, has a long talk with Ben Crawley, his partner in Robinson and Crawley Constructions, and in the evening writes the following letter.

My darling Betty.

Since I have made my feelings plain to you, there seems no point in repeating myself.

You know how I feel, yet you do not answer. I understand why, you are a good and honest woman, and I think I know how you feel. Not only are you married, with responsibilities to your sick husband, but I am your dear daughter's husband. That is my misfortune.

Still, as you can imagine, things have been pretty rocky around here lately without her, but I have recently had an offer of work from an ex-customer now living on the Costa del Sol. I have decided to accept the job, but of course, I'm concerned about my boys. They will come out and be with me for their summer holidays, but until then, Claudia has said she will move back home to look after them, as she has probably told you. I leave for Spain next week, and it would take a lot off my mind if you would be good enough to look in on them occasionally, make sure she's in good shape and that the boys are ok. I know this is asking a lot of you because you have your own problems to deal with, but if you could manage it, I would be most grateful.

You have my mobile number if you need me, I do so long to hear your voice, and my heart goes out to you my darling Betty.

I love you with all my heart and always will.
Joe.

Chapter Eighteen

Judy, the Agent

Autumn 2009

*S*he jumped me!" Marco whispers hoarsely into his mobile. He is crouching like a fugitive in the corner of his New York bathroom whispering to his agent Judy Pearl in London. On the other side of the door, Georgiana is reclining on his bed of shame, reading her reviews.

"I could hardly tell her to bugger off back to her own room. We'd just had this fantastic first night. She bought me a fabulous dinner, she got me new costumes made, what was I supposed to say? Fuck off, I've got a girl friend?"

"Perhaps not quite in those words," says Judy, dryly, sitting at her vast leather-topped desk in South Moulton Street, W.1, playbills and photographs of horses behind her on the wall. Judy Pearl has two obsessions in life, show business and horses. At her home in Guildford, she keeps stables and every morning rides one of her three horses before driving to her office in Mayfair. "It keeps me sane," she explains to anyone expressing surprise at her habit. To Marco she continues, "Would it solve the problem if your girl friend was with you?"

"Not half! But it's impossible, there's the baby. Anyway, we can't afford the air fare."

"Leave it with me. I have a call holding on my other line right now. Can you hold?"

"Sure."

Judy presses a button on her intercom and reconnects the New York call. "Sorry about that. Minor emergency. When would it suit Mr Scorsese to see him?… Wednesday, 12.30, St Regis, Manhattan." She makes a note. "Many thanks. I will make sure he's there. 'Bye for now."

She presses her intercom again. "Marco! Get yourself to the St Regis Hotel, Wednesday, at 12.30. Martin Scorsese wants to see you. And wear a suit."

"Bloody hell!"

"Meanwhile, keep smiling at your boss, and carry on being brilliant. I'll get back to you. 'Bye, darling, don't worry, leave it to me."

She disconnects and presses her intercom again. "Get me Marco Danieli's home number in Brighton." She writes on her pad, then:

"Hello, is that Cheryl Ashdown?"

"Speaking," says Cheryl.

"Judy Pearl, here, Marco's agent. I've just had a call from him in New York. He would very much like you to join him. He's having a big success and wants to share it with you. If I can arrange a flight for you and your boy from Gatwick tonight, could you make it?"

"Oh, my heavens! Good gracious! Um… Yes, yes, I suppose we could. How exciting. Yes, yes, we could be there."

"Great! I'll get back to you. Just take your passport to the desk at Gatwick. Have you got a passport for your baby?"

"No."

"Oh! Then, get yourself and your baby to your local passport office quick, and get one fast tracked. Let me know when they have issued it, and I'll arrange a flight. Meanwhile, pack. Good luck. Marco will be thrilled. Bye for now."

Cheryl puts down the phone and jumps for joy. "Thomas! Thomas! We're going to see Dadda in New York! New York! Hurray! Oh, Lord! Where's the local passport office?"

Part Two

Chapter Nineteen

Two Years Later

*B*etty wakes up and sleepily glances at the digital clock on her bedside table: 07:20 14/2/11.

Valentine's Day. Three years ago today, Rex Black proposed. A very black day indeed!

Two and half years have passed since Rex's heart attack, for Betty, two and half years of nursing, medicines, bedpans, exhaustion and misery. Her relationship with Agatha, if anything, has worsened. Agatha's hearing has diminished, which has necessitated the acquisition of a National Health hearing aid, consisting of a body-worn box containing a microphone with a lead connecting it to an earphone behind her ear. Agatha insists on holding the microphone in front of your mouth, like an interviewer, when speaking, which makes a relaxed conversation – never easy at the best of times – practically impossible. She listens to the television and her beloved friend, Joyce Heron's piano recordings, in the same eccentric manner, holding her microphone out toward the speakers.

Betty pushes back her bedclothes. Feeling the chill, she hastily pulls on her cosy pink dressing gown, and as usual, switches on the electric kettle in the corner to make a cup of tea for Rex.

What with Cheryl away in America, Joe apparently vanished off the face of the earth, Claudia on the verge of a nervous breakdown and Rex getting weaker every day, she has endured two and a half years of gloom, relieved only slightly by the glow of a surprising new friendship with Sophia.

Waiting for the kettle to boil she prepares the small tea tray and considers taking a cup of tea next door to Sophia, but decides against it, their relationship has not quite reached that stage of intimacy. Their conversations have centred around bland, safe things, like menus, flowers, plants for the garden and television, i.e. *Midsomer Murders* and *Poirot*, which, apart from the murders, depict a world they both know and recognise, unlike the world they perceive outside on their walks along the sea front.

The closest they came to something more personal was three weeks ago on a walk when Sophia abruptly asked, "Was your first marriage a happy one?"

"Very," Betty had replied, "I loved Sam very much."

"I'm glad, so glad," Sophia, answered, "I think that when you have loved someone and then lost them, you begin to understand what life is really all about."

Profound, Betty had thought, tempted to ask whom it was she had loved and lost. The conversation had led her to ponder on the whereabouts of the unobtainable man that she loved, Joe, her daughter's vanished husband. The constant weight of guilt and self-loathing she felt whenever she thought of him, which was too often, had, in a curious way, been diminished by his disappearance.

As she warms the pot, she recalls how her friendship with Sophia had begun… *on the morning Cheryl flew to New York… in the basement kitchen…*

"I met Cheryl on the sea front the other afternoon and invited her to tea."

"Oh, Sophia! I'm so sorry – she just telephoned to say she wouldn't be coming. It was very nice of you to ask her, and she sent her apologies, but she's flying to America this afternoon to join Marco in New York."

"Oh, I'm glad, she was worried about him, but oh dear! What shall I tell Mrs Hunt? Look," she said, opening the pantry door, "she's prepared all this."

On a shelf inside stood an appetising cherry pie and a plate of freshly cut cucumber sandwiches covered with a glass cloche, next to them a bowl of raspberry jelly with swirl of cream on top and a freshly made Madeira cake.

"Oh dear!" exclaimed Betty. "Well, you'll just have to tell her the party's off."

Sophia bit her lip. "Would you mind telling her? She's been a bit short with me lately."

"Of course, where is she?"

"Mary said she'd popped out for some milk. Oh, here she comes."

At that very moment Mrs Hunt came bundling through the basement door carrying her grocery bag.

"I'll disappear," whispered Sophia, vanishing.

"Oh, there you are Mrs Hunt," said Betty, "I'm so sorry, but my daughter has flown to New York today, so regretfully there will be no tea party this afternoon, after all."

"You mean all that in the larder is wasted?" said Mrs Hunt, bristling. "I made that special. Miss Sophia said she wanted it special."

"Well, I'm sorry, but what can I say? We can keep the cake, of course, it looks delicious, but the rest is well... I'm so sorry," and Betty swiftly followed Sophia up the stairs, fearful that Mrs Hunt might explode.

Which is exactly what then occurred. Betty heard the blast from behind the kitchen door.

"My daughter has gone to New York, indeed!" fumed Mrs Hunt, imitating Betty and throwing off her overcoat. "This is the last blooming straw, it really is."

Mary, who was coming out of the scullery, asked, "What is?"

"This sort of thing has been going on for too long, ever since mister Rex had his heart attack. What with three women at me every day telling me three different things, how to cook, when to cook, and where to serve, I'm the one who's due for the heart attack. Three mistresses in the house is never going to work. I knew that from the outset. No one ever sits down in the dining room no more. It's an unhappy house and I've had enough of it. I'm off!"

"What about poor mister Rex?"

"Poor mister Rex has three women at his beck and call day and night, which is more than I have. He'll manage very well."

"And with poor Doris up in her room with her leg, I'll miss you something terrible."

"You nailed your flag to the Madam years ago, but I'm telling you, Mary, she can't go on forever, no more than mister Rex can. So make tracks."

"Are you telling me to go, too?"

"I'm just saying, look after yourself. I shall go to me brother's in Somerset, don't you worry about me. He's got a cafe there: make me very welcome, he will. So I'll say cheeri-bye, and think on what I've said."

"Aren't you going to tell the madam?"

"Oh, I'm going to tell the madam alright!" And off she stormed to give the Honourable Mrs Agatha Black her notice along with a piece of her mind.

Since then, half a dozen cooks have passed through the kitchen, resulting in Betty eventually taking over the job herself, helped occasionally by a reluctant Sophia, who confessed, "Cooking isn't really my thing."

Only yesterday, Rex had grasped Betty by the hand as she was feeding him in bed saying, "You will take care of Sophia for me, won't you, after I've gone."

"Now stop that sort of talk, Rex," Betty had answered, refusing to go down that path, "Of course, I'll take care of her."

"I do appreciate everything you've done for me, Elizabeth," he said, looking into her eyes. "You do know that, don't you?"

"Get on with you."

"About my will."

"Never mind about all that now… "

"No, I want you to know," he insisted. "It's a bit complicated, but… "

"Do we have to go into this right now?" she'd asked.

"It's hard for me to tell you this… to admit… "

"Admit? Admit what? That you're leaving everything to the Dog's Home, or you haven't got a penny?"

Rex had looked at her dead pan for a long moment, then straightening his sheet, "I've arranged for whatever's left to be divided between the three of you, the house, the contents, everything."

"Thank you for telling me, dear. Now, can we please finish up this nice broth. Sophia made it."

Rex grinned, "Sophia can't even boil an egg!"

Betty stands thoughtfully warming the teapot. She pours in the water, and carefully carrying the little tray, crosses the room to Rex's bedroom.

Chapter Twenty

Victoria Falls

*R*ex's grizzled head lies on the pillow but his mind is far, far away, and it is long, long ago… Sunday, the 14th November 1962, a day he could never forgot.

At nineteen Rex was at the peak of his masculine beauty, tall and bronzed with crisp brown hair and a perfect physique. The winner of "The 1962 student most likely to succeed," at Cape Town University, a great deal is expected of him, and on this particular day he realises that big changes lie ahead. He stands on a cliff top gazing at his favourite sight in the world, the magnificent Victoria Falls in Southern Rhodesia.

Twice as high as Niagara, the thunder of water falling hundreds of feet below him into the Zambezi River is deafening. The blazing sun, high in the heavens, casts a perfect rainbow in "the smoke that thunders", hovering over the churning river below.

In his short-sleeved khaki shirt and jodhpurs, the hairs on his forearms glisten in the sun, even the bristles on his unshaven chin catch the sunlight. If handsome looks were the arbiter of happiness in this world, Rex would be one of the golden chosen ones, yet at this moment, tears glisten in his eyes, he is heartbroken. Angrily he brushes them from his cheek. He has just ridden over from the deathbed of his beloved father. He has been sitting by his side for the last sixteen hours.

"Rex, son, sorry about this… we had an adventure, eh? We've seen some excitement, eh? Afraid you'll have to go back home to England now, son… earn yourself a living… don't worry, you'll do well. You've got a good head on your shoulders. I made sure of that, you're well prepared with your undergraduate studies."

"Yes, Dad, you said."

"Did I? Yes… I did, didn't I. Well, it was important you were well educated when I brought you out here. Education is important in life, that's how you get ahead."

"Yes, Dad."

"You'll have to go back to your mother, now. We had our problems, but she'll be good to you. I have a big house back there, you know, do you remember it? Did I tell you?"

"Yes, Dad."

"Magnificent house it is, by the sea in Brighton. I let your mother have it when I came out here after the war, but it'll be yours now. All yours. Be kind to her, won't you. I never was. That's why I let her have the house. You'll have to sell up here, but you'll get a good price, this is valuable land. Maybe it's as well we're leaving it now, eh? We've had the best of it. The copper mine, the safaris, the hunts, the parties. What fun it all was. Seems it's all change for everyone now this Ian Smith fellow has declared us Independent. Still, none of my affair anymore… more important matters to see to. I've always loved you, son, tried to be a good father, a good man. They'll say I've been hard, but to get things done out here, a man has to be, has to be strong; but I've always loved you, m'boy. Give me a grand funeral, won't you? I'd like that. Tell 'em all what a fine fellow I was."

And I certainly did. Spoke for twenty minutes. Told them all about his copper mining days in northern Rhodesia, the jokes about us riding ostriches on the farm, saying good-bye to the dear old fellow. Saying good-bye to that beautiful country, too… over half my life I'd spent there, fifteen years. Had to start all over again in rainy old England, back to a mother I barely knew. Mother…

I stood in that square outside, in the rain, freezing, it was, looking up at the grandeur of it all, all that Georgian architecture, the whole square painted cream. I rang the front door bell shivering and quailing in my boots, what a kid I was. Wondering what sort of reception I'd get. I was like some prodigal son returning home. I was the heir, taking the house away from them. Mother's old butler opened the door and showed me into the library, I hardly remembered him, but he remembered me though. Then Mother came in wearing a long black dress. "We got your telegram," she said. Such a hug she gave me, she even wept... and over her shoulder, I saw her, little Sophia, smiling up at me.

"Who's this?" I said, knowing full well.

"This is your sister, Sophia," said Mother. "You knew her as a baby."

I hardly remembered her at all. She was new to me, and so pretty... big brown eyes, high cheekbones, fair hair, wholesome. Make a perfect wife for someone. I didn't know her, yet she was my sister, but a stranger. All the same, I gave her a kiss, and big hug. She felt so slim and fragile. I hadn't touched a white woman in months. With her tiny young body next to mine, I think I loved her from that very moment. 'Wow!' I thought, 'she's terrific.' Then I pulled myself together, 'Steady on, she's my sister. Something's not right here.'... but we certainly clicked.

"This is your grandfather, Lord Charles Sherwood," said Mother, carefully, introducing a big man, with a big smile and firm, dry handshake.

"How do you do, young sir?"

"How do you do, sir."

"Papa," said Mother. "You have to give Rex a job, and a good one. We can't afford to lose him again. Not now he's come home to us at last. He must never leave us again. Promise me, Papa?"

"Yes, Grandpapa," said Sophia, "Promise us. You can't allow him leave us again, can you?"

"I'm being ganged up on here!" cried the old man, grinning at me. "Seriously, I should be proud to have you in the company, young man. Very proud. Come up to town with me on Monday and I'll show you the ropes."

Indeed he did, bless the man. Made him a lot of money, I did, a lot of money. How could I have guessed it would all turn out so well? Work and love, love and work, that's all that matters, really. Sixty-eight years! It's all happened so quickly, flown by... How lucky I've been. Best of all was the loving, being loved... and family. My Darling Dad, Sophia, even dragon lady Mother, dear Grandpapa and young Sam... what a lad! Sam, so sad. But by and large it's all been grand. Except for this damned illness... and Eve. Poor Eve. Still, it's all long ago now, so long ago... should never have married her. Nice girl, but never loved her, not like I loved my lovely Sophia.

Forgive me, Sophia, my darling. Sophia, my angel.

... Sophia... Sophia... Sophia... Sophia.

Chapter Twenty-one

The Inevitable

14th February 2011

*B*etty knocks gently on the bedroom door and, without waiting for a reply, opens it. Rex is lying asleep in his magnificent double bed with his head resting on Sophia's sixty-five year old naked breast.

"Sophia!" Betty drops the tray, aghast.

Sophia cradles her brother in her arms and looks up serenely, "So at last. Now you know."

Betty rocks on her heels, ignoring the broken teacup and saucer at her feet, she is unsure what to do or say.

"He's mine. He always was," says Sophia, calmly. "He loved me always... and I've loved him," her lip trembles. "For forty years."

Thinking she may scream, Betty puts her hand to her mouth.

A sad smile hovers around Sophia's lips, "What are you going to do? Throw yourself off the Pier, like Eve? I don't think so. You have more sense. Eve was a sensitive little thing. You're much tougher... you and your son-in-law. That would make us about equal in the incest stakes, don't you think?"

Unable to move, Betty huskily cries out, "Rex. Say something!"

"He won't answer you. He's dead. I came to him last night and he died in his sleep. So you see there's nothing you can do." She strokes his white hair. "Nothing anyone can do anymore. It was quite peaceful, wasn't it, my love? A merciful release for you, dear brother." Looking up at Betty, she adds casually, "You can telephone the doctor and the funeral director, if you like. The numbers are by the phone in my room." Turning to Rex again, she murmurs, "They'll take care of you now, dear one. You're at peace now, aren't you?" She kisses his head, sighs, and in a matter-of-fact tone adds, "I'd better get up and tell mother."

Betty stands reeling.

"You may leave us now," says Sophia.

Staring at the extraordinary scene, Betty takes in Rex's dead face. All the lines and wrinkles that marked the passage of his life are smoothed away. He looks almost young under his white whiskers.

She sighs and leaves the room.

Once back in her sitting room, she supports herself on the door jam, her head spinning. *Lovers for forty years! Came to him last night. Eve? Did Eve find them like that and kill herself? That's what she implied. Oh, Lord! I can't think about this right now, there's too much to do. I must ring the doctor.*

On her bedside table lies a notepad with the doctor's telephone number and that of the funeral director. They have been there for months, so she has no need to fetch them from Sophia's room.

She makes the necessary calls, washes her face and dresses, choosing a black frock, and returns to the bedroom where Rex lies dead.

Sophia, now wearing a long dressing gown, is kneeling by the bed in prayer. Agatha, also in a dressing gown, is quietly weeping, supporting herself on the bedside table.

"The doctor is on his way," Betty says.

"Thank you, dear," says Agatha, holding out her hand in a rare gesture of affection.

Betty regards her hand, and grasps it; it is the closest she has ever felt to the old lady. *Did she know of this incestuous relationship? Did she condone it?* With her eyes downcast, she notices a tea stain on the carpet, but the tray of tea things she dropped earlier have vanished.

"Elizabeth," says Agatha, softly.

Betty turns to her, "Mmm?"

"Would you mind telling Robert and Mary?"

"Of course," she answers, and leaves the room.

Sophia kneels up and regards her dear dead brother's face. The hairs on his chin have grown down over his throat to mingle with the white hairs on his chest. She remembers a time when they had been fine and blond, the day she presented him with the gift of a slim gold necklace, she'd bought him in the Lanes.

"My dear, darling girl," he'd exclaimed, lifting the chain from the jeweller's box, "I could never wear a thing like this. Gold chains on men are for chaps from Essex! I would be teased unmercifully." Seeing her disappointment, he'd added, "Why don't you wear it instead. It will be much more becoming on you. It can be a secret covenant between us. But you must allow me to buy it, let me pay you what you spent. Here, let me put it on you."

He had kissed her and fastened the gold chain around her neck, and there it had remained, on and off, for almost five decades.

Even now, she feels the fine gold links round her neck.

Taking hold of Rex's right hand she tries to remove his signet ring. It does not budge. She puts his knuckle in her mouth, licks it, and the ring eventually slides off. She hands the item of cold gold to her mother.

"No, dear," says Agatha, "You keep it."

Sophia gasps and sobs on her mother's breast.

Agatha takes her in her arms, "There, there, my darling. Be strong. Try to be strong."

Half an hour later, the doctor and undertaker arrive simultaneously at the front door. There is a polite kerfuffle in the hallway. First, the doctor rides up in the lift to the master bedroom. He examines Rex, signs the death certificate, which, in the adjoining sitting room, he hands to Agatha, who passes it over to Betty, "You should take care of this."

The women leave, and the undertaker and his two assistants return to the bedroom. They place Rex's body in a black plastic bag and zip it up. On the count of three, they lift him on to a stretcher, which they carry out into the hall and the lift. On the ground floor, Robert waits by the front door. He opens it and with an enigmatic expression, watches his late master carried past him and inserted into the back of the undertaker's vehicle. He closes the door, and noticing a letter in the front door letter-basket, retrieves it, and takes it upstairs to Betty's sitting room.

"The post, madam."

"Thank you, Robert. Put it on the dresser, please."

Betty is looking out of the window, Rex's death certificate in her hand; she is staring out to sea, her eye on the burnt out West Pier sticking out of the water. *That ugly pier... Eve's suicide... How does everything come back to that? Rex always said it reminded him of Eve's death. I wonder if they're together now in some celestial somewhere? Maybe they don't want to be. Could she really have killed herself just because she found him in bed with Sophia? Bit extreme. I don't think I believe in those fairy tales about God anymore. I think it's all up to us, to make our own individual way as best we may.*

Absently she takes the letter from the dresser and looks at the envelope; she notices the stamp is foreign, postmark 'Mexico'. Opening the envelope with a frown, she discovers a lush Mexican Valentine card... in an instant she knows who it is from... the picture shows a hunky handsome Red Indian with a massive red-feathered headdress carrying a barely-clad unconscious maiden in his arms: it is a beautiful picture and undoubtedly erotic. On the back in small print, it says: 'According to Mexican legend Popocatepetl and Iztaccihuatl were star-crossed lovers bewitched into mountains.' Inside, the message reads, 'Te Amo'.

Despite only two hours having passed since experiencing the twin shock of discovering Rex dead, and in Sophia's arms, the corners of Betty's mouth curl up into a smile. Immediately she bites her lip and tears the card up into a hundred pieces, throwing them into the dustbin.

Chapter Twenty-two

The Tiger of Success

February 15th 2011

On the beach at Santa Monica, the blazing afternoon sun shimmers on the blue Pacific Ocean. Marco is enjoying himself diving into the waves of the foaming waters. Further up the beach Cheryl sits under a floppy sun hat wearing a snappy blue bikini, she is studying a film script behind huge sunglasses. Beside her, sitting on an orange towel, are her two sons, Thomas and sixteen-month-old new arrival, Antony.

Thomas solemnly pokes his brother in the face and waits for a reaction.

Antony cries.

"No, no, Thomas," says Cheryl, springing to her baby's defence, "you mustn't do that."

The sides of Thomas's mouth turn down. He is beginning to learn he no longer comes first in his Momma's eyes.

Marco wades ashore, running up to join them, seawater sparkling like sequins on his lean, hirsute body; he grabs a towel and vigorously rubs his head. "What do you think?"

"The gangland setting seems a bit sordid. I guess it's kind of thrilling though, if you're into all that."

"I am, and Danny Boyle don't make rubbish! I liked him a lot when we met. I have to work with these challenging directors. Judy says they start shooting next week. My guess is someone's fallen through. Still, I have to make up my mind quick. It's either that, or the other offer of third lead with Johnny Depp and Penelope Cruz in the next *Pirates of the Caribbean* thing."

Marco is riding the tiger of success: apart from film offers pouring in, wherever he goes he is photographed, interviewed, feted and profiled. This is his first day off in six months. Nominated for a Bafta and Golden Globe Supporting Actor award for his work in the Martin Scorsese film, he is on the cusp of becoming a star. *Screen International* tips him as being an actor destined for stardom on the big screen.

Two years ago, his reaction to Cheryl's arrival in New York was one of relief. Cheryl immediately noticed the connecting door to Georgina's suite, but tactfully kept her mouth shut, as she did about her luncheon with Georgina's husband, Michael, in Brighton. As Judy anticipated, Georgiana backed off immediately Cheryl appeared; she even changed tack and offered friendship, taking Cheryl out shopping to Macy's and Bergdorf Goodman on Fifth Avenue, buying her gifts of scarves and silk shirts to ease her guilty conscience.

After that, things went swimmingly, the Scorsese film came up, and Georgiana returned to London. Since *The Reluctant Vampire* closed, Marco's life has been a whirlwind. He and Scorsese clicked, so much so, Scorsese asked him to play the second lead in his next film opposite Leonardo di Caprio, whom Marco now counts among his friends. Peter Weir then engaged him to play the star part in a film of a bestselling period novel set on a boat. He filmed it on the island of Catalina, off the coast of California, where Clark Gable and Charles Laughton had made *Mutiny of the Bounty* in 1935.

Georgiana may be out of Marco's life, but her husband Michael is back in; at least Marco talks to him on the telephone two of three times a month. With Marco's success has come money, lots of it, he has suddenly acquired 'people', an accountant and a publicist.

Most of all, he needed a trustworthy financial advisor: Michael was exactly the right man to ask.

There have been expenses; a Harley Davidson motor bike and a home, with "Marco Danieli" written on the title deeds. It is a first floor apartment approached via a white wooden staircase from a backyard carport, with three bedrooms and a spectacular living room, with a veranda overlooking Santa Monica beach.

Another important expenditure was a ring for Cheryl following the birth of Antony. A gorgeous 4 carat diamond made by jewellery designer and celebrity favourite Neil Lane. Cheryl was delighted, *it looks very like an engagement ring*, she thought, but she was sanguine. "A single man in possession of a good fortune," wrote Jane Austen in nineteenth century England "must be in want of a wife." Yet Cheryl doubted Marco had changed his mind about marriage, she knew well enough that in twenty-first century Hollywood, Miss Austen's words no longer held true.

For all her modernity and 'girl of the moment' looks, Cheryl has a slice of her mother's more orthodox views. Miffed at the magazines articles describing her as 'Marco's live-in English girl friend,' she commented, "I hope I'm more than that!" So the diamond ring, as well as being a celebratory gift to commemorate the birth of Antony, was also a sop.

"Is it better to have a supporting part in a blockbuster," she now asks as she packs up the baby things and beach paraphernalia to head back to their apartment, "or the main part in a just okay film?"

"Good question," answers Marco. "Normally the blockbuster, but the Danny Boyle film will be a damn sight better than just okay. Actors take parts in his films without even reading the script. Besides the character has to sing a song, and I'm mad for that, who knows, it could become a hit. So I think I must do it. I'd get top billing. Anyway I suspect the *Pirates* franchise is running out. These offers can't last forever, y'know. I feel I hardly deserve it. There are a hundred guys out there just like me, so I must make the right choices, the right investments, too. If I slip, make a bad film, I know perfectly well there'll be hundreds of actors only too happy to see me fall. I've seen it with other guys riding the crest of this fame thing. In Hollywood they only want you when you're hot. It's all dandy till you slip, then when the next, so-called fashionable personality comes along, the press either ignore you or kick you in the crutch. They do in England, anyway. It does seem to be different here, though, I'll say that."

"What does Judy say?" asks Cheryl, carrying baby Antony on her hip.

"Says she's happy to leave the decision to me. Part of it would be shot in England, so we'd have to go back home for a while."

"We could see Mother and Claudia! Oh, yes, darling, do that one. Ma sounded so sad on the phone this morning and she hasn't even seen Antony yet. Yes, go on, Marco, do *do* that one. It would cheer her up no end, make her ever so happy."

"Some reason for a career decision!" he says, raising his eyes to heaven. "Make Mum happy!"

"I'm joking, but… "

"I know." Taking Thomas by the hand, he says, "We'll have another go at swimming tomorrow, okay?"

"Okay!" shouts Thomas, gleefully, waddling up the beach.

"We couldn't live at home in Brighton, though. The film's being made at Pinewood, that's in Berkshire; we'd have to live nearby in a hotel or something."

"Not a hotel, not with the children. Couldn't we stay in a country house or cottage? That would be lovely, then Ma could come and stay with us."

"I guess. I'll ask Judy if she can fix it up. They can only say "no". What do you suppose she'll do now? Your mother, now that

Rex has died? Will she stay in that great house? Maybe she'll want her old home back!"

"That's just what I've been wondering," says Cheryl, "I shouldn't think so. After all, now she's going to be stinking rich."

As the family sit round the table in the kitchen for tea, Antony up in his high chair, the front door bell rings.

Cheryl looks at Marco nonplussed. "Are you expecting anyone?"

"No. Maybe it's someone from the studio. I have some looping to do tomorrow; maybe they've brought some changes."

He gets up from the table, goes into the hall and opens the front door.

On the doorstep, lit by the late Californian sunlight is a bronzed and very healthy looking Joe Robinson. Grinning fit to bust, wearing a Mexican sombrero, he says, "Wotcher, Marco mate! How y'doing?"

Chapter Twenty-three

Dump't

15th February 2011

*W*here the hell is he? Claudia Robinson gazes disconsolately at herself in her dressing table mirror. *What a fool I was to walk out on him.*

Digging at her lank hair with her fingers, she tries to give it body, but it's hopeless. With her palms pressed on either side of her cheeks, she attempts a face-lift. She lets the flesh fall. *God, I look a hundred.*

Her reflection does indeed throw back a woman nearer forty than her own twenty-nine years. Dark circles under her eyes and a sallow complexion tell a story of sleepless nights and bad health. There is no doubt about it, Claudia looks and feels well and truly dump't.

This morning, after taking Peter and Paul to school, she had come home, called her supervisor, Sylvia, at the Liverpool Victoria Insurance Company, told her she had the 'flu (which was a lie), and gone back to bed. Now it is midday and she has already downed a glass of gin and orange.

This situation is not something sudden; it has been a gradual decline.

Two years ago, moving out of her basement flat and returning home, things had looked promising, but with hindsight, she made a fatal error. She chose to not to sleep with Joe in the marital bed.

"What's going on?" he'd asked, watching her make up the bed in the spare room.

"I want to sleep alone. Well, I've not exactly come crawling back to you, have I? You asked me. I've got used to my independence. Sorry, luv," she added with a smile, "but I'm a grown up now."

She was nothing of the kind, she was still the drama queen child she always had been. A week later Joe had flown to Spain to start his new job: and two weeks afterwards the boys joined him for the school summer holidays, and Claudia was back on her own.

Immediately she regressed to fun-loving teenager mode. Out every night to clubs with a hectic determination to "have fun", she started by having just a "wee drinkie to get me going" and on two occasions, finished by having casual sex with strangers, men whose names she now couldn't even remember.

Seven weeks later, when the time came for her to collect Joe and the twins from Gatwick airport, she was well on the downward path.

"Where's your father?" she asked, as the boys came through the gates.

"He's staying over," said Peter. "He asked us to give you this," and from his inside pocket handed her a letter.

Waiting at the baggage carousel, she read it:

Dear Claudia,
Enclosed two tanned and happy sons. They seem to have had a terrific time and, incidentally, so have I. My job here is almost done, there are a few outstanding problems I have to stay to deal with. There is also the possibility of another job, which I am considering.
I've bought the boys a Blackberry phone, so I can keep in touch with them. It's on my orange

account so I've given them a good talking to about not making expensive calls, and hope they've got the message. Hope all is well with you. Love Joe.

Driving home, she thought, *Not a word about when he's coming back. I don't believe he intends to. What do I care? So he's dumping me, but I dumped him first. Fancy giving them a phone! Probably so they can spy on me.*

That evening, after putting the boys to bed, she wanted a drink. Not yet having sunk back to keeping gin bottles in the house, she had two options; either to go out and buy one, or seek solace from a friend. Fortunately, with her sons asleep upstairs in bed and Woody Walsh's words 'it is alcohol**is**m, not alcohol-**was**m that is not going away' echoing in her ears, she had the good sense to choose the latter. That friend was her mother. She telephoned Betty, who immediately asked Robert to drive her over in the Bentley.

"He's left me!" she cried.

"So you said on the phone. But I rather had the impression you had left him, dear," replied Betty.

"I did, but… I'm not sure I can manage any more on my own. I'm not up to all this single parenting stuff, like you did." She had then resorted to tears, crying on her mother's shoulder for half an hour. Convincing herself Joe had left her for some woman he'd found in Spain, nothing Betty could say persuaded her otherwise.

At that point, Betty had the letter Joe had written to her in her handbag, so her feelings were complicated. Her maternal nature dominated and she comforted Claudia as best she could; yet at the same time feeling a sense of guilt, suspecting she herself might be the cause of Joe not returning home.

Claudia knew she was drifting back into alcoholism and fought to stop, but without Joe's support, she felt weak, cut in half, as if she were only partially present. It was quite different from the hope and euphoria she had started off with when she left him, and moved into her basement. Now she was scarcely able get out of bed in the morning, run the house or deal with the mundane problems of everyday life without a drink. A simple thing like folding double bed sheets caused her to burst into tears. Overwhelmed by life she came to realise she had to fill in the other half of herself, to colour it in, so to speak, like the picture in a child's colouring book, in order to function, if only for the sake of Peter and Paul. These two normally energetic boys appeared to be only mildly put out by their father's absence, missing him mostly on Sunday mornings when his habit was to take them to Queen's Park to play football.

As the days turned to weeks and there was still no word from Joe, Claudia decided to tackle his business partner, Ben Crawley.

"Ben, have you any idea where he is?"

Ben looked at her. Constantly in touch with Joe, but sworn to secrecy, he it was who had reported to Joe in Spain what everyone in the local building trade already knew, that "Tiger" Robinson's wife was back on the bottle, was sleeping around and available. "Ain't got a clue, Mrs Robinson," he replied, looking her straight in the eye, "and that's God's truth. True as I'm standing here."

She had guessed it would be hopeless and he would lie, Ben would never give Joe away, regarding it as a betrayal... *some sort of man thing, honour among two-timing bastards.*

She told everyone the dramatic tale. "Joe's still away in Spain. I think he's left me."

Her friends were sympathetic and condemned him, which was her intention. Most of them had been dumped themselves at some time or other, so were on her side. Their sympathy helped, for she was not equipped to change from 'teenager mode' to 'mother mode'. Without Nanny Elliot, she was dealing with work at the Insurance office, which she called, "Hell." Listening to claimants telling their tales of woe every day, and at home, dealing with two rambunctious kids. Gin was her answer, standards slipped and things began to slide again.

As she fixes her hair into a French pleat before the mirror, the telephone rings. Looking at the instrument as if it might bite, she lifts the receiver with a premonition of disaster. "Hello!"

It is the Headmistress of her sons' school.

"Mrs Robinson, nothing to worry you too deeply about, but I have to tell you it has come to our attention that Peter and Paul have been watching pornography. Another boy was showing it to them on his i-Phone in the playground. We have confiscated the phone, but don't know exactly what they saw. This is a completely new area for us, never having experienced anything of the kind before. This is the first generation of children exposed to this sort of thing. It seems you can get practically anything on these i-phone things these days. I just wanted you to be aware of the situation so you can have a word with them, perhaps explaining that what they saw is not a true representation of real life or for that matter real love. When you pick up your boys this afternoon, pop into my office if you have the time and we'll have a chat."

Claudia buries her head in her hands. *I'm not up to this. I can't deal with it. Oh Joe, where the hell are you? This is the sort of thing you should be talking to them about, not me.*

Desperately she dials up her mother's mobile.

"Claudia, darling!" Despite Betty's endearment, her voice sounds tense.

"Mother, dear, I must see you. Can I come round?"

"Not at the moment, dear, do you mind. Rex died in the night and I have such a lot to do. I'm at the Town Hall right now, as a matter of fact, registering his death."

"Oh Ma, I'm so very sorry. Is there anything I can do? Should I come round?"

"Tomorrow maybe. Give me a buzz then. I must ring off now, darling. 'Bye."

Claudia stares at herself. *Even dump't by Mum. I'm out of here. I'll have lunch at that nice beach bar where I met that man.*

The bar under the promenade looks directly out over the sunny beach just by the Palace Pier. She finds herself a high stool, sits at the bar, and orders some prawns and apple juice. Three drinking acquaintances, a blonde woman and two men in their late-twenties arrive and join her. One of the guys is the one she had sex with in the back of his car, whose name turns out to be Geoff.

"Well, hello, Gorgeous!" he says, eyebrows atwitter. "It's drinks all round, I think. What'll you have, luv? Gin and tonic, I know, I remember."

Then someone else buys a round... she has a double.

She buys a round herself, and some crisps. There are laughs and more drinks, and Claudia feels woozy and looses track of time.

Half past three, the time she should collect her boys from school, comes and goes. At half past five, she looks at her watch and suddenly remembers.

"Oh my God! My boys! I should have collected them." In a panic, she fumbles for her mobile and calls the school... but there's only an answering machine. She calls her mother again... another answering machine. "What the hell am I going to do?"

"I'll drive you to the school if you like," says Geoff.

"Would you? I'd be so grateful. I should have been there hours ago. I hope to God they're alright?"

"Have to be so careful with kids these days," says the blonde, "There are these perverts haunting playgrounds all the time, so they can groom them for sex."

Claudia can barely look at the stupid woman, "Thanks a bunch!"

Frantic and desperately trying to sober up she gets in beside Geoff, in the self same car they had sex in, directing him to Peter and Paul's school in Kemp Town.

Once they get there, they discover the school gates closed, locked, and not a child in sight.

"Maybe they walked home?"

Geoff drives her home.

Claudia unlocks the front door, calling "Peter! Paul! Are you here? I'm home!"

Silence, not a sign of them anywhere.

"Should we alert the police?" asks Geoff.

"Oh Lord! Yes, I suppose I should."

"Best be on the safe side."

"Alright. It's in John's Street just down the road. My husband has dealings with them all the time."

They dash back into Geoff's car. While sitting at the wheel, he asks, "How come your husband deals with the police so much? Is he a crook?"

"Of course not, he's a builder. He has to have permits for skips and things, check for criminal convictions of his employees. Actually, now I think of it, you'd better not come in with me, it might be a bit awkward."

"No problem. I'll wait for you outside."

Chapter Twenty-four

Sophia's Surprise

February 15th 2011

When Betty noticed Claudia's name come up on her phone, her conscience had pricked for neglecting to ring her last night after speaking to Cheryl, telling her of Rex's death. "Excuse me," she now explains to the clerk across the counter at the Town Hall, "my daughter. I had to answer it. Is there anything else I have to do?"

"That is all," he replies. "That green form is all you will need. Next."

Betty folds the green form, puts it in her handbag and heads for the exit. *Right, that's that done. Now, what else? I must go through his wardrobe. Oxfam is going to have a field day!*

Standing on the top of the Town Hall steps, she takes a deep breath. The sunny fresh air raises some blind in her mind. All the colours in the street suddenly look brighter, sharper, the people more in focus. *It seems as if something tremendous has just happened. Of course, I'm a free woman!* The full extent of her new situation suddenly hits. For the first time she realises she has inherited a fortune and is now a wealthy woman. With her head high and a spring in her step she walks along the High Road trying to hold back a grin. Noticing a Cash Point outside Barclays Bank, she inserts her Visa card. *How much have I saved from Rex's monthly cheque...* £33,500!

Impressed, she passes a dress shop and spotting an expensive dress in the window, toys with the idea of buying it, *I can afford that if I wanted… but I don't.* Continuing on her way, she asks herself… *Now my life with Rex is over, what am I going to do? I'm certainly not going to go on living in that house with Sophia and Agatha, that's for sure. I don't even want to go back there right now.*

Pondering again how Sophia and Rex had managed to carry on their affair without anyone knowing; about Cheryl's new life in America, wondering at Joe's cheek in sending her a Valentine, and Claudia's unhappiness, her feet lead her almost unconsciously through the streets she knows so well back to her old home in Holland Street.

Standing outside, she puzzles why she's here. *What a fool I was to give my house away. I wonder if I could I ask for it back?* She looks up at Rosa's windows next door and rings her bell.

Rosa opens her front door and beams with delight, "Betty, pet! What a surprise. How lovely to see you. Come on in, come in."

In the kitchen, she insists on opening a bottle of wine, and Betty tells her about Rex. "I'm exhausted, Rosa. Now it's all over, I don't know what I'm going to do with myself."

"Listen to me, my girl," says Rosa, wagging her finger, "After all these years of nursing this incredibly sick old man, of trying to be everything to his nothing, you've poured yourself out. Look at you, girl, you're shaking, you're a vulnerable wreak."

Betty looks down at her hands. Rosa is right: they are trembling.

"You need time to heal. Give yourself a holiday. You can afford it, after all, you're a wealthy woman now. You need a period to rebuild yourself." She scrutinizes Betty, "Are you hearing me?"

Betty seems absorbed in pushing back her cuticles. "I'm hearing you, Rosa, thank you."

After a while, she rings for a taxi and on the way home thinks. *A holiday, yes, that would be nice. Maybe I could go and visit Cheryl in America. But I must talk to Sophia first. How did all that with Rex come about? I must know... and what about Eve? I'm going to have to talk to her about it some time. I'll knock on her door and ask her straight out. 'Sophia' I'll say, 'I need to know'...*

Betty knocks on Sophia's bedroom door and waits.

She looks down the corridor toward the loggia and imagines seeing herself wrapped in Joe's arms, just as Sophia must have seen them years ago.

She hears laughter.

"Elizabeth!" exclaims Sophia opening the door. She has pinned up her hair and is wearing a full-length grey afternoon dress. "Good. We were just waiting for you."

Behind her, sitting on the window seat, a plate of tea things and books on a table before them, are Peter and Paul in their school uniforms.

Betty is astonished. No one is ever allowed in Sophia's room.

"Grandma!" they both shout, bounding towards her.

"Good Heavens! What are you two doing here?"

"Mumma didn't pick us up from school," they say, speaking at once. "We waited hours. The Head telephoned her, but her phone was off, so we texted Dadda."

"Texted Dadda? I don't understand. How?"

"He gave us this," Paul produces his Blackberry. "We're always texting each other."

"Always. Oh, are you?" she mutters weakly. "Well, what did he say?"

"He said to call you. We did, but your phone was on the answering service, too. So he told us to get in a taxi and come here. Auntie Sophia paid the driver. She's given us tea and showing us these fabulous pictures of Egyptian mummies. Look."

Betty glances at the illustrated books on the table and for the first time takes in the room. She has never been in here before and it is very surprising, astonishing. Part Greek temple, part museum, part Edwardian bedroom, the four-poster bed with heavily embroidered curtains is guarded either side by life-size Egyptian statues. Either side of the window are busts on columns and in a glass cabinet, artefacts and relics from a bygone age. A bookcase on one wall is overflowing with leather-bound tomes, on top of them are paperbacks lying on their sides.

"Well," she says, somewhat dazed. "Thank you, Sophia. You seemed to have saved the day!"

With a broad grin, Sophia says, "I've never been called Auntie before. I like it. It's been fun, hasn't it?"

Peter and Paul nod and grin back. Paul says, "Look at those fab statues. Gran, I've never seen them in a bedroom before."

Betty cannot resist asking, "So where was your father?"

"He's staying with Auntie Cheryl in America."

"Good heavens! Well… " Hiding her surprise, she turns to Sophia, "You must tell me how much I owe you for the taxi?"

"Forget it," she says, with a shrug.

"He's been halfway round the world," pipes up Peter. "He was in Mexico last week."

"Mmn, so I heard," she says weakly.

"And Peru, the week before. He was helping to build a skyscraper in Brazil."

"He said he crossed the Atlantic in a liner."

"My!" Trying not to appear flabbergasted, which she most certainly is, she adds, "Well, we'd better get you off to your Mum. She'll be worried sick. I'll go and ring her now and tell her you're here."

"Ask Robert to drive them home," suggests Sophia.

"I can easily call a taxi," says Betty.

"Nonsense, you'd like a ride in nice Bentley, wouldn't you, boys?"

"Yes, please," they say in unison.

Betty leaves the room to call Claudia. *I might have known it. Joe would never lose touch with his boys. He's a hands on Dad.*

Claudia's phone is switched on, and Betty tells her the children are with her.

"Thank God!" she cries, "we've been worried sick."

We? thinks Betty. *Has she got some new man in tow?*

Sophia stands next to Betty on the doorstep, waving goodbye to the twins.

Once they are out of sight, she turns to Betty. "When you came in to my room, just now, you didn't know the boys were with me, did you?"

"No, it came as a complete surprise."

"Then why did you come? That was the first time you've ever knocked on my door?"

Betty considers, and then answers. "I wanted a talk." She turns back into the hall and goes to the lift.

Sophia watches, joins her and speaks: "I thought as much. Shall we go back up to my room?"

Chapter Twenty-five

Sophia's Secret

Approaching Sophia's bedroom door, Betty glances down the corridor and once again remembers herself in Joe's arms.

"Come on in," says Sophia.

When the door closes behind her, Betty repeats what she has rehearsed, "I need to know about you and Rex."

Sophia regards her for a long moment. "I've been expecting such a question. Please," she indicates a chair, "sit down."

Betty has the impression that some ancient high priestess of Delphi is inviting her into her sanctuary, for Sophia's room is weird and worrying. A little patch of normality is the remains of Peter and Paul's tea things still on the table.

"You were his wife, after all," continues Sophia, "You have every right. I knew this day would come," she says, drifting to the window, her fingers playing with the gold chain around her neck. "Now that it has, it no longer matters." In gentler tones, she adds, "Rex was the love of my life. I shall never experience his like again."

Betty frowns, astonished, yet touched by her honesty.

"Do sit," Sophia repeats, half turning toward her. "Ask what you please."

"Are you sure you don't mind?"

"I have never talked to a living soul about this, but," she says with a half shrug, "like you now, I have the need. Someone else should know how it was."

"How did all start?"

Standing by the window Sophia stares out to sea. "On the day Rex came home from Rhodesia. A thrilling day. Mama hadn't seen him since he was five years old, but I knew she kept his baby curls in a box on her dressing table. I only knew him from his pictures in the photo album. I barely remembered him, well, I didn't really, not at all. Mama and Father had parted when I was a baby, you see, and that was when Papa took him away. So I never knew my brother, or Papa. Mama used to talk about Rex though. We used to get Christmas cards from him in his nice writing, and I used to write my name neatly at the bottom of Mother's birthday cards to him.

"When I was eighteen Mama had a telegram saying Papa had died and Rex would be coming home. She was overjoyed. I was curious to meet him, of course, but it wasn't that important. I was busy doing a Foundation course at Brighton Art College, wrapped up in what I thought was a grand passion for one of my classmates. It was just a schoolgirl crush, really, calf love, but he was a sweet boy. An American called Elmer Hurwitz. Strange to say he was keen on me too, can you believe? But when Rex came home, all that changed, poor Elmer never stood a chance. Before Rex, I never knew what it was like to be in love. To be swept out of control by my emotions.

"I first saw him from the staircase. I'd just come downstairs and he was standing in the library looking up at all the books. He looked totally lost, poor love, afraid, almost. Sunny brown hair, he had, and so tanned and tall, just beautiful he was. Mama hugged him, held him tightly for ages. I think she'd thought she would never see him again. He looked at me over her shoulder and smiled. Then he took me in his arms and we hugged. He was a complete stranger but our bodies fitted perfectly and we just held each other for ages. It was strange. I didn't know the man and yet here we were so physically close, closer than I'd ever been to Elmer. He kissed me and I kissed him back. I felt so drawn to him, it was as if he was the person I'd been waiting for all my life.

"We showed him his bedroom and he unpacked, showing me all the little things he'd bought home. Carvings the native boys in Rhodesia had given him, and animals he'd carved for us, for Mother and me. He gave Mother a great wooden salad bowl he'd made from one piece of wood, with two salad servers made to look like giraffes. We used them for years, there're still downstairs in the kitchen somewhere."

"What did he give you?"

"That lion, over there."

In pride of place on the mantelpiece is a miniature lion carved in pale wood about five inches high by seven inches long. Betty picks it up, her fingertips tracing the tiny marks Rex had made as a young man with his knife. "I'd no idea he could do such delicate work."

"Did you know he was brought up by a black woman?"

"Good heavens, no."

"Papa was busy working with the menfolk all day, so, before he went to boarding school he was looked after by a nursemaid, like an Indian Ayah. He told me she was the only woman he had ever loved before me." She opens her bedside drawer, takes out a handkerchief and dabs her nose. "Those first weeks, we spent every single second together. Like kids we were, couldn't keep our hands off each other. Nothing happened for ages, but then, one thing led to another… on the Downs, one sunny afternoon. We felt no shame, no guilt, because we loved each other… it was wonderful. We weren't harming anyone… we were grown-ups. Still, we had to keep it secret. No one could ever know. Mother came in here and discovered us one morning when we were in our dressing gowns. We'd forgotten to lock the door. Rex was lying on the bed there.

"'Rex! What are you doing here at his time in the morning?' she asked.

"'Just looking at these history books,' he answered, casually.

"If she suspected anything she never showed it. I often wondered if she guessed, but if she did, she kept quiet about it. I have an idea she thought she might lose him again if she made a scene."

"Lose you, too."

"Yes, I suppose so. We felt this uncontrollable urge, you see, to keep hugging each other. Mama said to me once, 'Will you put him down,' and we all laughed.

Betty gives a half smile. "Did you never think what you were doing was wrong?"

"We didn't see things in those terms, right or wrong. We were just trying to deal with this new, strange, yet wonderful situation. My feelings were so all consuming they obliterated every other consideration. Rex was my closest family and my natural family, so it felt right being with him. But then, things don't go on forever, do they? They change. I discovered I was pregnant."

"Yes, Rex told me you had a child… "

"Mm… " Sophia regards Betty in silence. "Elizabeth. What I have to tell you may be difficult for you."

"In what way?"

"We told everyone the father was Elmer Hurwitz. There had been talk of an engagement between us." She shrugs, "There never actually was, but it was easier that way. Elmer had been drafted back to America by then and wasn't around to deny it. Rex was frightened the baby would be deformed or something, that God would punish us, but when he was born he was just perfect. The most beautiful baby boy."

"A boy? You had a little boy? Rex told me it was a girl."

"Well, he would, wouldn't he? He didn't want to upset you."

"Why should that upset me?"

"Because my son was Sam, your first husband."

A vision of Sam's face appears in Betty's mind. Searching for some genetic similarity, it merges with Sophia's face, with Rex's. Are they alike at all? Yes, Sam was tall, like Rex, and Sophia's white hair was once fair, so Rex told me. Yes, Sam was fair. What colour were his eyes? Oh God! I can't remember!

Try as she may she can't… not to remember the colour of the eyes of the man she loved above all others is pitiful. In a panic she clasps her hands to her head, crying, "I can't even remember the colour of Sam's eyes."

"They were brown," says Sophia, "like Rex's."

"Yes, of course, of course they were." Stunned, Betty stares at her. "My Sam… was your son?"

"Yes." Sophia looks away, back in to her own thoughts. "I didn't deserve to have a child. I never wanted one. I'm not the maternal type. I didn't deserved to be a mother. I would have made a terrible hash of it. Unlike you. You seem to me to have been the perfect mother. I told Rex we should have it adopted, and he agreed, so did Mama. 'Yes,' she said, 'I think that would be best for all concerned.'

"You see," Sophia says meeting Betty's eye, "to have an illegitimate child in those days would have meant social disgrace, for me and the whole family. I think that was Mama's principal thought. 'If people find out,' she said, 'your reputation will be ruined.' That sort of thing mattered so much more then than it seems to nowadays. So she arranged everything. She was on the board of some local Women's Church Union that had connections with an adoption agency. She was able to cut through the red tape and arranged it. Then I discovered that the woman… the woman who was to adopt the boy, was someone I'd known at Rodean

Girl's College. A girl called Roberta, a nice girl, I'd liked her, she had married a man called Ashdown... "

"That used to be my name."

"Of course."

Betty looks at her unable to speak.

"Roberta had been unable to conceive a child of her own and wanted to adopt, so... they took my baby away from me. Not Roberta personally, Mother arranged it all, very discreetly. Afterwards, I must have had some sort of post-natal depression; I sort of shut down, went a bit potty. After that, things somehow went wrong between Rex and me."

"In what way wrong?"

"We stopped having sex. He said we should try not to. He was busy by then working up in London for Grandpapa, so I only ever saw him in the evenings. Even at weekends, Grandpapa took him off to stay in country houses, being social with all his wealthy grandee friends. I missed him dreadfully. I did become a bit eccentric, I suppose. People always said I was odd. That was when I got into all of this, Graeco-Roman history. The dynasty of incestuous Kings and Queens of Egypt, Ptolemy, there, and his sister Arsinoë II," she indicates the statues either side of her bed.

Betty looks at them in awe. "They're very impressive. Where on earth did you get them?"

"The shop at the British Museum, they were ten thousand pounds each. Rex bought me Ptolemy and I bought Arsinoë II, myself."

"She looks a bit intimidating."

"I think she probably was, but I love her. I sort of buried myself, my unhappiness, in learning about their lives. You see, I'd always been rather an insignificant person. Arsinoë II and Ptolemy were gods, they had made a success, a triumph of their relationship, whereas Rex and I had become as nothing. One day, I saw Roberta walking along the sea front with my little baby in the pram. She passed by me without a word. I thought I should go mad. Mama said it was my frustrated maternal instinct surfacing, but I doubted that. My baby symbolised what had happened to Rex and me, what we'd once been. Now it was gone, lost forever."

Betty doesn't know what to say. One of the thoughts in the back of her mind is: *Can I tell the children Sophia is their grandmother?* What she actually says is: "Yet, you must have kept in touch with your friend, Roberta, how else did you come to know so much about Sam and me?"

"Ah! That was Rex's doing. Roberta's husband, Stephen, I think his name was… "

"I never met either of them, they died before Sam and I were married."

"Yes, I know. Anyway, Stephen Ashdown was a member of Rex's golf club, and Rex befriended him. He sort of monitored what was happening to Sam. Stephen Ashdown never knew Rex was Sam's real father, of course, he was just, well, a casual chum from the golf club. We learnt when Sam had the measles, when he went to Brighton College, and even when he took up cookery. Rex said we were like his guardian angels.

The first time I saw him was when he was fifteen. He was playing cricket, dressed in white flannels on Brighton College playing field. Rex took me there one Saturday, I don't think it was Speech Day, just some match with another public school, and I met Roberta again. It was all very social, distant and polite and she never knew. Sam was such a handsome boy, tall, like Rex, with blond hair, like mine used to be. After that I didn't see him for years. I didn't really want to. I found it too emotional, too upsetting, though Rex took him out quite a lot. He didn't mind, he got a kick out of keeping the secret, a kick out of being with his son.

When we heard he was planning to get married, we asked him over to dinner so we could meet you."

"To check me out!" says Betty. "So, all these years you've been my mother-in-law?"

"Mm," she grins, "and Claudia and Cheryl's grandmother."

Betty nods. "That's why you invited Cheryl to tea that day?"

Sophia nods, smiling. "And gave my great, grandchildren tea this afternoon. It was such a delight. A great pleasure."

"Tell me about Rex's wife? How long after Sam was born did Rex marry Eve?"

Sophia's smile freezes. Eve's cold dead hand reaches out and clutches her heart. She shuts her eyes and sinks onto the bed. "That was dreadful, at least, for me, in the beginning. I thought he was betraying me. Childish, I know. I hated her."

"Like you did me."

"No, Elizabeth," she says, inclining her head. "I never hated you. I just didn't like the idea of you. I thought, oh no, not again! You see, Rex never told me he was ill, never told me you were a trained nurse. He never said he was marrying you to make our lives together, his and mine, easier."

"Is that what I was doing?"

"You knew that, surely? He told me it was an arrangement between the two of you."

"No, my dear." Betty thinks for a moment. "Though it was an arrangement of sorts, I suppose."

"He married Eve in 1966. That was Grandpapa's doing. Rex said he suspected Grandpa had heard some talk, some rumour about the two of us. Grandfather's chauffeur was very keen on one of our maids at the time, so I suppose it was possible. Anyway, Grandpa said it was time Rex got married. He insisted, in fact, said it was vital. He was planning a big merger at the time with Witherspoon, the steel people. Eve was Mr Witherspoon's daughter, so… it was business thing, the daughter of the boss marrying Sherwood Incorporated. Grandpapa promised to make Rex his heir if he married her. It was a condition. So he did it, and Eve came to live with us. I dreaded her, but I couldn't hate her. No one could, she was nice, a well brought up young lady. Everyone liked her, she was the asset Rex needed in business. We ended up becoming quite pals. The sad thing was she actually fell in love with Rex. She adored him. He became fond of her too. Well, she lived with us all for twenty-three years.

"He did come back to me though, after a while, but in a different way. He used to sneak in here for a cuddle whenever they had a quarrel. It was like in the old days… almost. The sex side of things had died long ago, but part of him was still mine, and of course I still loved him.

"When we received your letter telling us Sam had died in that skiing accident in Austria, I was heartbroken. Rex came in and showed me your letter. I sobbed and sobbed. We held each other close and he stayed with me here. We were on the bed there. We just held each other like we used to in the old days. Eve came in and saw us. She just stared. We weren't ashamed. But she got the wrong idea. Well, it was the right idea really, of course. She ran out. I got dressed and followed her. She ran down to the front, along the prom to the West Pier. I caught up with her and tried to explain. She said she'd always thought Rex loved me better than her. Suspected we were lovers all along, and now she knew it for certain she was going to report us to the police. I told her she was crazy, told her not to be so melodramatic, told her it was all in her imagination, but she went on and on, and in the end, I admitted it. 'You're right,' I said. 'Rex and I do love each other. We always have done. We heard this morning that our son has died and we were comforting each other.'

"'Your son!' she cried. 'You and Rex have a son? I don't believe it. You disgust me! I can never look you in the face again. Either of you, you're both vile, I hate you.'

"I left. I walked around for a while not knowing what to do, then I came home. Eve never did. We found her body under the pier the next morning. She must have thrown herself off after I'd left her. I blamed myself for telling her, but then, we could never have gone on living together, not after that. I've heard people say the past is dead and cannot trouble us, but it's not so, the past rules us, imprisons us. It has me. Made me what I am today, an under-achieving eccentric old maid."

"Sophia, please, don't say such things." Betty holds out her hand, "You have me now, as a friend. We'll always have each other."

Sophia looks doubtful, hesitates, then grasps Betty's hand. "It would be nice. It's funny, isn't it, about time? Rex and I were lovers for such a short time, not even a year, yet it has been the most important part of my life. Everything that's come since has been as nothing."

"Our memories define us."

After a moment and in a brighter tone, Betty adds, "But you and I are both going to have happy years from now on. I'm determined." She stands up. "First, we have to deal with this funeral, endure it, rather, then we'll go away together, just the two of us, have ourselves a ball. What do you say?"

"Oh, Elizabeth, do you really think we could?"

"Of course. But one thing, Sophia, I must say. I do think after all these years it's time you called me Betty. Only people who don't know me very well call me Elizabeth."

"But Rex always called you Elizabeth."

"I know. I did ask him to call me Betty once, years ago. He said he preferred the name Elizabeth, so… " she shrugs.

Sophia grins, "Well, I'll call you Betty, from now. To mark our new friendship."

"We'll be two middle aged ladies out on the razzle. We'll find somewhere very exciting to go. How about a cruise to the Caribbean?"

"Or up the Nile. I've always wanted to do that."

"Of course, the Nile! We'll get brochures and make plans. Oh, Sophia, I'm so glad we've had this talk."

"So am I… Betty."

And the pair laugh.

Chapter Twenty-Six

The Will

February 22nd 2011

Rex Black's funeral draws to a close in the bare brick chilly chapel of the Woodvale Crematorium in Lewis Road. The three women in Rex's life stand next to each other in the front pew. Agatha is barely visible behind a heavy black veil, Sophia's frail features are stained with tears, Betty's nostrils dilate slightly as she stares at the coffin disappearing slowly behind a blue velvet curtain.

Outside, the weather is cold and bleak, the trees bare and black. A group of mourners hover around waiting for the service to end so theirs can begin... burial on a conveyor belt.

Suddenly an attendant appears and holds back the chapel doors. Agatha, leaning heavily on her walking stick, is the first to stagger forth, accompanied on either side by Sophia and Betty, all three dressed top to toe in black. Claudia follows them with Peter and Paul, both smartened up in their best suits.

She hugs her mother. "Darling. We must spend some time together soon, when you have a moment?"

Betty shrugs wistfully, "Of course, my dear."

"I need your advice."

"What about?"

"I'll tell you later," answers Claudia, flapping her hand dismissively. Gently taking Agatha's hand she says, "I'm so very sorry." Smiling at Sophia, she adds warmly, "Thank you so much for looking after these two the other day."

"It was my great pleasure," says Sophia, smiling at the twins.

Rosa comes over and gives Betty a hug. "Luvvy! Lovely service. Pop round again soon, eh? Be like the old days." She blows a kiss, "God bless!" and totters off in the direction of Robert, the chauffeur.

Brighton and Hove's most senior and respected citizens slowly emerge from the chapel. One of the most impressive and certainly the largest is Rex's lawyer, Mr Henry Williams.

A man of vast proportions, he takes up most of the back seat in the Bentley returning home. Normally he would have requested his clients to attend his office in Hove High Street, but in deference to his friendship with the deceased, and his long association with his mother, the mountain, for such he appears, comes to Mohammed. The glass partition between the passengers and Robert is closed. He leans to Agatha and nods at chauffeur. "He should join us for the reading."

"What?" asks Agatha, holding out her microphone box and fiddling with her earpiece.

With exaggerated enunciation, Mr Williams repeats, "The staff should join us for the reading."

"Sophia, you take care of that."

"I've already done so, Mother."

Still wearing their funereal hats, Gladys, Mary and Robert (holding his chauffeur's cap) sheepishly assemble in the library on the ground floor. The wintery sun breaks through the clouds, dust particles swirl in a sunbeam.

"Do please sit down," says Betty, trying to put them at their ease.

Looking and feeling self-conscious, Gladys and Mary perch gingerly on the edge of the high-armed leather-studded sofa. Robert, behind them, prefers to stand.

Betty sinks into an armchair while Agatha and Sophia, both with straight spines, sit side by side on the opposite sofa.

Mr Williams arranges himself in Rex's old captain's chair behind the desk, opens up his briefcase and removes the document.

Despite the knowledge of how Rex wished his estate divided, Betty is experiencing a certain tension. An avalanche of money is about to be distributed. Over the last two and a half years, she has had ample opportunity to ponder how inheriting Rex's wealth will change her life. She has dreams of owning her own home, buying a flat overlooking Hove sea front, near Cheryl and the baby, perhaps taking the family for a holiday on a Greek island. Having read countless detective stories, and seen films and television plays depicting scenes of Will readings, she is aware that a split inheritance is always tricky and surprises often occur. She arranges her face for whatever may transpire.

"First," says Mr Williams, polishing his spectacles, "as a friend of the family," and here he bestows a smile on Sophia and Agatha, who is still holding her microphone out to him like a begging bowl, which in the circumstances is oddly appropriate. "I feel it my duty to inform you, regretfully, that contrary to popular opinion, Rex Black was not a wealthy man."

Slowly a bank of cloud casts a shadow over the room. The three servants exchange looks. Silence, like a shattering scream, echoes around the room.

Mr Williams clears his throat. "Most, if not all of his properties have had to be sold over the years to cover the huge losses incurred by the bank crisis of 2007, followed by the Icelandic, then the RBS and Irish bank crashes in 2008. With the exception of this house, which he was at pains to protect for his family," and here he favours Betty with a glance. "However, I will deal with the matter of the house privately with the family afterwards."

He opens the first page of the Will and flattens it out on the desk with his palm. "There is an insurance policy which will cover the funeral expenses, a few minor bequests, otherwise, I fear… " and here, he trails off. Clearing his throat again, he continues, "I do not propose reading all seven pages of the will, just those paragraphs relevant to those here present." He peers at them all over the top of his spectacles, and begins. "'I, Rex Franklin Black of Brunswick Square, Hove, hereby revoke all former wills and testamentary dispositions made by me and declare this to be my last will. I appoint George Henry Williams of Williams and Sons, Solicitors of Hove High Street, Hove, to be my Executor and Trustee of this my will.

I give the following specific legacies absolutely:

1. To Gladys Simpson, of 18, Portslade Villas, the sum of £5000.

2. To Mary Davies, of 12a, Ventnor Villas, Hove, the sum of £5000.

3. To Robert Taylor, my chauffeur and friend for many years, the sum of £10,000.'"

Expressions of suppressed exuberance appear on the faces of those here named, their happiness obvious.

Betty gives them a tight smile and turns back to Mr Williams.

"'4. All the remainder of my chattels and effects of personal domestic or household use or ornament as defined by the Administration of Estate Act 1925, as are not hereto otherwise specifically disposed of excepting money and securities for money to my Mother, Agatha Dorothia Black, and my sister, Sophia Alexander Black, and my wife Elizabeth Estella Black in equal shares to be divided among them as they shall agree.'"

Sophia and Agatha sit like stone effigies, the latter with her hand extending her hearing aid with the expression of a petrified gecko.

Betty looks at them. *How am I ever going to get my third? I'm going to be trapped in this house with these two women for the rest of my life.*

"I should now like to speak with the family in private," says Mr Williams, pointedly to the servants, "So if you will be so kind as to leave us. You will all be hearing from me in good time. Thank you."

Gladys and Mary tentatively rise. Robert opens the door for them, they nod politely, mutter "Thank you," and depart.

As soon as the door shuts Mr Williams speaks, "I regret having to do that, but as this is a somewhat delicate matter, I feel it appropriate we should be private. I hope you will agree."

"Henry," says Agatha, "Your discretion is, as always, irreproachable."

"Thank you," with a further clearing of the throat, he continues. "Now then… "

Sophia looks down calmly and clasps her hands. She knows exactly what is coming. It is a secret she has kept for years. During their pillow talks, Rex had confided his financial troubles and discussed with her how to solve them long before he instructed Henry Williams. She had sympathized, understood and concurred with his decision.

"… Three years ago, against my advice I might add, Rex took out an Equity Release plan with the Norwich Union. At the time, he confided to me that 'Sherwood and Black Consolidated' was in trouble and as a result, his personal finances were not as healthy as he wished. The Norwich Union valued this house at £1,500,000, and offered a release of £622.500, at an annual interest of 8.5% compound, which Rex, possibly aware his days were numbered, accepted. I fear this arrangement has considerably reduced the size of his estate. I have had a word with the Norwich Union informing them of Rex's death and they will now be obliged to put the house up for sale."

"Sale! Did he say sell the house?" demands Agatha.

"I'm afraid so," says Mr Williams.

"No, no, there must be some mistake," says Agatha.

"I fear there is no mistake."

"But… "

Sophia puts her hand over her mother's, and Agatha subsides.

Mr Williams resumes, "Allow me to explain. The deeds of the house are at present in the possession of the Norwich Union. On completion of a sale, they will reclaim their original loan from the proceeds of the sale, plus the interest incurred, which I might add is considerable. Only then will they distribute the remainder. I will then distribute the legacies, which amount to £20,000, and retain a certain amount for legal expenses and fees. The remaining sum I will then divide equally between the three of you, as was Rex's wish. However, I feel it only fair to warn you, there will not be much collateral left, especially taking into account the recent housing slump."

A wave of cold horror creeps over the women.

Agatha realises her worst fears. *They will put me in a Home.*

Well, thinks Sophia, *I've been rich and miserable most my life, now I shall be poor and hopefully happier.*

Betty realises the truth. *So I'm not a wealthy widow after all, and now it appears, I'm going to be homeless.*

"I don't mean to paint too black a picture," says Mr Williams, "I anticipate the chattels and house effects will realise a goodly sum."

There is silence.

Agatha looks at Sophia aghast. "Does he mean we have to auction the furniture… the paintings? Are we to display our belongings, our memories, for money? Are we all to be thrown out on the streets?"

"Mother, please… a cosy little home might be very nice."

Agatha looks at her daughter as if she has gone mad. "Nice!"

Betty bites her lip. "May I ask, on behalf of my mother and

sister-in-law, how much is it that the Norwich Union are owed?"

"I have their account here," says Mr Williams, extracting a letter from his brief case. "I did anticipate such a request. Let me see now… " he opens up his pocket calculator. "If the house is sold for, let us say, one and a half million, which was the valuation four years ago… " He presses buttons. "Minus the loan of £622.500, at an annual interest of 8.5% compound… " he presses more buttons. "Mm. That would be the first year's interest… " more button pushing. "that the second… the third year would be… yes. Divided by three… roughly, I would say, you are looking at a figure of approximately £250,000, each." Meaningfully he looks at each of them, his fat face contorted with something like remorse. "Even less, for there will be death duties."

Chapter Twenty-Seven

Providence

Wednesday, February 23rd 2011

There was no sleep for Betty that night. *What the hell am I going to do? Why didn't he tell me?*

Providence having supplied her with a third of Rex's estate, it is, to her, as nothing; for with her share, even with the £33,000 she's saved, she knows it is not sufficient to buy herself a house, at least not a house in Brighton. *This is my comeuppance, a just reward for my avarice. Before I married him at least I had a home! It's karma. Life is paying me back. I have to suffer for my greed. I've rolled the dice and if not lost, I've certainly come unstuck. Fate, the Gods, or whoever, have spun my life web, twisted it, and sent me plummeting into the abyss.*

She gets out of bed and makes herself a cup of tea. *Unlike my darling Cheryl, she's always so happy when we speak. Motherhood has improved her. If the Gods have dumped me, then they have mercifully sent her to some happier place, some seventh heaven where the exalted angels dwell. I'll have to ask her for my house back.*

After barely an hour of sleep, she goes down to breakfast and absently looks through the morning post. *Cheryl's handwriting!*

Inside the envelope there is a post card of Grauman's Chinese theatre in Hollywood with a photograph of Bette Davis' handprints and signature written in cement: on the back:

Mamma darling. Thought you'd like this picture of your heroine's hands, like you, a woman of strength, character and beauty. Marco is contracted to make a film at Pinewood, so we will shortly be coming back to the UK. We will not be staying in our old home that you so generously gave us, the producer has arranged for us to have a house near the studio, so you can come to stay and meet your newest grandson, Antony. I'll call you immediately we arrive. All Love Cheryl.

Much elated, Betty puts the card on the mantelpiece in her room and discards the envelope in the waste paper basket... the torn pieces of the Mexican Valentine she discarded have vanished. *How awful of Joe to send me such a thing. Does he expect me to betray my own daughter? Wicked, really... What an insensitive monster he must be to do that to Claudia. Oh, goodness, I promised I'd go and see her.*

She speed dials Claudia's number and waits.

"Mumma, darling. Thank God! I have to talk to you. Can you come round?"

"Why whatever's the matter?"

"It's about the boys. Can you come over? You said you would. They've been looking at pornography stuff on some boy's i-Phone at school. I'm at a loss as what to say to them."

"Good heavens!" Feeling guilty for not contacting her earlier, she says, "I could come over now, if you like."

"Oh Mother, would you? I'd be so grateful, and if you could talk to them."

In the Bentley on the way over, as Robert is driving, he asks, "Might I enquire if the family have made any plans yet, Madam?"

"Everything is up in the air at the moment, Robert. It seems the house will have to be sold."

"I suspected as much."

Betty looks at him surprised. "Why did you suspect such a thing, Robert?"

"I heard Mr Rex talking on his phone. I don't think he noticed me sitting here half the time."

"He always knew you were there, Robert, believe me. If he talked frankly, it was because he trusted you."

"I'd like to think so. Anyway, I ask, because Gladys, Mary and I were talking… It seems we've all had the same idea at the same time. We would like to give notice. To take advantage of this bequest he's left us. On the other hand we don't want to inconvenience the family at such a difficult time."

"That is most thoughtful of you, Robert. I'll explain to Mrs Black and Miss Sophia. Meanwhile, you go ahead and make your plans. Tell Gladys and Mary to do the same. Things are going to be very different now for all of us."

Arriving at Joe's house, Claudia opens the front door in a fine froth of fury. "Thank God you're here!"

By the look of her eyes, Betty recognises she has been crying. "Mamma's here now, Pet, don't fret." She gives her a kiss and smells liquor on her breath. "Calm down, dear. Isn't that what that Michael Winner man says in the telly ad?"

"I'm fine now," says Claudia. "Really, I am. But I have to tell you I've come to a decision."

"What's that, dear?" she says hanging up her overcoat.

Claudia closes the front door and stands with her arms akimbo, waiting to give the full impact to her dramatic announcement.

Betty turns round. "Well, what?"

"I've been to a lawyer! I'm getting a divorce. I don't love him anymore. I'm glad he's gone, you hear me? I refuse to allow him to bugger up my life anymore. I should have jumped ship years ago," she says, leading Betty down the hall. "It was only ever sex between us. Since he's stopped fancying me, he's been off with other women all over the place. And look at the place," she says with an extravagant gesture opening the door to her stylish but comfortable living room. "Just look at it. None of it's me. Joe did all of it, everything, decorated every inch of it, never allowed me to do a thing, not even make the curtains. He was the one to measure up and order them. Everything is his taste, there's nothing of me reflected in the place. I should have gone years ago, been free, and that's just what I'm going to be now, I've decided."

"Well, Claudia, that is quite a speech," says Betty, clutching her handbag. "I seem to remember hearing something of the kind two years ago."

With the wind somewhat taken out of her sails Claudia mutters, "I wasn't brave enough to go for a divorce then," adding forcefully, "but I am now."

Betty regards her daughter coolly. "You used to tell me you loved what Joe had done to the house. Loved Joe, too, and what a wonderful husband he was, even when you came out of rehab."

"Well, I had to, didn't I? That was guilty conscience talking… he'd done a lot for me, I admit. I felt I owed him something. But it was a lie. Now, I can't stand the sight of him, I hope I never have to set eyes on him again. He's been the cause of so much unhappiness. I'd have left him years ago if it hadn't been for the boys. And did you know he's been talking to them all the time on the phone? Texting them. Never a word to me. I'm going to be much better off and much happier without him, I know it. We had our time together and some of it was good, I admit, but now it's over. And now that you're going to be on your own, there's something I want to you to do for me."

Betty reads her eyes. "I think I know what it is."

"I want you to look after the boys for me."

"Look after the boys?"

"While I'm away."

"While you're away," she repeats, sinking onto the arm of the sofa. "Where might you be going, dear?"

"No idea. The other side of the world! Australia, Africa, anywhere to get away."

"Darling, can you afford to do that?"

"Yes I can. Joe's always been good to me with money, I'll say that. If you can take care of the boys for me, I won't worry. After all, now Rex has gone, you have nothing else to do. I thought it would fit in perfectly for you. What do you say? You can either take them to live with you in that vast great empty house of yours, or you could move in here, if it suits you better. That would certainly make things easier for the boys, but it's up to you. What do you say?"

Betty puts her hand to her forehead. "As a matter of fact, Claudia, Rex's house is going to be sold."

"Oh, well that's just perfect. It fits in beautifully. You can move in here."

"I was planning to take a holiday."

"Holiday! How can you be so selfish? This is a crisis, Mother! Can't you help me out? If Cheryl were to ask you, you would."

"That's not true, dear."

"So will you? Please, say you will."

"Looking after two bouncing boys will certainly take my mind off my own troubles."

"Troubles? What troubles have you got?"

Betty sighs, looks around at the shelves filled with Joe's books, at an arrangement of Staffordshire pottery on the mantelpiece, a shepherd and shepherdess she knows Joe gave Claudia as a present. "No troubles, dear."

"I should think not. Rex has left you all his money, for goodness sake. You're a wealthy woman."

Betty looks up into her face. "I'll be glad to look after the boys for you, dear."

"Darling, you're a saint. Bless you. Let's go and tell them. They're upstairs. They'll be thrilled. I've told them you were coming."

"First," she says, taking her hand. "When are you thinking of leaving?"

"I don't know where I'm going yet, let alone when. Why don't we say this time next week? Move in then. Let's go and tell the boys."

Betty follows, worrying about how she is going to break the news to Sophia.

Peter and Paul are lying on their beds reading when Claudia opens their door. They both spring up, shouting, "Gran!" and give her a kiss.

"Goodness, what a welcome. Hello, darlings."

"Sorry about Granddad," says Peter.

"Yes, sorry," mutters Paul.

"Come and sit down. I want to have a talk with you." Glancing at her daughter, she adds, "Are you going to stay, dear?"

"No, no. I'll leave you alone. I've loads to do downstairs. Now, you two, listen to your Grandma." So saying, Claudia closes the door and leaves.

Betty looks at them both and takes their hands. They settle on the beds, Peter and Paul both facing her. "Now what's all this I hear about you watching rude films on someone's i-phone at school?"

"We knew it was a bit wrong," says Peter sheepishly.

"You were right. Were there pictures of naked ladies?

"They weren't exactly ladies," says Paul.

"No, I'm sure they weren't. You know that all that sex stuff in those films isn't real, don't you. It's greedy old men wanting women to be like that. You should never treat women like that when you're grown up. What you saw wasn't real life. Those women are so poor they do it for money. It doesn't represent reality, it's not real love."

The boys look at their knees and nod. "We know."

"Good. Well, that's all right then, as long as you know that, no worries. Do either of you have any questions?"

Paul looks up and brushes his fringe from his eyes, "Why are Mummy and Daddy divorcing?"

Betty takes a moment. "Has Daddy not told you?"

"He says that we will stay with him and not to worry, and that he's earning enough money so the three of us can always be together."

"Mummy won't say," chips in Peter.

"The thing is, being married is sometimes hard and a person's feelings change, even mummy's and daddy's. Can you understand that?"

"When I get married," says Paul, "and have a family of my own. I'll never leave them."

A pang of something very like pain pierces Betty's heart.

Chapter Twenty-eight

Kuala Lumpur

Saturday, 26th February 2011

*O*f all the cockamamie things Claudia did next, she flew to Malaysia. Online, she found a "special offer", flight and hotel for £699. Typical of her impulsive nature she grabbed it, such recklessness ranking alongside her devil-may-care immersion in gin, or inviting a total stranger into her home for a beer... which was Joe, ten years ago while he was mending the road outside on his pneumatic drill. Now that she admits that was a mistake, now that she is "love free," as she calls it, and her marriage over... her solicitor said divorce would be a formality now eighteen months had passed since Joe had left her... Claudia is disporting herself in a new pink swimming costume beside a glittering pool on the rooftop of the Hilton Hotel, Kuala Lumpur.

Lying on a tropical sun deck, hidden behind vast sunglasses, she is admiring one of the most beautiful young men she has ever seen. He looks Malaysian, about nineteen, and is diving and splashing around the pool, apparently with the object of impressing his girl friend, another one of the beautiful people.

She noticed him when she arrived yesterday, although then, he was with another girl; they had looked the perfect couple. She is uncertain if it is the same girl today. *Is he a guest, one of the staff, or a pool attendant?* A wet beach ball comes hurtling toward her from the pool; narrowly missing, it bounces onto her lap.

The Malaysian boy comes bounding up to her laughing. He

stands before her, his slim, swimming costumed brown body bulging with muscles in all the right places. Bowing slightly with his hand over his heart, he says, "Excuse, missy."

Charmed by the sight of him, she notices he has sexy eyes as well as a beautiful body. She throws him back his ball.

"Thank you. Americano?"

"No, English."

"Ah, London, yes?"

"No. Brighton."

"Brighton? Ah yes. I have heard of Brighton. By the seaside, yes?"

"Yes, beside the sea."

He promptly sits on the sun longer beside her. "How long you stay?"

"Two weeks."

"From London. With friend?"

"No, I'm here on my own, actually. You ask a lot of questions. Shouldn't you be getting back to your girl friend over there?"

"She is my sister." He throws her the ball. "You like me fetch you mint julep?"

"Do you work here?"

Deeply offended, he flinches, "No. I am not waiter," then proudly, "I am member."

"Member? I don't understand, of what, the hotel?"

"The gymnasium."

"Oh, I see."

"You like mint julep. Yes?"

"Yes, I think I would. Thank you, thank you very much."

He runs off to the bar and Claudia takes the opportunity of reaching for her bag. She finds her make-up compact and opens it up to look in the mirror; she lifts her sunglasses to check her face. Over the rim of the compact, she notices the boy's sister, her face over the edge of the pool watching her, their eyes meet, woman to woman.

The sunglasses fall back on her nose. She tucks her compact away and lies back in the sun, waiting. *I've turned into a cougar!*

At the clink of ice cubes, she opens her eyes. The boy is holding two highball glasses with sprigs of mint and a straw in each. "Missy London. For you. Happy landings!"

Claudia laughs and takes the proffered glass. "Thank you. Happy landings!" and she drinks. It is cold but there is more bourbon in it than she expected. It is very good. "What is your name?"

"Harry. Like your Prince Harry."

"Harry. Thank you, 'Prince' Harry, this is delicious."

"And you, please, your name?"

"Claudia," she extends her hand.

Politely bowing, Harry shakes her hand. "Claudia. You very beautiful lady. Why you come to Kuala Lumpur?"

"For the sun. In England now it is very cold and wet."

"Rain in K.L. too, but mostly sun. I would like to go London very much."

"London is not far from me in Brighton. Just an hour away on the train."

"I come to Brighton with you and we go to London, yes?"

Claudia laughs. "Well, yes, that would be nice, but... "

"First we go to dinner. I take you on the town, to see Kuala Lumpur. We get to know each other. You come with me, yes?"

"Tonight?"

"Of course."

"Well, that might be very nice, but... "

"No buts, please. I arrange everything. What time you like to eat, I take you nice place. What time I call for you?"

"Well, now. This is all very... How about eight o'clock?"

"Eight. Where? What room number?"

"Room 462, but perhaps it would be better to meet at Reception?"

"No, no, Reception know me as member. Better, I call at room 462. You please excuse me. Now I have to take my sister home."

"Of course. Where is she? She was here just now."

"Downstairs in changing room. It is pleasure to meet you, Missy from Brighton, London. We meet eight o'clock, room 462. Good bye, please. Excuse." He bows delightfully and runs off, leaving his glass on the table.

Claudia watches him with a smile, *Mm, if he turns up, I might well eat him up alive*. Finishing her drink, she puts her glass on the table. Noticing his, half full, she picks it up and finishes it.

Chapter Twenty-nine

Weekend at Pinewood

Saturday, 26th February 2011

"*I* love it," declares Georgiana Barrington looking over the guest bedroom, "It's cute and chintzy, exactly as a country cottage should be."

"The studio people told us Marilyn Monroe stayed here while she was filming *The Prince and the Showgirl*," says Cheryl.

"Good heavens! Do you suppose she had a bath in there," Georgiana inquires, peering into her en suite. She is a picture of unpretentious good taste, wearing a spangly necklace over a black and white patterned top, and black trousers over neat boots.

"It's possible, but there are two other bathrooms. Mother will be having the room next door and my nephews the end room."

Georgiana turns with a frown.

"You met them at the christening, remember?"

"Of course. So, we're going to be a full house?"

Cheryl nods and smiles.

Georgiana bends down to look through the low cottage window, "I see you have a tennis court, too."

"Yes, Michael and Marco could play if the weather was better."

"Just as well it's not. Michael's dreadfully competitive and I know your dear Marco just loves to win."

When Georgiana had received Cheryl's weekend invitation, she had been delighted, for it proved to her beyond any doubt that her dalliance with Marco in New York had remained a secret, and that

Cheryl had accepted her hand of friendship. The truth was slightly different.

Marco's agent, Judy Pearl, had negotiated a fee for the movie far exceeding anything he had anticipated. Anxious to invest it wisely, he needed Michael's advice. After discussing the matter with Cheryl, who appreciated that a meeting rather than a phone call would be more appropriate to discuss such an important issue, she overcame her prejudice against the Barringtons and issued the invitation.

"Do you have help with the garden?" Georgiana asks, "It looks charming."

"A gardener comes twice a week and a maid every morning, so we're very lucky."

"Leaving you free to manage your boys, well, three boys now!" she laughs delving into her weekend bag. "My dear, you're wonder woman!"

"I'm hardly that, the studio people found it for us. Look, I'll leave you to unpack and freshen up. Come down and have a drink when you're ready."

"Oh, I'm ready for a drink right now. Just let me hang this out so it's not creased for this evening."

"Use this," Cheryl opens a cupboard door and passes her a coat hanger.

"Thanks." Georgiana shakes out her little black dress.

"Killer L.B.D!" exclaims Cheryl, feeling the material.

"That's magazine talk, girl. You've grown up a bit since New York!"

Cheryl laughs. "Who is it?"

"Giles Deacon. It has these divine bat wing sleeves, see."

"Fabulous! But I'd look stupid in anything like that."

"Nonsense, it's just a style thing. You look delightful in whatever you wear. Michael was just saying the pair of you are both looking terrific. Success obviously agrees."

"That's down to you. Marco always says if you hadn't cast him in that play, it would never have happened."

"It's sweet of him to say so," she says, following Cheryl into the hall and down the stairs into the living room, "but with his talent it was inevitable sooner or later, with or without me."

Downstairs by a burning log fire, Marco, Michael and 'Tiger' Joe, are chatting over their drinks, all three wearing sweaters. Marco in a figure-hugging V-neck, displaying a tanned neck and chest; Michael, a navy cashmere with a blue shirt underneath; Joe in a crew-neck cable knit. Joe's hair has more salt than pepper in it these days, Marco's new name for him is 'Silver skin head'. He stands up politely as he sees Cheryl and Georgiana descending the stairs towards them.

"Darling," calls Michael to his wife, "You have to hear this. Joe here was just telling us, he worked his passage across the Atlantic. Got himself to Buenos Aires and visited Machu Picchu in Peru!"

"Goodness! We've always wanted to go there, haven't we? Was it as amazing as they say?"

"Fascinating," answers Joe. "Incredible really. It's a ruined Inca city perched right on a ridge in the Andes. There's a palace, a temple to the Sun and cultivated terraces. I found the place extraordinary and strangely spiritual."

One of the three mobile phones on the coffee table trembles. Marco picks it up and passes it to Cheryl. "It's yours, Honey."

"Mother, darling!" says Cheryl, turning away slightly. "Where are you?"

Joe watches her eagle-eyed.

"Fine," continues Cheryl, "Then you should be arriving in about half an hour. I'll get Joe to meet you at Slough station... Take care. See you soon. Can't wait. Bye, darling." She clicks off and turns to Joe smiling, "Go get 'em, Tiger."

Joe puts his glass down, grins at Marco, gives Cheryl a peck on the cheek, and dashes out pulling on his tweed jacket, "Excuse me all."

Cheryl explains. "You'll have to pardon Joe. This is the first time he'll have seen his sons in over two years."

Georgiana raises her eyebrows, "How come?"

"He's been working abroad. Last week he turned up out of the blue on our doorstep in Santa Monica!"

Cheryl and Joe had had many long chats on the balcony while Marco was filming at the studios. Overlooking the beach, over beer and too many cigarettes, he had told her of his not-so-high adventures over the past two years.

"I built a bar-come-cafe in Fuengirola, right on the road facing the beach. Stayed in this fantastic four-bedroom apartment with a swimming pool, courtesy of my boss. When Peter and Paul came out, we had such a ball. They were in either the pool or the sea every day. I took them to visit the Alhambra in Granada. Being with them 24/7, I saw sides of them I'd never seen before. It was just great."

He stopped short of explaining why he made the decision not to return home with them, how his partner, Ben Crawley, reported Claudia was sleeping around making a fool of him in Brighton. He did confess to the pain it had cost him to send his boys back to her, and school. "I hadn't bargained how it would be without them again. I had this hollow feeling inside me. I used to text them every day. Tell them what I was up to, and they'd text me back."

He did not admit to the change in his attitude to sex. Many señoritas would have been open to advances from "guapo hombre, Joe", but somehow, something always stopped him. Joe was now forty-five and the desire to seduce women no longer seemed so important. It just didn't bother him that much. *Perhaps I'm slowing down*, he thought.

On the celebratory opening night of the bar he'd been working on, he heard of the building boom going on in Buenos Aires. How it was the fastest growing economy in the world, in shipbuilding and motor manufacture. How everything from fabrication and electrical engineering to training was required, and just how much money workers could make.

It was exactly the adventure he craved.

With a mate he boarded MSC *Magnifica* at Malta, and as a maintenance plumber and electrician, worked his passage to Buenos Aires. Once there he joined AHF, S.A. a structural engineering company with 14 building projects on the go.

"One day I picked up a magazine with Marco's great ugly mug staring up at me. Well, I knew then where my next stop would be. But I have to tell you one thing, luv, I will never go back to your sister."

The most important thing he did not confide was the yearning he still had in his heart for Betty. For the sight of her special smile, for his longing to hold her in his arms again.

So even now, Cheryl remains ignorant of his true emotions in going to meet her mother at Slough railway station.

Chapter Thirty

Meeting Up

Saturday, 27th February 2011

"Auntie Cheryl says your Dad is coming to meet us at the station," says Betty, switching off her mobile.

Peter and Paul grin excitedly from across the carriage and carry on playing with their toy, a miniature mummy in a sarcophagus.

Betty glances at the doll; she knows it is a gift from Sophia. *Macabre sort of present if you ask me...* but no one had asked, it had just arrived in the post. Just before she moved into Joe's house, Sophia did ask though if she could take the boys up to London one day to the British Museum. She had answered vaguely, "We'll have to see."

I can never tell them Sophia is their great grandmother.

Betty looks out of the window. The countryside passes, the suburban houses with their little gardens, some well kept, some with sheds and little ponds, others messy and untidy. She notices nothing.

She is deeply concerned about spending the weekend in the same house with her son-in-law. How should she behave towards him? Joe is the man who so shamefully sent her that letter and damned Valentine card. When Peter and Paul told her where he was, and Cheryl confirmed his reappearance during their next transatlantic call, she had had mixed feelings. Admittedly, she'd been relieved he was alive and well, joyful, almost, consequently not entirely confident she had conquered all those unhealthy thoughts she'd harboured; she was also surprised that Cheryl's layabout boy friend should be doing so well that he could afford to give him a job.

"Marco *so* needs an assistant that he likes," Cheryl explained, "someone he can trust, instead of some stranger the studio foists on him. So it's all turned out rather well. When you come and stay with us in Pinewood, Joe will be with us, too, won't that be grand? And perfect for the boys. I haven't told Claudia yet, whether you do or not, is up to you."

"Under the circumstances," replied Betty, "I rather think not."

Since listening to Sophia's tale of incestuous love for her brother, she has inclined not to be so hard on herself for her earlier feelings for Joe. Her crime, as she sees it, pales into insignificance by comparison: it is not as if she and Joe were of the same blood. Indeed, as she had argued to herself, if they had met each other first, as Joe had joked, they may indeed have got it together. They are certainly closer in age than he is to her daughter, and now that Claudia has admitted that she no longer cares for him… *Nevertheless, it's an impossible situation. What would people say? One simply does not do that sort of thing. Happiness is all very well but one must obey one's conscience.*

Joe scans the station indicator to discover on which platform the London train is due. As he hurries to platform 4, it occurs to him that Slough railway station is hardly the most romantic place in the world for a lovers' reunion. *Not that we were ever that.* He asks the guard if he can wait on the platform.

"No, wait at the barrier, please sir."

Hearing the train approach his heart beats faster. He tells himself it is because he is about to see Peter and Paul again. Will he recognize them? Will they like the colourful Mexican toy dolls he has bought them, or think them too babyish? But the images in his mind are of kissing Betty, holding her in his arms, hugging her, seeing that fantastic smile again. *Will she feel the same?* "Is this the Paddington train coming now?"

"No, the fast train to Falmouth Docks. Yours is next."

Eventually the train arrives and Joe scans the passengers as they alight. With a leap in his heart, he spots his sons. They see him simultaneously, and run towards him, "Dad! Dad!" But without their tickets they have to wait at the barrier for Betty. As she approaches, her eyes are not on Joe but on opening up her purse. She hands the tickets to the guard and boys rush past her into Joe's bear hug arms.

"Peter, Paul! Dear darling boys! Just look at the pair of you. You're so tall! Oh, how grand it is to see you." Over their heads he looks at Betty

Standing squarely, she meets his eyes. With her hands firmly grasping her handbag, she says crisply, "Joe, how nice to see you again."

Joe realises in an instant she is not at all pleased to see him. The smile he remembers so well has vanished.

Chapter Thirty-one

Eastern Promise

Saturday, 27th February 2011

*S*ince Claudia boarded the plane two days ago, she has successfully put her sons, her mother, her sister, and definitely her husband out of her mind. She imagines herself to be a different woman. Having spent a lifetime thinking she didn't fit in anywhere, in the exotic east, with a little help of three more mint juleps by the pool, and a third of a bottle of bourbon from the mini-bar in her bedroom, she has at last found herself.

At 6.50p.m., in the persona of some imaginary jet-setting sybarite, she is in her luxurious, open plan, marbled bathroom with the rain shower, rubbing moisturiser onto her arms (as all glamorous women do after sunning themselves abroad). Seeing her reflection in the mirror, she grins, *There are no two ways about it; tonight you're going to lay that cute "Prince" Harry. Either before or after dinner, I really don't care which.*

"Shameless, that's what you are, girl", she tries to ignore her mother's voice in her head, "giving him your room number like that." Betty had taught her being "shameless" with a boy was just about the worst thing a girl could do, which was probably why she had been shameless most of her life. She giggles to herself. *But he did seem keen on me. Definitely gorgeous. But what was all that 'London, London' stuff? Probably wants me to take him there.*

On the dot of seven o'clock, just as she finishes zipping up the back of her new topless sundress, there is a knock on the door. She fluffs up the back of her hair and checks her image in the mirror: *Eyes a little droopy, but that's sexy, seductive. You're looking good, kid.*

She slips aside the peephole, and sure enough, there stands Mr Gorgeous.

"Prince Harry!" she cries, flinging open the door.

"Good evening, Miss Claudia." He wears an open neck white shirt, dark trousers and a worn, slightly shabby jacket, but he has brushed his hair and looks very handsome. Bowing slightly he presents Claudia with a pink hibiscus.

"How lovely! Thank you, Harry. You're exactly on time. Come in. I shan't be a moment." As she goes to the table to fetch her handbag and pashmina, Harry closes the door and saunters in a macho fashion toward the window.

"You have excellent view. You can see the lights in our famous Petronas Towers. It was tallest tower in world until Tapei 101, but still tallest twin towers in world," he smiles. "You have excellent room, you are very rich, I think, to afford such a room."

Not wanting to disillusion him by admitting it was a Thompson last minute deal, she says, "Do you live in K.L.?"

"Over there," he says, pointing. "You see lake here, my family have er… apartment, five miles behind those skyscrapers."

Walking toward him, she catches a sad look in his eye and noticing his worn jacket suspects his neighbourhood is a poor one. Moving close behind him, she puts her hands on his hips. "So where are you taking me out to dinner, young man?"

His body stiffens and he turns to face her.

Their faces are close.

Claudia takes in his slanting, sexy brown eyes, his black lashes, his full purple lips; she holds his face and tenderly kisses him.

He responds greedily.

Quickly he finds her back zipper and undoes her dress. Pulling her towards the bed, he passionately strips off his own underpants and lies on top of her.

Claudia meekly luxuriates in his young, smooth body.

Passionate, he may be, but he is not a lad for lovemaking. Harry requires instant gratification, there is no foreplay, no necking, chat or any endearment, just a murmur of "London, London," in her ear as he grinds away. Swiftly he reaches his orgasm, wailing deliriously, "LONDON! LONDON!"

Stifling a laugh, she realises he is a child and she will have to remain unsatisfied.

After a while, lying naked on the bed, she repeats, hoping to amuse him, "So where are you taking me to dinner?"

Lazily he turns his head. "Pasar Malam all night market? Chinatown is near. We can go there."

"I must go to the bathroom," she says, kissing his shoulder.

Washing, she grins at herself in the mirror, *short but alas not so sweet!*

Returning to the bedroom, she is surprised to see him wandering about in his underpants talking on his mobile. She cannot understand a word he says, presuming it to be Malaysian. She dresses while he talks.

Standing by the window, he waves to someone outside.

"Harry!" she reprimands.

"My friend," he explains, "he has binoculars."

Dumbfounded, she sits by her dressing table with her bag and shawl on her lap waiting. *He's boasting of his conquest of the woman in room 426.*

"He sees me!" he shouts, jumping up and down and waving.

"I'm so happy," says Claudia, peevishly. "Can we go to dinner now?"

He disconnects his phone and vanishes into the bathroom with his clothes.

Waiting for his return, she opens the mini bar and pours herself a slug of bourbon. A bubble of doubt surfaces in her mind. *Do I really want to spend the evening with this child? What on earth are we going to talk about?* Not having left the hotel in two days she thinks it is about time she discovered the town, and seeing it with a "local" will be better than going alone, besides, she tells herself, *it will be an adventure.*

He emerges from the bathroom fully dressed. "Ready?"

"Ready and waiting," she replies stifling sarcasm, and they leave.

In the lift, he places her arm through his and winks. As the doors open, he walks in his macho fashion across the marble floor. Strutting, cocksure, past the front desk he arrogantly nods to the Receptionist.

So Claudia leaves the safety of the Hilton Hotel and steps into the balmy night air, making her way, with Harry as her guide, into the noisy, teeming streets of Saturday night in Chinatown.

Chapter Thirty-Two

A Light Lunch

Saturday, 27th February 2011

"*I*'ve only done a light lunch, tomato soup, and cheeses," announces Cheryl taking her place at the head of the dining table, "Tuck in."

Peter and Paul don't have to be asked.

Joe regards them fondly as they spoon soup politely into their mouths.

Marco and Michael continue the conversation they were having in the living room about which car Marco should buy.

Georgiana leans in confidentially to Betty. "I was so sorry to hear about your husband's death. "Please accept our condolences."

"Thank you," says Betty.

"Will you continue living in that fabulous Georgian house we went to after the christening?"

Betty hesitates.

"Sorry, it's none of my business," says Georgiana, sensing she's struck a nerve. "You probably haven't had time to decide what to do yet."

"No, no, it's not that," she answers, embarrassed at having to talk about it in front of Joe and Cheryl, whom she hasn't told yet. Planting on a smile she says, "We are going to sell it, as a matter of fact. It's much too large for just the three of us." She glances across the table at Cheryl. Since coming to realise just how wealthy Marco has become, it has occurred to her that Cheryl may not wish to return to her old home in Holland St, in which case what will happen to it? Should she ask, or will they offer?

"How interesting," replies Georgiana. "It must be worth a fortune. It is one of the finest houses I've ever been in. Michael, do you hear that, darling?"

"What's that?"

"Betty here is selling that fabulous house we went to."

"Who to?"

"No one's made an offer yet," answers Betty, not wanting to discuss it. "It's not actually on the market yet, but it will be soon."

"Perhaps," says Michael, turning Marco, "you should buy it as a property investment. Turn it into flats. You could make the penthouse your English pad. What sort of price tag are you asking?"

"I'm not certain," says Betty, shocked at the turn in the conversation, "the lawyer said, well over a million." *That'll put a stop to that!*

Joe pipes up. "That's what you were planning to do in the beginning, do you remember? Turn it into flats?"

"Well, yes," Betty replies, annoyed. "Rex did consider it at one time."

"You asked me to do the conversion, do you remember?"

She smiles mechanically, not quite daring to look him in the eye.

"How many flats were you going to turn it into?" asks Michael.

"Six or seven," answers Joe.

"What a fantastic idea!" says Marco. "Could we really afford it, Mike?" Explaining to the rest of the table, he says, "Mike, here, is my financial wizard."

"Of course," says Michael, "you'd have to take out a mortgage, but with the income from the flats, you'd soon pay that off. Afterwards you'd have an income for life."

"Have what Humphrey Bogart called 'an F.U. fund'. I could pick and choose scripts on their merit, not have to do rubbish to pay the bills. Great! Let's do it."

"It would cost a fortune to convert and refurbish," warns Joe.

"The man is making a fortune!" says Michael. "We could easily work round that one. One film and the mortgage is paid off. Your whole family could live there, in separate apartments, if you so wish. You could rent out the others. Yes, I think perhaps we should to look into this." He turns to Betty with a smile.

Betty returns his look, hardly believing what she is hearing. "Steady on there, young man! This is not my decision. There are my in-laws and Rex's lawyer to consider."

"What's his name?"

She has good reason to remember the fat man. "Henry Williams. Hove High Street."

"Leave him to me," says Michael, smiling brightly. "Not to worry. I'll contact him, I'll arrange everything."

Betty savagely tears a crust off the French baton and spreading butter on it rather too thickly, adds a slice of cheddar, munches, and idly pursues the thought of Marco as owner of Rex's house. *Unbelievable! Cheryl and the children living and romping around in that grand house. Thomas and Antony... Sophia's great-grandchildren! How odd. Come to think of it, it would be quite fitting. One day, who knows, it might even be theirs.*

Chapter Thirty-Three

Chinatown

Saturday, 26th February 2011

A mass of Oriental faces press around Claudia; Petaling Street is ablaze with vibrant electric night-signs and red Chinese lanterns, pedestrians clog the walkway. Cycles and scooters whizz dangerously close by, tempting cooking smells come from noodle carts and eateries crammed between hawker stalls selling a myriad of goods on either side of the road. The whole place is a grungy chaos of people and business.

"It's packed!" says Claudia clinging to Harry's arm, the noise of the swirling ghetto assaulting her not entirely sober senses, colours ebb and flow out of focus in her head.

"There are two bus stations over there, so everyone comes. This is best place in K.L. Food stalls open all night. You like to eat proper restaurant? Inside? Sit down? I have friend works at "Nam Heong", we go there."

"I would rather sit down, yes. What is 'Nam Heong'?"

"Hainanese Chicken Rice, best in town."

"How far is it?"

"Close by."

Thank God. I can't take much more of this.

Jostling through the crowds, vendors at metal tables selling drinks, tourists haggling over counterfeit name-brand goods, they make their way past endless Chinese restaurants, eventually reaching the yellow and red hoarding of 'Nam Heong' and Harry's waiter friend, Chai.

Chai greets Harry effusively and makes a great fuss of Claudia, clearing one of the outside tables and offering them seats. "Regret inside is full."

The table, like many others, is balanced half on the pavement and half in the street, with the gutter running in the middle underneath. Relieved it is a dry night Claudia shrugs, and accepting the proffered table, sits in the chair in the road.

"You do the ordering," she says, relieved to be sitting and reluctant to admit to feeling woozy. "I'll have that chicken thing you told me about. I'll have a drink, too, how about you?"

"Tiger beer," says Harry to Chai.

"Yes. Me, too," says Claudia, determined to enjoy herself.

When Harry finishes ordering, Chai leaves and they are alone. As alone anyone can be sitting in the middle of a bustling busy street. She puts her chin on her hand and regards Harry. "So tell me, what it is you do, Harry? What is your work?

"I have no work. I very good at football. One day I play for Harimau Mayaya."

"Sorry, but what is that?"

"Mayayan Tiger, national team of Malaysia."

"Oh, I see. Well, that's splendid! My boys... " she peters out. About to tell him about her sons, who both love football, she checks herself. *Tales of Peter and Paul, who are not much younger than he is, might not go down too well.*

Harry takes out his mobile and for a moment she thinks he is about to chat with one of his friends again, when he asks, "What is your phone number? I programme it in my mobile. Then I tell you when I play, and you watch me on television, yes?"

"That would be delightful." Charmed by the idea, she delves into her bag for her mobile. "I can never remember my number, crazy, isn't it? I can remember my mother's but never my own."

"Then I come to see you in London."

Oh dear! Abruptly Claudia reconsiders giving him her number. *Perhaps I could give him a false number. No, no, how could I be so awful?* Opening her phone, she presses buttons. "Ah! here we are. Ready?"

"Go."

At that moment she hears cries behind her and the noise of an approaching engine. She glances around. Heading up the street are two youths on a motor bike. People are scattering out of their way, leaving a path leading straight toward her. Instinctively she rises to get out of the way, but her head is foggy. As she stands, she stumbles, the motor bike skids and crashes into legs, smashing her into the table and chairs and squashing her body against the shop front wall, fracturing her ankles, skull, several ribs and clavicle.

The last thing she remembers is seeing her mobile phone flying in the air.

Chapter Thirty-Four

The Call

Saturday, 26th February 2011

"Are those boys in there quite serious?" asks Betty, standing by the sink washing up.

"You've no need to do that, Mother, there's a washing machine just here, look."

"I'm happier doing this; it gives me something to do. I'd no idea Marco could afford that sort of money."

"Well, he has been doing rather well lately, darling. This will be his fourth consecutive movie in a row and third starring role." Taking a tea cloth she starts to dry a glass. "*Attitude*, you know that gay magazine, voted him the 14th sexiest man in the world last month."

"Good heavens! How on earth would I know such a thing?"

"It's crazy, but fun; apparently he's become a gay icon. Oh, I forgot to show you this." She extends her hand, showing off the ring Marco had bought.

"Yes, I noticed it before, but didn't like to say," says Betty. "It's beautiful. Does it mean you're getting married?"

"No, darling, it was just a present." She finishes drying the glass. "Don't you like the idea of us buying your Brunswick Square house, then?"

"No, no, I mean, why should I mind? On consideration, I think it's quite a good idea. It's just so very surprising."

"I think it would be fabulous. All that room, and an income for life! Before you arrived, they were bandying about the maddest notions. At one time they were talking about buying Battersea Power Station!"

"Besides, it's hardly my house; at least I don't feel it is. It belongs to Sophia and Agatha."

"And now you, darling."

Betty gives a faint smile and hands her a wet plate.

In the ambulance, the paramedic is writing something down on his clipboard.

"Missy Claudia! Missy Claudia!" calls Harry, crouched beside her. He is feeling responsible and dishonoured that such an accident should befall his fine English lady friend. Tentatively he slaps her hand. "I am so sorry, Missy? Please be okay, lady, we go to London together. You must be okay."

Claudia's eyelids flutter open, her lips move... "Mumma!"

"You want your Mama?"

She nods. "My mobile."

"Nokia? I have it, see," says Harry, holding it up. "I caught it. Don't worry. You just be okay."

"Mumma," she says faintly. "Press one. Number one."

"Number one?" Harry repeats, "This one?" and he presses it.

"Tell her... tell her... " Her eyes close and she loses consciousness.

Seeing 'Mum' appear on the screen, Harry, who is Nokia savvy, adds the U.K. dialling code to the number and presses the green connect button.

Joe is sat at the dining table marvelling at Marco and Michael still arguing about the merits of a Jaguar XF, cost £33,900, against a Junior Executive BMW, cost £26,680. Marco is favouring the purchase of the more family friendly BMW, when the sound of

Betty's phone buzzing on the dresser distracts Joe. He picks it up.

Coming into the kitchen, he gives it to Betty. "Your phone, I believe."

"Ta," she says, not looking at him and drying her hands, then pressing a button. "Oh, it's Claudia! Hello, darling. Where are you?... What?"

"Is that Miss Claudia's Mumma?"

"Hello, yes. I am Claudia's mother. Who is this speaking, please?" she frowns at Joe and Cheryl. "It's a foreigner."

"I am Harry, friend of Miss Claudia. She is hurt."

"Hurt? Why, what's happened? Where are you? Can I speak to her?"

"No, no. She is not conscious."

"Unconscious? Why, what's wrong with her? Oh my God! Has there been an accident?"

"An accident, yes. A motor bike crash."

"Motor bike! Lord! Where is she hurt? Can you tell me where she is hurt, please? Where are you speaking from?"

"Ambulance."

"Ambulance! How badly is she hurt, please?" She turns to Joe, "There's been an accident? Where are you, please? Can you tell me where are you taking her?"

"Hold on. I will ask."

"Where are you?" she looks at Cheryl. "The man's gone! Hello?... Hello."

"Hello, please!"

"Yes, Hello, I'm here," says Betty, "Where are you taking her? Where are you?"

"Kuala Lumpur."

"What? Where?"

"Kuala Lumpur. K. L."

"I can't understand a word the man is saying."

"Give it to me," says Joe, holding out his hand.

Betty hands him her mobile. "She's hurt," she says to Cheryl, "in an ambulance somewhere."

"Hello!" Joe calls down the phone. "This is Joe Robinson speaking, Claudia Robinson's husband. Where are you calling from, please?"

"Husband? Oh my! Yes, sir! I am so sorry, sir. I am just friend of Miss Claudia. Paramedic say we take her to Kuala Lumpur Hospital."

"Kuala Lumpur!" He turns to Betty, "Good heavens, she's in Malaysia!" then into the phone again. "Kuala Lumpur Hospital, you say? In Malaysia?"

"Yes, sir. I am so sorry, sir."

"Tell me, how badly is she hurt, please? Can I speak to a doctor?"

"One moment, sir."

"He's passing me to the doctor."

"Tell him to give her my love," whispers Betty, her hand clasped to her mouth.

The mobile crackles, "Hello, yes, I speak English," says a different voice.

"Ah, Doctor!"

"No, I am paramedic."

"Sir, I am the husband of your patient. Can you tell me, please, how serious is her condition?"

"I cannot say for certain, not at this time, but very serious, we think. We take her to General Hospital in Kuala Lumpur. She is in excellent care, rest assured. General Hospital is well-resourced to meet challenging situations."

"Thank you. Will you tell her, please, that her mother sends her love."

"Her mother?"

"Yes. My thanks to you, sir. Goodbye." He hands the phone back to Betty. "She's on her way to the General Hospital, Kuala Lumpur. The paramedic fellow says it's serious."

Betty clicks off her phone and looks at Cheryl. "I must go to her."

"Yes, darling," says Cheryl, clasping her hand. "Perhaps you should. We'll take care of the boys, don't worry. Let's get online and find you a flight."

Joe stops them. "Betty!" he calls, "I'll come, too."

Betty regards him steadily for a moment. "No, no, Joe, you must stay with your boys. They'll need you, especially if... I'll be fine."

"I have to see her, Betty. I must. She's the mother of my sons. It might be for the last time. You have to let me come with you."

Taking a breath and biting her lip, she shrugs, "As you please," and she follows Cheryl into the living room.

Joe stares at the empty doorway

In the living room, Georgiana and Betty look over Cheryl's shoulder at her laptop.

"The flight takes twelve hours!" she says, studying a flight list on a Cheap Flights web site.

"Heavens! So long?" exclaims Betty.

"I can't stand travelling, either," says Georgiana. "The stress! Whenever I go near an airport, I have to take a valium. For long journeys, I always take sleeping pills. Do you want some? I have some upstairs."

"There's a plane at 6 o'clock this evening leaving from Heathrow," reads Cheryl. "It's cutting it a bit fine; you'd have to leave in an hour. Are you up for that? It's £455, stopping in Hanoi, Royal Brunel Airlines, for two, that's £910. I'd better book a hotel, too. There's an advertisement here for the Hilton, shall I go for that?"

"Book it," says Joe, over her shoulder.

"Two rooms," calls Betty, a little too loudly.

Joe fights a grin and says, "Use my credit card." He fishes in his pocket for his wallet, extracts the card and passes it to Cheryl.

"I'll settle up with you later," says Betty.

"No need," says Joe.

"Joe," answers Betty firmly, "there is every need. I insist we pay our own way." Her tone and expression imply a great deal more, but she leaves it at that. "Georgiana, I think I'll take you up on that offer, if you don't mind. I'm beginning to feel a bit wobbly already."

"You poor darling, as if you haven't got enough on your plate. Come with me, we'll find you some 'soma', isn't that what Aldous Huxley called them?" and she makes her way up the stairs.

"I'd better fling some things in a bag," adds Betty following her. "Thank goodness, I brought my passport. I had some vague idea we might all fly back to California together. Oh, well!"

Joe goes to Marco's side and places his hand on his shoulder. "You can manage without me for a few days, can't you?"

Marco shrugs; he is not a happy bunny. "It is my first week! It's vital I have someone."

"Sorry, man. I didn't think you'd mind."

"I'll have to accept some dumb-arse trainee from the studios."

"I'll help you out."

Surprised, they both look across at Michael sitting in an armchair with a newspaper.

"What's involved exactly? Driving you to the studios? Making tea? Can't be that bad."

"Mickey!" says Marco, "it's a full time job. Calling people, arranging stuff, I'm in the front line, my head is in a different place. You have to think for me. I'm learning lines, in costume and make-up, working stuff out, and I still have to finish the song.

You'd have to be Mr Fixit behind the scenes, the hard man."

"You mean what I do for Georgie every day?"

"I guess," smiles Marco.

"Honestly," says Michael. "I'll be happy to do it, be like old times."

Marco regards him ruefully.

Since his wariness of Michael three years ago, he has moved on. These two old school friends who experienced their first secret love share an experience woven deep into their psyches. Now that they are equally successful and enjoying happy heterosexual relationships, they are finding an agreeable piquancy in each other's company.

"In the old days I used to fag for you!" says Marco.

"Ah ha," grins Michael evilly, "but now I hold the purse strings."

An hour later, Cheryl is at the wheel driving Betty and Joe to Heathrow.

Sitting next to her Betty pops the first of Georgiana's Mogodon. "All I can think of is my poor girl lying there alone in a strange country. What must she be going through?"

As they wait at the Check in, Joe is as attentive and courteous to Betty as he knows how. "Can I get you anything?"

She shakes her head.

Flying halfway across the world to see a woman he no longer loves so that he can sit next to a woman he does love, does not strike Joe as deceitful. On the contrary, as far as he is concerned, he is, in the words of Noël Coward (a man he greatly admires), "grabbing every scrap of happiness" he can. Even being solicitous and helping with her luggage gives his machismo a frisson of pleasure. However, while they are in the lounge waiting to board, Betty pops two more of Georgiana's sleeping pills.

Things are not looking too promising for Joe to go a-wooing.

Chapter Thirty-five

Arriving

Sunday afternoon, 27th February 2011

"*I*n a few minutes we shall be landing in Kuala Lumpur," announces the chief flight attendant. "We hope you have enjoyed your flight with Royal Brunel Airlines and look forward to welcoming you again soon."

"I'm dreading what we'll find," says Betty, squeezing in beside Joe. Since leaving Hanoi, she has hardly spoken, but now, after a long sleep, and a freshen-up in the toilet, she is ready to face the worst.

Joe is not. The only moment of pleasure he experienced during the long flight was when Betty's head nodded, in sleep, onto his shoulder. That such a simple act should produce so much happiness astonished him. Since then he has been experiencing a morbid sense of guilt. *Am I masquerading as a loving husband?*

He has, or so he imagines, made it clear to Betty that he is only making this trip to make his peace with Claudia… should the worst happen.

"I'll get a taxi straight to the hospital," says Betty, as they are coming in to land, "if you can take care of the luggage?"

"Good idea," he says, "I'll check us into the hotel and join you as soon as I can. It'll be good for you to have some time with her alone."

"Thank you," she answers, sitting back preparing for landing.

The Pantai Hospital Kuala Lumpur turns out to be the flagship of the Malaysian Ministry of Health. It has an impressive entrance with a long list at the door of the wide variety of clinical services available. So comprehensive a list and so spotless is the Reception area that Betty is confident Claudia is in capable and professional hands.

At the desk, she explains to a woman her own age wearing a Muslim headscarf, who she is and asks where she can find her daughter.

Referring to a computer, the receptionist directs her to, "Block C. Ward 2. Follow the signs, please."

Walking along the long corridors, she notices nearly all the nurses wear the hijab. Eventually she reaches Ward 2.

"Where can I find Mrs Robinson, please," she asks a nurse behind a counter. "I'm her mother."

"Ah! The English lady," answers the nurse smiling and showing Betty the way. "She came out of surgery this morning, so should be coming round soon." Leading her to a small side room with blinds over the window and an empty bed, she draws aside a curtain and there lies an unconscious Claudia with her head on a pillow. Her face is visible through bandages wound around her head and under her chin, beneath the sheet over her body is a hoop to protect her legs. High on a shelf to her right is an electrocardiograph machine showing Claudia's heartbeats on a monitor.

Betty gasps. Looking lovingly at her daughter she touches her hand and slowly sits beside her.

At the Hilton Hotel, Joe checks in, and collects his key.

"Which is Mrs Black's room please?"

"The room next door to yours, sir," answers the Receptionist.

"Thank you." One of the first things he does when he gets there is to check whether there is a communicating door.

There is not.

When he joins Betty in the hospital room, Claudia is still lying unconscious.

"She hasn't moved since I arrived," whispers Betty. "I've been sitting here reliving her entire childhood. What a little devil she always was. Oh, and I left a message on Cheryl's phone to say we arrived safely."

Silently going to the other side of the bed, Joe cannot resist gently touching Claudia's hand, the one wearing his wedding ring.

Her eyes open.

"Hello, Honey," he says softly.

She studies him and slowly smiles. "Joe."

He nods and grins. "Hello, Lovely."

"Joe." Smiling at him for a long time, gradually her lower lips starts to tremble and tears fill her eyes.

"Now, now," says Joe. "None of that. You're going to get better, do you hear, and soon." Indicating Betty, he adds, "Look who here."

With difficulty, Claudia turns a little. "Mumma!"

"Darling!" says Betty, going to her side and taking her hand.

Her voice croaks as she tries to say something…

"Here," says Betty, pouring water from a carafe into a glass. Carefully she brings it to her lips. It is difficult for Claudia to drink, so Betty puts her fingers in the water and moistens Claudia's lips.

"They're quite clean. I just washed them."

"You've come all this way."

"Of course."

"Are the boys all right?"

"They're fine. They're with Cheryl and Marco."

They look into each other's eyes and again Claudia's eyes fill with tears. "I'm so sorry."

"Whatever for, my darling?"

"Being so bad. I was always such a worry. You wanted to go on holiday, I made you stay."

"Well, you've succeeded in getting me abroad now, haven't you?" says Betty with a lump in her throat. Smiling, she caresses her daughter's hand. "There, there, my darling. There's no need to talk, don't talk."

"Where's Prince... ?"

"Prince?"

"Prince Harry? He's not really a prince... Did you speak to him?"

"No, dear."

Joe asks, "You mean the guy who telephoned us?"

"Oh yes!" exclaims Betty, "I should have thought. The nurse said earlier that there'd been someone waiting. A Malaysian boy. She said only next of kin were allowed so she sent him away. Do you want us to get him a message?

"Thank him for taking care of me."

Betty glances across the bed to Joe, "Of course."

Joe looks on, feeling he must say something. "Marco's making a big film at Pinewood, he's asked me to work for him, to be his Personal Assistant."

Claudia turns a little to see him, but her neck hurts. "Sit by Mumma, then I don't have to turn... "

Joe crosses below the bed and stands beside Betty.

"That's better. You both look so nice... together. You match." She smiles at them a while. "Better than you and I did. I'm so happy to see you, Joe," she says, tears welling up again. "You should have married Mumma. She'd have made you a much better wife than I did."

"Nonsense," says Joe, without much conviction.

"Nonsense," echoes Betty, self-consciously.

Claudia closes her eyes.

Betty and Joe sit silently avoiding each other's eyes and wait beside the bed.

Chapter Thirty-six

The Arrangement

Monday morning, 28th February 2011

Michael is working in Marco's spartan star dressing room at Pinewood film studios, his phone earpiece in his ear, his laptop open before him, a notepad and pencil in his hand.

"Good morning, Michael Barrington speaking. Is that Mr Stephen Wilkie of the Norwich Union?"

"It is. Good morning. How may I help?"

"I have been given your name by Mr Henry Williams, solicitor of the late Rex Black, of Brunswick Square, Brighton. I understand from him that you are handling the sale of Mr Black's property in Brunswick Square, is that correct?"

"Yes, that is so. I have just spoken with Mr Williams."

"My client, Mr Marco Danieli, the film actor, is interested in acquiring the property and is prepared to make an offer of one million, two hundred and fifty thousand. It would be an immediate cash transaction. There are no mortgage arrangements to be made, and, of course, you would have no commission to pay estate agents."

"I see. Well, that would certainly seem to be a… " he hesitates, "appropriate. Could you give me a moment, please?"

"Certainly." Michael doodles on his pad. After a few minutes, Mr Wilkie returns.

"Mr Barrington?"

"Mr Wilkie?"

"Yes, indeed, that would seem to be an acceptable offer. Could I take some details, please?"

"Certainly."

It was that easy.

Of course, it would take a little time for Michael to liquidise the £625,000 required from his own investments, which was to be his personal loan to Marco; but as the mortgage broker, he would then have Marco in his pocket, which was exactly where he wanted him.

At that moment Marco walks in, covered in mud (fake mud – porridge and gravy browning), having just led twenty-five Chechen refugee children (from the Sylvia Young and Barbara Speake Stage Schools) heroically to safety through a filthy underground sewer (a glass-fibre tube). "I'll take it from here, thanks, Fred," he says, closing the door on his dresser, "Many thanks."

"How was it?" enquires Michael.

"Four takes, not bad, considering all those kids messing about." He sits on the bed, snatches his Blackberry from the table and speed dials Cheryl. Waiting for her to answer he starts to undo the laces of his muddy boots.

Michael unplugs his earpiece. "I made the deal for the house in Brighton. It's all yours!"

"You're kidding me?"

Michael grins sleepily, shaking his head. It's his cool way of accepting praise.

"Mickey! Wow! You're brilliant."

"Hello," says Cheryl's voice on the phone.

"Hi, Honey! Any news yet?"

"Nothing since the message yesterday. There're eight hours ahead of us there, though, remember."

"Yes, of course. How are you managing with all those kids?"

"Loving it. How's Michael doing?"

"He says he's just bought us the Brighton house."

"You're not serious? What about the mortgage?"

"She says, what about the mortgage?"

"You owe me a fortune," says Michael, still grinning, but the sparkle in his eye has a little more steel than usual.

"We owe him."

"Heavens! Georgiana will be more impossible than ever!"

"But we'll have a classy home and an income for life, Honey." Coving the mouthpiece, he asks casually, "Take my boots off."

Michael, who has been watching him as if mesmerized, slowly gets on his knees and one by one prises off Marco's mud-caked boots.

"But where will my Mother live while Joe's fixing the house up?"

"Presumably where she is now, in Joe's house looking after the twins." Covering the mouthpiece again, he adds, "And my socks."

Michael looks up at him sharply.

Marco meets his eyes with his green-eyed smouldering look.

It is an expression Michael recognises... and not just from Marco's screen close-ups.

"If Joe's going to be doing the building work on the Brunswick Square house," says Marco, still holding Michael's eyes, "he won't be much use to me as a P.A. Still, Mickey's managing very well here. He just loves it. Don't you, Mick?"

"Just love it, Marco," Michael replies, peeling off a hot sock.

Chapter Thirty-Seven

Early Hours

28th February, and 1st March 2011

Claudia lies groaning, "It hurts. It hurts so much"

"Where?" asks Joe.

"All over. Can't they stop it? There must be something they can give me. We're supposed to be living in a modern age, for God's sake." Looking into Betty's eyes she asks, "Am I going to die?"

"I don't know, my darling. I do hope not."

"I'll find someone," says Joe. "They should be able to do something." Leaving the room, he sees a nurse by a night light sitting at her desk. "My wife is in great distress. Could you not give her some painkiller, please?"

"I'll see. Leave it with me, sir."

Back in the room, Claudia is saying, "Mumma, you will take care of Peter and Paul, for me, won't you, with Joe… "

"Don't talk that way… " says Betty. "Please. Yes, yes, of course I will."

"And take care of Joe, too."

Betty bites her lip. "I'll try."

Joe pushes open the door, and goes to Claudia's side.

"Joe! Promise me you'll take care of Mumma for me, you will, won't you?"

"Of course," he says, looking into Betty's eyes across the bed.

"She *so* needs someone to look after her. Promise me."

"I promise," he answers, choking up. "I promise to take care of Betty."

For a while, no one speaks.

Betty sits with her mouth tense, praying to a god that she no longer believes in to make Claudia well.

Claudia groans and whimpers.

A white-coated, chic Malaysian lady with short black hair comes in. "How's the patient? I am her doctor. May I have a word?"

In a small office just off the main corridor, she explains, "I can give her something to stop the pain, but it is dangerous after the trauma of such an operation. I should not like to take the responsibility. You must make that decision."

"No pain," says Joe. "I don't want her to suffer, but," he looks at Betty, "it's your decision."

"Do all you can, please. Give her the morphine, or whatever it is. I can't bear to see her in such pain."

Hours pass. The electrocardiogram on the shelf by Claudia's bed shows her heartbeats are becoming more and more infrequent.

Betty holds her hand.

Claudia eyes roam, finally she stares at her mother.

Betty smiles back unsure if Claudia can really see her. *Yes, I think she's still there. My face was the first she ever looked into, now I think it will be the last.*

The monitor, like some hypnotic cobra, impels Betty and Joe to keep looking up. For three hours, they watch Claudia's life slowly, so slowly, ebb away before them on the screen. Blip… such a long pause… blip… another pause… blip… blip…

Sometimes they walk around the bed, sometimes they sit down, accepting the inevitable, silently meeting each other's eyes, wanting and not wanting it to end. They keep their vigil until the electrocardiogram comes to a stop with a constant low whine.

As she holds Claudia's hand, Betty's body shakes with uncontrollable sobs.

Joe puts his arms around her shoulders to comfort her. Holding her body, he feels a curious bittersweet happiness.

A nurse comes in and switches off the electrocardiogram. She covers Claudia's face with the sheet and it is plain the time has come for them to leave.

Slowly, with his arms still around her, Joe leads Betty out into the corridor. "This should never be," she sobs, "this should never have happened. She shouldn't go before me. It's not right. I should go first."

"My darling," Joe rubs her back. They walk a while down the long corridor. "It's nearly four o'clock, Monday morning! I tell you what: we'll get a taxi back to the hotel, try to get some sleep, and meet up for breakfast, well, let's say brunch, at midday, okay? We have to decide about the funeral, and I have something to say to you."

"You'll have to do everything, Joe. I don't have the energy. You take charge."

"Very well, my dear, I will. You can count on me. You can always count on me."

With his arms around her, they continue their way down the empty corridor.

Chapter Thirty-Eight

Low Tide

Monday, 28th February 2011

A lonely figure carrying a bag wanders along Brighton beach. Sophia is feeling wretched, bewildered and a little frightened.

Mr Williams, the lawyer, had telephoned earlier: "Can I speak to your mother?"

"She's gone to Worthing for the day. Can I take a message, please?"

"I just wanted to tell her that I have just heard from the Norwich Union that a buyer for the house has come forward. I know how concerned she was. You can tell her the sale should be complete by the end of the month. I thought you would both like to know, to put your mind at ease."

Mr Williams' call had done completely the opposite.

A moment of agonising nausea had overtaken her… wild panic. *Where shall I go. What about Ptolemy and Asinoe? Where will they go? I must have them with me. Rex! Rex! Mother! Betty!*

With such big changes happening Sophia is utterly at a loss as she ambles along over the wet sand. Without her family to talk things over with, she is lost.

Last week Betty promised to get travel brochures, to make plans to go down the Nile. She did say later, she had to look after her grandchildren, but since then, nothing. She would help, I know it, if she knew. She never condemned me when I told her about Rex. What am I supposed to do? Contact Auctioneers, house clearance people? What about all my things? Where am I going to live?

To add to her worries Agatha has been talking a great deal lately about her retired concert-hall pianist friend, Joyce Heron, in Worthing, who, only this very morning Robert had driven her over to visit.

She seems to have realised that she must move and grasped at the straw of her celebrity friend in a similar position. All yesterday afternoon she was playing one of her CD recordings. "My dear friend Joyce," she said, "used to take her piano stool to all her dress fittings. Can you imagine it? So that she could see in the mirror the line of her dress from the back, you see, while she was at the piano playing her concerts. She used to spend, oh, as much as ten thousand pounds on one dress. Of course, she could afford that sort of money, she was very successful, used to give concerts all over the world. She asked me to join her as a companion on one of her English tours. I did for a while but... " Agatha shrugged, a seraphic smile on her face, "I was a home bird, never the travelling type. Yes, Joyce is real quality, someone I should be proud to spend my last days with."

Sophia believes the two of them are hatching a plot to go and live together in some grand expensive nursing home.

Robert is probably driving them around to look at some right now. Where shall I go then?

Being low tide, the burnt out remains of the West Pier ahead mars the seascape more than usual. The black iron girders covered in barnacles, the horizontal crossbars shrouded in dripping wet seaweed. Considered an eyesore by most of the residents of Brighton and Hove, to Sophia it is a haunting reminder of that dreadful morning twenty-three years ago.

Those dark wet shadows underneath where they found Eve's body.

Since confiding her tale of Eve's death to Betty... well, her version of events, which after all these years she has come to believe is the truth... she is beginning to have doubts. *Is that really the way it happened?*

Seeing Eve's astonished face at the bedroom door.

Getting dressed quickly.

Catching up with her just as she was turning onto the West Pier. Running beside her.

"Leave me be," she said, in that dainty highly-strung way she had, "you disgust me! Wretch! Keep away from me. You, who call yourself my friend. With your own brother, you horrify me."

"I can explain," I said, running beside her trying to hold her back, but on she went, past the little oriental houses and bandstand.

"You revolt me! The pair of you. I suspected you were lovers from the start, from the very beginning, but I refused to believe it. Now I know it for certain, I'm going to report you to the police."

"You're crazy, Eve. Don't be so melodramatic. There are no policemen here on the end of the pier, look, there's no one." We were past the concert hall now, at the very end. "Come home, come and have some breakfast."

"He never loved me. It was you. Because of you. He never loved me, not as a man and wife should. He promised me children but we could never have any. You took him away from me."

"Eve, this is all in your imagination."

"In that case," she said, turning on me spitefully. "What were the two of you doing in your bed this morning?"

"Alright, I admit it," I said. "Yes, you're right. Rex and I do love each other. We always have done, ever since he came home from Rhodesia. We just heard this morning that our son has been in a terrible skiing accident. He died and we were comforting each other."

"Comforting each other! Your son!" she shrieked. "You and

Rex had a son? I don't believe it," and she backed away from me cringing against the rail. "You disgust me! I can never look you in the face again, either of you. You're vile, to make up such wicked lies."

She was standing by one of those red fire hose cabinets attached to the rail. I went up to her, and she leant against it, almost sat on it, so she was higher, cringing away from me.

I looked into her glowering eyes, her crimson face. "It's not a lie. I did have a son, and he was beautiful." A sort of blind rage rose up inside me, "and now he's dead and I hate you," I said. "I always have done, ever since you first came into our house, spoiling our lives with your hoity-toity ways. How do you think I've felt all these years watching you, knowing my son was alive and that he never knew me. Now he's dead, like you should be,"… and I gave her a good shove, sending her toppling over the rail.

One moment she was there, and the next she was gone.

I looked around. Not a soul. No one had seen us. She hadn't made a sound. I looked over the rail. I couldn't see her. She'd vanished into the sea, down into the deep. Yes, I killed her. I went home and didn't say a word to anyone.

We found her body the next morning underneath the pier, everyone was sad, except me. No one guessed, except maybe Rex, but he never said, never even asked me.

All those questions the police asked us afterwards: Was she depressed? Was she unhappy about something? Is there any medical evidence of her state of mind? Had she ever threatened to commit suicide?

Rex's gruff answer, "She wasn't the type to wear her heart on her sleeve."

Mother saying, "She was such a frail creature."

Rex said, without even looking at me, "She had just had a bout of the 'flu, and was feeling run down, if that's anything to go by."

"Yes," I said quickly, backing up his fib. "She was depressed after having the 'flu."

Just as Mother was about to contradict us, she caught a look from Rex and kept silent.

The policeman looked at us doubtfully, "Depression after influenza?"

Hardly a convincing reason, but they swallowed it.

At the inquest, that was the motive put forward, just like in a 'Poirot'.

Really, I suppose, I should go to the police now and tell them the truth. Confess. I wonder if they'd believe me after all these years? Yes, that's what I'll do. I'll confess. Then they'll have to find me somewhere to stay. Where is it? I remember, in John Street somewhere.

Chapter Thirty-Nine

Conclusion

Monday, 28th March 2011

Waking late in the morning, Betty feels desolate. She orders a room service breakfast, leaves a message for Joe cancelling their lunch appointment but suggesting dinner instead. After showering, she decides on a walk to clear her head. Putting on sunglasses, she ventures out, but the sun is so hot, she doubles back to the hotel boutique to buy herself a cheap but fetching straw hat. Setting off again she makes her way through the manicured parklands beside the hotel, past a beautiful artificial lake, to a pathway beside a modern freeway leading to skyscrapers in the city ahead. She follows it feeling a bit like Dorothy on the way to the Emerald city of Oz.

Eventually, she reaches an arcade with music playing. She goes in. It is a vegetable market, with fish, meat and spices displayed on open stalls. The place is a teeming mass of dazzling, throbbing activity. Vendors and shoppers alike, all races, all colours, creeds and ages, are packed together, bargaining, eating and drinking, laughing and embracing life. Preordained on enjoying themselves, apparently without a care in the world.

Yet it all clashes with her sombre state of mind. *I must get out of here. I am out of tune with life. But everyone has problems to deal with. Troubles to rise above. I must do the same, get a grip, woman. No one is going to help me but myself. No supernatural God is coming to my aid. It's Claudia life that's come to an end, not mine!*

On the roof garden at the Hilton, the still surface of the underwater-lit blue swimming pool perfectly reflects a full harvest moon hanging low in the sky.

Perched lightly on a stool by the bar, Joe waits for Betty. He lights up a cigarette and blows the smoke out into the warm evening air.

It has been an odd sad day recovering from the emotional vigil of last night. With help from the hotel manager and the hospital, he has arranged for Claudia's funeral, a cremation, to take place tomorrow morning. Even though her travel insurance would have covered the cost, he made the decision not to fly her body back home and have a funeral in Brighton, because he did not want to prolong the grief and pain, but he is now concerned about telling his sons. He has not yet spoken to them.

He had run into Betty on her way back from her walk wearing her new straw hat. Raising his eyebrows, he teased her, misquoting Noel Coward: "'In the Malay states /There are hats like plates /Which this Britisher *will* wear.'

She'd smiled, but only half-heatedly.

He went on to tell her of the funeral arrangements he had made. Fortunately, she accepted them without demur. "I don't believe in God anymore," she'd said. "Besides, burial is for the living not the dead."

"No smoking in the bar," beams a merry Malaysian barman. "Sorry, sir."

"That's okay, mate," says Joe, moving out into the garden, wandering past the spot where Claudia had met Harry two days ago.

Joe had enjoyed sex with a good many women in his life, but he has loved only two, his wife, and Betty. What had started out as admiration, over the years became an obsession, now it has flowered into a passionate love. *What else,* he asks himself, *could have impelled me to undertake this long, painful journey? The question is, what does our future hold?*

Several floors below him in her bedroom, Betty is wondering much the same as she carefully applies her lipstick. Packing for her stay with Cheryl and Marco, she had had the foresight to include what Cheryl, when she helped her unpack, described as 'a killer L.B.D.'. Perhaps it is not quite that, but the black silk jersey certainly has an understated glamour, and, thinks Betty, as she examines her reflexion in the mirror, well worth what she paid for it. Dining in a sophisticated restaurant with a handsome man she has feelings for, is an experience Betty has almost forgotten. She collects her handbag and drops in her mobile. *It must be lunchtime in England. I must call Cheryl and the children to tell them. I dread it, but Joe will help.*

The lift doors open and Betty appears.

Joe rises to greet her.

They lock eyes, and she walks toward him.

There is in their look a pleasantry, even a joy, combined with relief from a great sadness or great danger. They greet each other with a kiss.

To an outsider, it would seem to be a perfectly natural and charming greeting for an attractive middle-aged couple.

For Betty and Joe it is a momentous milestone. Still holding each other's eyes, they link arms and with a shiver of anticipation, move off to the poolside restaurant, passing a sign, The Tropical Oasis, written in gold.

Seated alfresco at a table with views, through the high glass barrier, all over the city, the wine waiter offers Joe a wine list. Wine is big in Malaysia; the long list he has to negotiate is mind-boggling.

He chooses what he knows best and orders smoothly, "The Pinot Grigio, please."

Then the food menu:

To Betty's surprise, Joe says, "I think I'll have the Lobster Bisque."

Exactly what Sam ordered on our first date. Regarding it as an omen, she asks, "I don't suppose you have a Dover sole, do you?"

"English Dover sole, no, madam, but we can offer you a Dutch Dover sole."

"Thank you, yes, I'll have that."

The waiter pours the wine, and they clink glasses.

"To Claudia," says Joe. "May she be happy at last."

"To my beloved Claudia," says Betty, drinking. "Do you know," she adds carefully as she places her glass on the table, "I was always afraid I never loved her enough. She was always so much more complicated than Cheryl. I think that's why I made this journey. To prove to myself, as well as to her, just how much I did love her. I'm sure that must sound strange to a man who was an orphan, but curiously her death seems to have set me free, set us free, do you know what I'm talking about?"

"Betty, luv, I know exactly what you're talking about."

"All day I've been thinking about her and about us. It's as if, by her death, she's given us permission. Given me permission. She blessed us, you and me, Joe. Her death has certainly removed a weight of guilt from me... my shame. A world of judgement seems to have been lifted from me."

"Shame?"

"The shame of loving my daughter's husband. The shame and dishonour I felt toward Claudia. The shame of loving you, Joe."

Joe grasps her hand across the table, "Betty, love."

"Oh, Joe. These last years... what an agony."

"I know, I know. I've thought of you every day, you know? I think of you all the time, it's awful."

"Thanks!"

"All through that time I spent in Fuengirola in Spain, working in that bar, every day I wondered if you might walk in, wasn't that crazy? On that damned liner I worked on, and in Buenos Aires. When we get back home, Betty, come and live with me."

"Live with you?" She withdraws her hand, but Joe holds her fast. "But… what about the children?"

"They love you. Love their Grandma, they told me."

"I did promise Claudia I'd look after them."

"And I promised her, I'd look after you. It was an easy promise to make. Let me take care of you, Betty?"

The tone in his voice, the expression in his face, the touch of his hand, calms any of her doubts; she grips his hand, her heart full. Smiling across the table, she is about to speak when the moment is spoiled by the sound of her phone buzzing. "Lord!" she says, reaching for her bag, "I'm sorry. That must be Cheryl. I've not told her yet. Hello!"

"Hello, is that Betty?"

The line is remarkably clear, the voice instantly recognisable. "Sophia, is that you?"

"I'm sorry to bother you, Betty, but I didn't know who else to call. Mother's gone to Worthing for the day, you see, and I didn't want to speak with Mr Williams, again. He rang up this morning to tell us the house is sold. I don't quite know what to do about it. I've lived there all my life, you see, so I'm at the police station."

"What on earth are you doing there, Sophia?"

"I told them about Eve."

"What about her?"

"I pushed her off the pier, you see, and I thought they should know. I've been here for a while. I've tried to explain. Now they say they want to interview me again, but I should have my solicitor present, but I'd rather it was you. They've let me telephone you. Could you come and be with me, please?"

Betty covers the mouthpiece and looks at Joe in astonishment. "It's Sophia, my sister-in-law. She's gone dotty! She's at Brighton Police station confessing to murder."

In a flash, Joe says, "Ask if you can speak to the officer in charge."

With her eyes glued to Joe, she says, "Sophia dear, can I speak to the officer in charge?"

"Hold on."

Joe frowns. "The Chief of Police came to your wedding with Rex, remember? Geoffrey White. I did some work on his daughter's flat in Kemp Town."

"I don't think I'm up to dealing with this," mutters Betty, holding her hand to her brow.

"Here," demands Joe, holding his hand out for the phone, "If it's John Street Police Station, I know a lot of the guys there." Talking into the mobile, he says, "Joe Robinson of 'Robinson and Crawley Constructions,' speaking."

"Not 'Tiger' Joe Robinson?"

"Yes, who's that?"

"Sergeant Aled Jones, Brighton and Hove Police. I've not seen you around for a bit. I heard you'd gone AWOL, abroad someplace."

"I did. I'm in Kuala Lumpur."

"Kuala Lumpur!"

"Yeah, in Malaysia."

"I know where Kuala Lumpur is. What have you got to do with all this?"

"Long story. Listen, Aled, Miss Sophia has recently suffered a bereavement. Her brother Rex Black died the other week. He was a close friend of your boss, Geoffrey White. She's upset, as you can probably tell. We, that is, her sister-in-law, Mrs Black and myself, will be back in Brighton on Wednesday. If you could get her home, Aled, I promise you we'll bring her to the station on Thursday morning in person and sort this out. Does that help at all?"

"No problem, 'Tiger'. There seems to be an element of confusion here. This concerns something that happened twenty years ago. We will need more information. If you can undertake to bring her back here Thursday, that's good enough for me. We'll go into it then. You wouldn't believe how many people we get in here confessing to this sort of thing. I'll hand you back to the lady."

"Thank you, Aled," Joe hands the mobile back to Betty, and gives her a thumbs up sign.

Thank you, she mouths. "Sophia?"

A strained little voice comes on the line, "Hello?"

"Sophia, my dear. Listen, you're not to worry. The police officer will take you home and I'll see you on Wednesday. We'll deal with all this then. You take care now. Are you alright?"

"They said they want a psychiatric report."

"Well, that should be interesting. Interesting for you to talk to a professional, I mean. You'll enjoy that."

"I think they all think I'm potty. The police officer said 'Kuala Lumpur. Why are you there?"

"My daughter Claudia was in an accident last night and died."

"Oh no! Not my grand-daughter."

"Yes, of course, I'd forgotten for a moment. I shouldn't have told you. I'm sorry."

"She was the mother of Peter and Paul. She forgot to fetch them from school."

"Yes, yes, she did. Look, I'll try and arrange for you to meet the boys again when we get home, you'd like that? You said you wanted to take them to the British Museum."

"Very much. Oh, yes, that would be very nice."

"Good. Well, we'll arrange it. Look, I must ring off now, Sophia. You take care, now. See you soon. 'Bye."

Betty clicks off her phone and sits back. "You're brilliant, Joe. Thank you, so much."

Joe winks.

It gives her a surprising twinge of pleasure. "What the hell am I going to do about her? Now Marco is buying the house, she says she has nowhere to go. I think she's lost it, bless her. "

"Do you like her?" asks Joe.

"Very much. She's a bit eccentric, but yes, I've come round to being very fond of her. She's the one who caught us kissing when you came to fix the platform over the stairs all those years ago, remember?"

"How could I forget. She could come and live with us, if you like."

"Joe, you're not serious?"

"Why not? There's a great 'Granny' flat at the back. When I built it, it did occur to me that it might be for you one day! She could stay there."

"A Great Granny flat! Oh Joe!" Betty laughs till the tears roll down her cheeks, not so much because of the joke, but because for a split second she's happy, tangibly happy, despite everything that's happened: for a moment she glimpses, in the far distance, a possibility of happiness. "Joe, you are a saint. You don't know just how appropriate Sophia living in your great 'Granny' flat will be."

Frowning and smiling at the same time, he asks, "How's that?"

"Sophia Black is Peter and Paul's great-grandmother."

"How the blazes do you work that one out?"

"Well, it is rather complicated. It started long before I married Rex Black,… "

At this point, the waiter arrives with Joe's Lobster Bisque and Betty's Dutch Dover sole.

Over dinner, underneath a pinprick of stars and an orange harvest moon, she tells him the whole story.

Acknowledgments

I owe a great debt of gratitude to Louise Stein for all her help and advice, also thanks are due to Hilary Johnson for her words of wisdom. My heartfelt thanks go to all my supportive friends, to Jan Waters, Josie Kidd and Vivien Mills, to Genevieve and Michael Walker, David Weston and to Neil Robson, for his advice on money matters. Special thanks go to the inestimable Jennifer Liptrot with Jeremy Thompson and all at Matador Publishing for their help. It goes without saying that any errors are my own and not theirs. An extra special thanks to my loving friend Paul Linn, for taking the photographs on the front and back cover.